The Hippie Cult

By

Len Thomas Cabela

Contents

Preface:

To God, Wordsmith of the Utmost Order. May Every Word Be the Perfect Word. In Jesus' Precious Name. Amen.

For my beautiful wife Jessica, my family and friends, neighbors, acquaintances, anybody who ever believed in me, even when I didn't, and everyone who purchases or reads this entire book or book series.

To say this work has been almost 50 years in the making would not be too much of an exaggeration. Mom would read me Little House on the Prairie, Curious George, and Dr. Seuss books. I always loved to read, before I even started school, Mom taught me simple two and three-letter words and I tried reading some in children's books and the Bible. Even so, my brothers warned me repeatedly that I would hate school. Grandpa Boes, however, always told us school was fun, every chance he got. My mother said I might have butterflies in my stomach, and that described how I was feeling on my first day of kindergarten. It was a unique feeling that I hadn't had before or since that year. I had to remember to take in milk money. I cried my eyes out after school that day and ate almost a whole bottle of chewable vitamin C. At Ida Elementary School, my kindergarten teacher was Mrs. Spots, and the teaching assistant was Ms. Ringle. Mom was insistent they did not enroll me in ITA, the Initial Teaching Alphabet, and true to her notion I turned out fine, unlike the others in the ITA program who were so confused when they actually had to learn words the right way. I stayed with

phonics. For First, Second, and Third Grade, my teacher was Mrs. Luft. Besides Mom, it was her I probably owe the biggest debt of gratitude to for a literary or artistic career, (and Mr. Strickland in college). She always encouraged me, was loving, and never gave up on me. In fact, she believed so much in her class students, that she insisted on keeping us as long as possible. When the school board wouldn't let her keep us again for Fourth Grade, she discussed it with her husband and retired that very year.

I awoke early one morning at 4 AM. I walked out into the living room and picked up my youngest older brother's copy of Animal Farm by George Orwell. I read most of it by the time he woke up and had to take it to school for a book report that was due. He said he would let me finish reading it soon when he was done with it, but for now, he would give me Lad, A Dog, by Albert Payson Terhune. I read it cover to cover. The book my sister brought home, Hiroshima by John Hersey, I didn't get to read until more recently by buying through eBay. I remember thinking that the mushroom cloud on the cover looked like a wicked old lady cackling with an ugly necklace and a big bouffant hairdo. But as I tried to write my own little book to take into school, I came up with the idea for Funny Farm, a little more than a pamphlet with a few of my drawings added to it, the little book with laminated construction paper cover told my fictional story of being mistakenly imprisoned in a lunatic asylum for being sane, and my inevitable escape and exile. Mrs. Luft had me read it in front of the class. Everyone loved it. She said she would bring in a

thing called the Young Author's competition. My fellow students requested me to read it again and again. Later on, I suspect, to take up more time so they wouldn't have to do other school activities, as days went on. I went on to get the blue ribbon for my school, and I think at least one more blue ribbon for regional participation. Mrs. Luft also read us books like *All I Really Need to Know I Learned in Kindergarten* by Robert Fulghum.

As I was achieving a near cultlike status with my writing, a group of schoolmates asked if I wanted to hold a little symposium during recess to figure out how to write better. I supposed it would be a welcome break from the usual game of Tag-Tackle-and-Pummel in which we would form a line, where I always ended up in the front, and they would all chase me around the playground. It was during one of these early chases that I wound up unwittingly in a bit of trouble, as the playground aide, who happened to be the boss's wife later when I worked at Carl's Hideaway as a dishwasher, grabbed me and said, "Here he is!" She asked if I was the one who had splashed mud on a little girl's dress. I said no because I had no recollection of doing such a horrendous thing. I looked over at a little girl who had been crying and she pointed at me identifying me as the one. Then I had to stand in the corner of the playground alone, while the others were beckoning me from a few yards off on the next chase. I just shook my head because I didn't want to get in trouble again.

Another year I wrote another story for Young Authors, this time School Days. I only got the

Second-Place red ribbon for that, and it was downhill from there, but I had by then learned to flesh it out to more pages, using more descriptive words, such as adjectives. I also learned not to use cuss or swear words, instead putting a box with 'Censored' in it, or symbols such as @#$%*. I understand the advocacy of free speech by Lenny Bruce and George Carlin, who my brother loved. However, any moron with two brain cells to rub together can use cuss or swear words for emphasis, but I wanted to make my literature accessible, friendly, and available to all audiences. Plus, I rather came to realize as time went on that besides differentiating my writing from all the rest who do use expletives, I could make more of an impact with more selective choices of words, sort of like when Charles Manson used the menacing snarling, "AWE HECK!" in a song. It was much more expressive than any bad words.

I later gave up on those book concepts when the movies Funny Farm with Chevy Chase, and Spike Lee's School Daze came out in 1988. That is when I should've originally graduated from high school, had I not dropped out, opting for the GED, Adult Education, and dropping back into school at Clintondale High School, Mount Clemens, Michigan instead. But back in Mrs. Luft's classroom, she had us learn to write haikus. I had written and rewritten what I'd begun to call Morning Haiku or Twilight Haiku. It was chosen to be published in the Monroe Evening News paper sometime in the mid-to-late 1970s. I was not able to find it as an adult at the gigantic Monroe County Library System's Ellis Reference and Information

Center on microfiche, but I suppose it went like this; *Cold dew on the grass/Light breaks on dawn's horizon/Hear faint sounds of birds*. I learned from this to be brief and concise, rather than longwinded. I also learned that I could do better within the confines of definitive restrictive parameters because I would uncover solutions to make great work while following rules and laws, even up to later work of driving a truck in the city, one of the choices of career day at school. (Monster truck, too).

The library was a great influence. I remember the sound my shoes made climbing up to the second floor on the metal steps and the buzz of the fluorescent lights. It was just like the library scene in *Something Wicked This Way Comes*, by one of my favorite authors, Ray Bradbury. I remember my neighbor friend inviting me to take my stash of library books out to his backyard shed to read them. The sound of the rain pouring down on the metal roof, as I took out a book about dog breeds with plenty of pictures and excitedly examined and read through it. The school library was one of a series of single-wide trailers set up on blocks, with skirting all around, behind the school. I remember climbing up the steps and finding a few good books. They enrolled me in the speed-reading program that year. It utilized a viewer machine that was on a little desk. There were a bunch of them in a row. I sat on a chair and placed my eyes up to the viewer's lens. Each line flashed as my eyes zipped across left to right trying to absorb the information before the next line appeared. At the end, I had a short comprehension test to see how well I did. If I did well, I could advance next time to a slightly higher

rate. If not, I would go slower again. My chart looked like mountains with many peaks and valleys, sometimes growing to new heights, (before diagnoses of ADHD, OCD, and dyslexia were even considered), I thrived despite all this.

Mrs. Luft had printed out tons of sheets of paper with fun learning activities for over the summer vacation months, probably wearing out the school's Xerox machine, giving us each a huge stack of papers about ten inches high. When it was her last year teaching us, there was a farewell card going around and all the students were writing a little note, like thank you for helping me with this and with that. I started writing, "Thanks for…" I hesitated, trying to think of the perfect things to say but was being rushed. Kids were saying, "Hurry up, she's coming!" and "Just write something." So, I just scribbled 'nothing' and signed my first name. As soon as she looked at it, she called me up to her desk, asking me why I wrote that. I was so embarrassed, saying "Just an extra thank you in case…uh…" Words failed me. She said to me, "You cross that out and write something nice." This time I had more time to think about it in depth before writing some very specific things she had helped me personally with. Unfortunately, I had written it in pen, which we were so used to using a pencil that we often wore out the eraser right away. One memorable learning experience was when the teacher brought a small pencil with an extra-long eraser on the end.

My brothers had warned me of a strict mean teacher they had, named Mrs. Mathis. But instead of her, I

got Mrs. Cronenwett, for Fourth Grade, who didn't seem that bad, but a little bit stern. Later in middle school, I had Mr. Jones who was in a wheelchair, but my brother had said he was his favorite teacher. When I was able to have typing class in school there was a classroom full of old clunky typewriters. The teacher there was an older lady like Mrs. Cronenwett, but I'm not sure if this was her. She said to everyone, "Don't crack your knuckles, they'll get big as a barn!" Everyone laughed. I eventually got an electric typewriter at home. For the report on caffeine, I did mostly on articles dug out of filing cabinets in the middle school library, I edited by literally copying by hand or cutting with scissors and pasting them back into the right section of blank notebook paper in the upstairs of my sister's rented house in Dundee, Michigan. This was before home computers became common in the early 80s, and the only computers they did have out were maybe the Apple 2e which I wasn't even interested in having at that point. I got an A+.

One of my new teachers in English literature class had us do an initial writing assignment on a topic we picked. I chose to write a paper on conscientiously objecting to the use of blood transfusions and abstaining from blood on religious grounds versus the possibility of saving lives. The day after grading them she talked to the entire class raving about how one of us in the classroom had done such an excellent job as to warrant a higher grade than she had ever been able to give in her entire career, an A+. She said she would not reveal who it was to the entire class but would after class was dismissed for the day. While everybody was

walking out, she motioned for me to stay behind. She let me know that I had achieved the highest grade and congratulated me on my fine work. She hoped I would keep it up, but the very next paper I did was a bomb, and I got a terrible grade. She asked me what had happened because we both thought I would do better. I learned that if I wrote what God wanted me to write I would be successful. If it wasn't what God wanted me to write, it wouldn't be successful. In an English Literature class in middle school, or maybe even high school, we did a collaborative writing exercise called Ad Libs, which in my family as I grew up mom called Consequences. Somebody wrote a slightly funny beginning, I wrote the middle portion, and everyone laughed a bit, reading that, another kid wrote a hilarious ending, which made everyone laugh uncontrollably and hysterically! I mean we had tears running out of our eyes, and we couldn't stop. I learned if you aren't willing to take it just one step further, the next person who tries will. For another class I took at some point, I wrote about all the possible different dimensions I could conceive of. The teacher said he was fascinated by the topic and would like to read more on the subject.

All of us in the family had a penchant for words, and art class was one of my favorite classes in school, although I could do math, but was better in Social Studies classes. I will see if I can add some samples of my cartoon drawings at the end of this book, the ones that I saved. But I didn't apply myself and missed a lot of school telling my mom I was sick. I would be absent at least one day a week, most weeks. Eventually, in middle school, they

allowed me to go into the gifted class, but there were a lot of kids who weren't doing as well, and they had hoped I would rub off on them. So, they'd have a spelling test with simple words for them. I made up a story of why I was late again, telling Mr. Donaldson I had been hitchhiking and was almost abducted. I thought it was so funny that it was obvious that I was joking, but others were telling me I was taking it too far. When he wrote it up and sent me to the principal's office, I had to relent and tell them it was all made up to get out of that class, which was essentially another boring study hall, because he was about to contact the police.

Later on, when I found out I was successful at college; in one of my introductory Psychology classes I kept falling asleep during the lecture and since they jumped around for the weekly tests, I often studied the wrong chapters but passed it with the minimum of a C anyhow. I remember thinking this was for me! I had always thought it was ridiculous for people to go to college and study when I was younger. My personal college experience made the basis for much of the inspiration for this book. I even wrote an article that was published in the Florida Villager, whose editor contacted me first to ask. I also studied Journalism for a work-study program in community college. I didn't have to pay for it, but it was not for credit either. They published one of my articles in the school paper, The Agora. It was about the modern music scene going into the turn of the millennium. However, the next paper I was invited to write about the various plants in the college greenhouse was a wild goose chase. I spent a lot of time

photographing them with a digital camera only to find out that it was never published.

I had a capstone paper published online on the website: academia.edu. I admired my favorite authors and was inspired to write by the work of James Patterson. Also, Stephen King who was such a prolific writer; he seemed to crank out a new thick book every few months, and when I read about J.K. Rowling becoming the first billionaire author to write fantasy fiction, starting out as a broke housewife, and becoming legendary with the Harry Potter series, I had this as my goal too. Although I had the concepts, and initial characters started to develop in my head, and I began to write it during a difficult career transitional period, I couldn't have written it years ago. I wish I could have, but the ideas just weren't all there yet. It lacked much direction. I enjoyed reading the book The Giver, recommended by a close friend, in the hammock in the side row of trees in the front yard one summer before I moved and noticed two more books by her formed a trilogy. That's when I seriously considered making this into a trilogy series. Since then, she made another book, and it became a quartet of books. I recently read the second one, Gathering Blue. I wanted to write a book that I, myself, would want to read if I were the reader, in effect following the Golden Rule. When 2019 rolled around and they started controlling the public with the "pandemic," I had it stored away on my computer, not knowing where to go with it due to writer's block. This worked in my favor, like the example of Stephen King writing vigorously for about three months, and then putting it away in the drawer for a few months

while it ferments in his mind, then he comes back with a fresher perspective. And I had a few poems I put up on poetry.com over the years.

As I was browsing YouTube, earlier this year, I was contemplating the band's material for the CA Quintet's A Trip Through Hell. I contacted a surviving member, Ken. I asked if he'd like me to write their story for them, he asked at first if I had anything to send him as an example of my work. I hadn't even completed the first three chapters yet. He said he was thinking about continuing the story he had begun himself, but that it might be nice to send each other our completed works so that we could compare. I felt as if dark forces were trying to get me to give up on the goals I had been attaining. When I got to the part in the second chapter, about where the sunrise was about to begin, it was page 13. Despite being very careful and getting in the habit of saving my progress often, I spent one Sunday writing at least five hours. I was also working on other projects, but when I got a chance to write again, in a week or so, I noticed that at least seven pages had disappeared, prompting a massive rewrite of the missing material. The pastor at our church had a similar experience with his sermon, and instead of continuing to waste time trying to retrieve it, we both just went ahead and wrote it again from memory, this time better. Less boring, more interesting, and more exciting. This writing has been almost therapeutic, and cathartic, writing in the flow. When the inspiration hits you, even with songwriting, or artwork, it is only valid for that moment. When I go back to try to recreate something later, it doesn't seem as good as when I

first thought of it. The moment will pass and then you are a slightly different person than you were before. The moment's gone. If you tried to remember your song, continue with the same inspiration, or feeling later, it would likely be inferior and lackluster, less than stellar consequently.

The concept of limited and unlimited talent comes into play with intellectual property. Those who are more concerned about somebody stealing their ideas have a limited amount of talent to begin with, and they would not be able to keep it up if others tried to copy them. If someone has unlimited talent, they would be inimitable.

What I love about being creative, especially art and writing, is that you're literally creating something out of nothing, like when God created the heavens and the earth after there was nothing. Even if you own nothing at all, and you ask, someone might give you a pen or pencil and a pad of paper, and you could eventually make a book. Good writers can become millionaires or better.

I'm not writing biographically, although I am inspired by my own experiences quite often. I do often use actual places, not made-up towns, or addresses. I don't like it when movies, or books, use made-up presidents. I'm not writing fantasy such as going back in time, or even something possible but very highly unlikely. Sometimes truth is stranger than fiction, so in those cases, where you just can't make this stuff up, my truthful experiences inspire my fictional story. The characters are purely

fictional. Any resemblance to actual people is purely coincidental and unintended. Names of characters in this story were devised to be different from anyone I have met in case anybody who reads it may be offended by their similarity to them. None of them are actually me.

Therefore, without any more delay, as I feel I owe this to you, and that there's always been someone, somewhere, out there who has needed my help, but I didn't know who it was or where they needed help. The truth is that there are lots of people out there, as well as animals who need all the help they can get, every day. It's always been important to make a difference in the world. Take a stand, be there at the right place, at the right time. I can promise you this one thing as you read this; you will be thoroughly entertained. Not just mildly amused.

Chapter One, Coaxis:

Monday, July 6th, 1998

His name was Mortimer Murray, and he had traversed afar. He motored south on Interstate 75 out of Michigan and over the drawbridge north of Oregon, Ohio on 275 and down 420. His 1972 Buick Skylark, GSX convertible went around each turn and a tumbling and groaning sound came from the trunk. It was a bright, gleaming GM white, with a glossy black, contrasting, new top, and original wheels, with brown vinyl interior and dash underneath repainted copper-tone. The motor was a 455 with stage 2 heads, so it could be mighty fast. There was a Cobra radar detector suctioned onto the windshield and turned on so he could stay out of trouble.

Unfortunately, there was not enough room for a good sound system, as there was an original factory speaker in front and rear behind the back seat. His big bushy hair was a bright neon yellow, blonde, and straight with light frizz. He made it to route 20 and out to County Road 175, just east of Clyde Ohio[1], which was a crossroads of sorts, for a strange meeting. It was back in the day at a building called Staff of Life. But don't bother to go look for it now, as it is long since gone. It had been torn down shortly after this encounter to make way for a modern Shell station.

---

[1] Anderson, S. (1960). *Winesburg, OH.* Viking Press.

The next one to show up was a fellow quintessential hippie named Deere Muff, coming from out West, along the Ohio Turnpike, before which he had driven Route 66. Well, about that time it had started raining, and he had been driving up in his 1962 VW (flower-power) Microbus USA model, listening to "Love Everyday" by Boyce and Hart. The song made him sad, and he started to cry. So not only were the windshield wipers wiping, but also those upon his weird-looking glasses activated to wipe away his fretful tears. But then he stopped and composed himself in time to hop out.

Two other guys popped in out of nowhere and were suddenly on the scene to join them too. One had an orange 1970 Mercury Cougar Eliminator, with black stripes. Man, that thing was sharp! He was Tom Bumblewood. He came out of the South, up from Florida. He had driven along I-75 North. Then there was an olive green 1975 Dodge D100 van with a gold design saying "Badlands Vans," an iron cross, and "WFW, Always Bookin'" on the sides. (People thought at first glance that it said WTF and had to look twice) His name was Fred Dumbeaux, from out East, New York to be precise, along Route 20.

They all walked into the light blue steel building. Inside the shop, there were different hippie items such as incense ("The Smell of Incense," by Southwest FOB started playing in the background) and soon they started reminiscing about automobiles and browsing through old J.C. Whitney catalogs, and Hemming's Motor News. Fred remarked that J.C. Whitney was always a major source for VW parts, Karman Ghia, and even Jeep, and they now had a website. "Far Out, Man!"

said Deere Muff. There were snacks like Funyuns, Munchos, Andy Capp's Hot Fries, and Pringles, and lots of different teas and soft drinks.

There was a plethora of candies such as Pearson's Nut Goodies, plus their Nut Roll, and Bun, and gums such as Cloves and Beeman's, Teaberry, Blackjack, and of course Wrigley's, Big Red, and Juicy Fruit. It was a big room that reminded them of a time capsule. Nostalgic candy such as Chuckles, Razzles, M&M's, candy cigarettes, Pop Rocks, Necco wafers, Sugar Daddy, and Marathon bars, Red Hots, Boston Baked Beans, and Dots in a box, and Pixy Sticks were available. "Cool," said Tom.

Candy bars such as Snickers, Payday, Almond Joy and Mounds, York Peppermint Patties, Zagnut, Charleston Chew, Zero, Clark, Mars, Milky Way, 3 Musketeers, Mr. Goodbar, Hershey's, 5th Avenue, Twix, as well as Mary Janes, Tootsie Roll, Raisinets, Goobers, Whoppers, Crows, Atomic Fireballs, Jujyfruits, Bottle Caps, Jujubes, Chick-o-Sticks, and Lemonheads. "Dig it!" exclaimed Fred.

Presently, there was an assortment of lava lamps, Himalayan salt lamps, drug paraphernalia, and assorted historical items, along the back row where Mr. Muff was gazing into the wonder of a fiber optic lamp listening to the Doors' "Crystal Ship." It reminded him of a cross between The Head Shed (a head shop) and Spencer Gifts. On the wall were plenty of vintage posters by M.C. Escher, a poster of a stoned Mickey Mouse that read "AM I SEE, KAY HEE WHY, AM OH YOU AS HE." There were a few black lights and black light posters with naked chicks, magic mushrooms, and

one with a marijuana leaf. "Awesome!" remarked Morty.

A guy showed up in a doorway leading to the back room holding a stack of records and asked Mortimer if he needed help. Mortimer looked over to the counter and saw a name. The owner said, "Just call me Bob." "Wait a minute that nameplate says Harry," Mortimer turned his head to look again, and Bob shifted his weight to the right to knock the plate behind a box under the counter with the back of his hand. "Hairy What?" asked Fred. "Not What, Harry Who?" snapped Tom. "Who??" asked Deere. "Oh, you're looking for The Who records? Certainly, you know I saw *them* in concert once, well actually a bunch of big-name groups all playing together." Bob was seriously searching through his collection of records, but the rest kept distracting him. "It might have even been the Fillmore East… or was it The Fillmore West? Hmmm…"

"Who was on first?" asked Mortimer.

"Wow! You saw Them in concert? That is one of my favorite bands!" someone chimed in.

"Yes," replied Bob. After several seconds Fred said, "Oh, so you saw Yes in concert too?"

Bob: "Uh…no, I did see Yes but at a different venue."

Tom: "Who opened for them?"

Bob: "Guess Who!"

Tom: "I don't know…The Association?"

Bob: "No. I just told you the band!"

Fred: "The Band?"

Bob: "Yes…now let's see, where was I?"

Mortimer: "Who was playing when the doors opened?"

Fred: "*Love*… the Doors!"

Bob interrupted, "The Guess Who, I said, and I don't have any Love records, just recently sold out."

"Almost all music is about love," remarked Deere. "No, I said that I love the Doors," said Fred, "So Who opened?"

Bob: "The Guess Who"

Tom: "I did guess who."

Bob: "Wait, What?" It was silent for a few seconds, so he explained, "Guess Who opened for Who."

Tom: "I did guess."

Fred: "I, myself, would like to know more about The Band; you know they're from Canada!"

Mortimer: "Who are we talking about now?"

Bob: "The Who are from England, stupe…uh Sir."

This witty banter and repartee went on for quite a while. Morty was getting a little bit peeved as he had been waiting in line now for what seemed to be forty-five minutes to buy a bag of Skittles, Starburst, and other assorted junk food snacks. By now all he was hearing was "BLAH, BLAH, BLAH!" He zoned out for about ten or fifteen more minutes with their endless chatter.

Fred: "Woah, So the Guess Who, The Who, Them, Love, The Doors, Yes, and The Band?"

Tom: "Wonder Who…" Mortimer was fuming. It almost looked like smoke was coming out of his ears, but no one was looking.

Bob: "The Wonder Who was just an early incarnation of Frankie Valli and the Four Seasons."

Fred: "More like the Blunder Who, they were a big mistake."

Tom: “The Wonders were a great made-up band.”

Fred: “Ever see the Wonder Years?”

Suddenly, Mortimer flew across the room with a shovel he had found that had been used at a famous groundbreaking ceremony, hitting Bob upside the head, and knocking him out cold. The others looked at him lying sprawled out on the floor, with their jaws gaping open. The records he was looking through were all over the place. “What to do?” Fred said. “Does anybody know CPR?” Tom asked. “Check his pulse!” replied Deere. Fred went over behind the corner of the counter and started checking Bob’s pulse.

Mortimer had already thrown a gob of cash down on the table and headed for the door. Tom ran over and grabbed him by the neck, “Oh no you don’t, Bucko!” He was strong and intimidating, like a bodybuilder or professional wrestler. “If we have to stay here and help, you do too! It was your fault in the first place!” Mortimer replied, “Hey! It was an accident!”

There were no vital signs. Deere tried some chest compressions and blew some air through his hands into the guy’s mouth. “Anybody have a defibrillator?” Tom said.

“Oh yeah, let me just pull that out of my…”

“SHUT UP, Jerk!”

“Trunk,” said Mortimer. “It’s in the back of my car.” He went out there and took several minutes rustling around all his stuff. “I couldn’t find it,” he said as he came back in. Tom was surprised he hadn’t already tried to escape. “I guess he’s dead, so it doesn’t matter anyway.” At this time, it was sundown, and there was a beautiful sunset

outside. The four men dragged the body around the far side to the back of the building, taking care the coast was clear. There was a field to the west side of the building. They brought the shovel but needed something more to make the hole deep enough. Mortimer went again to his trunk to get a pickaxe.

As time went on, Bob started making noises. "I'm not dead yet!" he wheezed as they extended their ears toward him. Morty was coming around the corner with his pickaxe. They told him what had just happened. "I don't believe you." But they insisted. "It's true!" So, they pushed him forward to listen after he had dropped the pickaxe on the ground nearby. Mortimer leaned his ear up close to the man's mouth because his eyes were still closed, but his breathing wasn't readily apparent. "OWWW! MY HEAD HURTS!" Bob screamed, still in the resting position. Mortimer was reeling from the volume, as he reared back.

"Just hold on a few minutes, I was sure I would die soon but I didn't know how it'd happen… until now." Tom quickly asked, "You mean you are clairvoyant?" Bob stated, "Or intuitive, something like that. But you know it's like I always thought I'd be late to my own funeral, but it turns out I'm super early. Ha-ha-ha-ha-ha-ha-ha-ha-ha-hah!!!" Nobody else laughed, just stood there with unamused gazes. "Here, let's help you get up. Take hold of my hand," said Deere. Lifting his arm was like lifting the arm of a corpse, cold and clammy. "I, I can't move. I can't move my…arms, my legs. I can't move anything. I'm paralyzed…um, from my neck down, I guess. How'd that happen?" He felt a tremendous headache. "You really don't remember?" asked

Mortimer. "Remember what?" replied Bob. "Hmm," said Mortimer, rubbing his chin.

"Just go ahead, I know you're thinking of it, my wife has an insurance policy, it's a quarter of a million dollars, keep digging, and when I am finally dead, I mean when it's my time, I'll let you know, and you can start filling in the dirt over my head. Sound fair?" They dug for over an hour in the tough empty dirt, as it got darker and darker out there. One of them had to go in, look for a flashlight, and grab a few things like rope, matches, and candles. "Ain't It Nice in Here," by Barefoot Jerry was playing on the stereo system. He thought it strange because for such a long while it had seemed to be silent. When finally done digging, they had it big enough, and gently, slowly lowered Bob into the hole in the ground and waited. The batteries for the flashlight were dead already. After so long, though, with mosquitos biting, and slapping maniacally on their skin to save it, they began to call Bob's name, quietly at first to avoid drawing much attention, and then louder. But finally, they had to send someone in to check on the status. Tom insisted on sending Morty since it was his fault. Mortimer reluctantly assumed the role of a search party and jumped down. He found nothing at the bottom of the grave but a dirt floor. Although he had a flashlight in hand, just to make sure, Tom demanded he dig around a bit more to do a complete and thorough investigation. "I don't see anything; he didn't dig anywhere with his pointy claws!" Mortimer yelled. Tom was about as frustrated and tired as he could be, extremely exhausted and fatigued. He grabbed the ceremonial shovel and started filling the pit with dirt. Of course, Mortimer shrieked, "What are you

doing?" To which Tom erupted, "DIE, BUM!" But Morty soon easily climbed out. "Don't you cross me!" Tom slammed the shovel down and looked around for Bob, pacing back and forth.

They couldn't believe it. "We've been HAD!" Tom screamed at the top of his lungs. "That goofball had us going all this time! I can't believe he pulled that one on us! Well, shoot, fellas!" He flung his hat and ultimately forgot it there in what seemed a vast wasteland. The rest of them just quietly got ready to go. Out to their vehicles, they went. Mortimer suggested they might as well go in and grab some more loot, because let's face it, they were dirt poor.

Soon everyone was back inside, "Hip Death Goddess," by Ultimate Spinach was playing on the sound system. "How do you turn this dang thing off? Dumbeaux fumed. Tom fired a few shots with his Smith and Wesson where the sound was coming out of the ceiling. But it refused to stop. "I'm not gonna waste any more bullets." They grabbed up any food they could get, and it was mostly MRE and shelf-stable products that could be put in any prepper pantry, and sugary candies and snacks. Deere Muff grabbed up any novelty items and Hippie memorabilia or toys to play with. Mortimer grabbed everything that would fit into his arms. They all were in a daze. Lightheaded. Bob never came back.

Eventually, they got into their vehicles and were hesitant to go. "You know what? I'm almost on Empty. Did anyone notice where the closest gas station is?" Nobody did. Another asked where the closest hotel or motel was, before realizing they didn't have much money left for one. "Hey, I don't

usually offer this," Mortimer volunteered, "but you guys need a place to rest your head, you can always crash at my place, well one of my places."

They all began to follow his Buick down to Route 224, to a rickety, run-down, dilapidated, very old, haunted, beastly house he called "Hideous House."

Chapter Two, Hideous House:

The Buick and all the other vehicles pulled into the dirt pathway to a vacant house that looked abandoned. There was brush and trees around it, so they fit their vehicles around back, as per Mortimer's waving hand sticking out from his driver's side window, beckoning them. The address was 1243 U.S. 224 in Nova, Ohio.[2] The house had virtually no paint left, but from the trim it appeared that it used to be painted white. It had some quaint ornate carved transom woodwork above all the doors and windows. The windows and doors were boarded up, but as they rounded the corner there was a door wide open out of view from the road. The guys were reluctant to get out of their cars.

Mortimer opened his car door and gingerly stepped out, his eyes adjusting to the lack of light. There was no electricity hooked up to the premises. He grabbed a broom, a lantern, and a light blue sleeping bag out from the back seat. He headed in, and since there were no lights available, he turned on his camping lantern setting it down on the porch. He beckoned them to come in. So, one by one, they stepped out of their vehicles and carefully walked up to the porch toward the doorway.

"Watch your step," Morty said quietly. There were loose and dirty floorboards, with many gaps in the floor. He started sweeping as he put down his sleeping bag nearby. "I don't suppose you have a…bathtub?" Fred said. "This place doesn't

---

[2] https://www.mansfieldnewsjournal.com/story/news/local/2015/12/22/fire-destroys-haunted-nova-farmhouse/77743170

have running water. That all costs money," Morty replied without looking up. Everybody was casually scratching themselves from mosquito bites and other skin irritants. Morty finished sweeping and whisked the pile of dust and dirty particulates down another hole in the floorboards. Someone coughed. Then he unfolded the sleeping bag and laid it in the middle of the floor, he started getting in it and making himself comfy. "Where are *we* gonna sleep?" asked Deere. "I don't know," Morty responded with much yawning, "Don't you pack a sleeping bag?"

"Well not typically." "Why would we do that?"

"You're a squatter, aren't you?" Tom quickly discerned. "Uh, *yeah*!" Morty sarcastically answered. "Did you think I'd actually pay money to live here?" "We'd be better off sleeping in our vehicles," Fred said. "Yeah, I'm not sleeping in such a horrible place," said Deere, "on the *floor*?!?!" Without another word, Tom turned around to sleep in his car, whispering "*thanks for nothing.*"

"Suit yourself," Mortimer shrugged, as he laid back down to go to sleep in his sleeping bag. He was tired from a long day of driving and activities. They all were. Suddenly before they got to their cars, there were loud banging and creaking noises. "What was that?!?!?" Tom swung around, pivoting on the sole of his shoe. There was no answer from the bag, then a slight muffled snoring sound. "Hey! Did you hear me?" Then Tom went to the bag and pushed lightly with his foot. The others were right behind him, looking down as Morty's head appeared from the front of the bag and one eye

and then the other began to flutter open. "Huh?" Mortimer grumbled. "Did you hear that?" Tom asked. "Hear what?" he responded a little miffed. "The *sounds,* dimwit." "What are you talking about?" he said slowly and calmly. "I'm going back to sleep. Do whatever you want." The light from the lantern cast an eerie glow through the wreckage of the house, which had probably been vacant around 15, or 20 years. Above the front door was a stained glass that was a ghastly red in color in the moonlight. There was much broken glass, and everything seemed inhospitable except to vermin, insects, and undesirables.

The other three walked to their vehicles again. Tom asked, "Hey, either of you have a pillow, or say covers, sheets, blankets?" Deere, since he had the microbus offered, "I have a couple extra pillows." "I might have a blanket or two," hollered Fred since he had the badlands van. It wasn't raining at all, but it did get a little chilly outside. A couple of times Tom, Deere, and Fred woke up and saw orbs and strange apparitions, which were like a mist rising from inside and around the house, but Morty never came out from the comfort of his sleeping bag. Some weird voices came out of the house just before morning, and then strong winds picked up blowing the trees and then shaking the vehicles. Other than that, though, they slept pretty well, only getting out a few times to pee.

The guys in their cars started waking up at daybreak. The 1975 Dodge D100 only had a few windows, so Fred had curtains put up and pulled them tightly together before going to sleep. Deere's 1962 VW Microbus Deluxe USA had a lot of

windows, letting the light of day in. Deere walked over and knocked on Fred's driver's side door to wake him up. Tom sat on the hood of his car looking out at the beautiful new sunrise drinking a beer. Orange. Pink. Gold. Lilac. He had a cooler with a case of Old Milwaukee. Deere and Fred walked over and introduced themselves to Tom, smiling. "Beer for Breakfast! You know I got the idea from the movie, 'Lions for Breakfast.' I got more in the cooler in the trunk. Want some?" Deere said, "Why not?" Fred said, "Sure, hey thanks, buddy!" Tom said, "You're welcome. I always try to keep some on hand."

They stood around talking, small talk, and about the night and dreams they had, drinking more and more beer all morning until 10:00 AM when they decided to go wake up the guy in the house in the sleeping bag. Tom, then Deere, then Fred gingerly stepped up on the porch, walking over to the sleeping bag. Tom bumped the bag with his shoe a couple of times rapidly. Morty stopped snoring and popped his head out with disheveled hair and instantly opened his bright eyes. "Good morning," he said. "I don't believe we've introduced ourselves. My name is Tom, Tom Bumblewood." Fred introduced himself, then Deere. "Ha! That's a unique name. Here's my card," Mortimer reached into his pocket and gave the guys each one. It just had his name, a tentative address, and a few phone numbers. "Mortimer Murray," Tom cooly read, "Looks like you have quite an uncommon name too." Fred read it and snickered, while Deere just glanced at the card and slipped it into his back pocket. "What, what's so funny?" "Murmur, heh-heh, your first and last name

have murmur in it. I'll call you Murmur, that'll be your nickname," said Fred. "Well, let me show you around," Murmur said, "watch your step."

By now they had enough light to see all the chunks of plaster on the floor as obstacles, and a lot of holes in the floor. In some areas, there was no subfloor but only floor joists to step on. The walls were not in good condition, and had a lot of graffiti on them, some of which was obscene. There was a pantry area. They could see where the bathroom was, a long closet, and what probably were the living rooms. The railing of one of the staircases was gone and several steps were missing. Some illumination filtered in from the holes in the roof on the upper floor. They went down toward the basement and quickly looked inside and then came back up toward the way they came in. They looked down at a hole in the ground underneath the joists in the back of the house, which looked like a kitchen area. It was bricked in like a well with sides that tapered outward. "That seems odd," Tom said, "is this a well?" They looked down into it with the light from Murmur's lantern. "I can't see the bottom," remarked Deere. "From the looks of it, I'd guess it's a portal to hell," noted Fred. "It's probably just a thing they used to cook on in the early days before they added on here in the back. You know kind of like an earthen grill," stated Murmur.

As they were done inspecting the house, they all gathered on the front porch. Tom was standing on the corner edge and caused a board to creak. Suddenly, they saw him animatedly whirl his head around, maniacally slapping at himself yelling, "Ow! Ow! OW!" He ran several yards toward his car, ripped off his clothes, and stomped on them.

"Those are my pet bees," reported Murmur calmly. "They're no honeybees, these are ground hornets from that hole over there by the house," yelled Tom with an angry face. After he made sure they were all dead, he showed the others all the ground hornet carcasses. "Don't you have any wasp and hornet spray, or better yet Ortho Seven Dust?" Murmur said, "No, I don't usually carry that around." "No, I don't," said Fred. "I don't either," said Deere. "Better check again. Double check in your vehicles, let's have a look in your trunk, Murmur," insisted Tom.

Murmur said "OKAY," and whipped out a round trunk key on his keychain. He swiftly inserted the key and turned it to the right, popping open the trunk lid. There was nothing inside except a tire iron, a jack, and a spare. "How do you like my GM spatter paint? Just like the original." "Groovy," Deere exclaimed. "Very clean," added Tom. "Far out," marveled Fred. "Check out my van," said Fred, inviting them over. Fred opened the back doors, and they all looked inside. There was a can of carburetor cleaner, some paint cans, and a few very high-end home stereo speakers. "Now you see why I try to keep it locked when I go anywhere." Some neat posters were hanging on the side walls and a little mattress. No bee killer. Tom complimented him on the van, "Neato!" He said, "Thank you very much!"

Deere decided to show off his bus next, "Hey check it out, dudes! I got a real collector's item here! It's a 1962 VW Microbus Deluxe USA model! You can all fit inside." They got in the side and closed the door. "Roomy!" "Wow! Super cool! Great color scheme." "Righteous, Man!" Deere

said, "Glad you like it. Dig these sounds!" He played all his Chocolate Watchband albums for them really loud over the car stereo system. He passed around some joints and offered the rest of his flask of whiskey. When they finally got out, Tom showed them his Orange Cougar, they opened the hood and trunk and sat inside, played the radio a bit, he played the 13th Floor Elevators including Kingdom of Heaven.

Tom said, "Well, guys, it's been fun, but I really got to get going. I have a lot of things to do." Murmur intuitively knew he didn't really. But he was parked right in front of Tom, so he said, "Hey but check out my GSX," He opened the hood and showed Tom the motor. "I put in the 455, added Stage 2 aftermarket heads, and updated to the dual exhaust." Tom had heard about them, having a classic muscle car himself. "Only 678 cars were built in 1970 and 44 in 1972. But you'd be better off with the 1970, it's faster, this was right before they started tightening up on the emissions standards by the next year."

"I know but I only paid 300 dollars when I lucked out and found this, just had to find the original air-scoop hood. Then swap out the 350 cubic inch motor for the 455 V8 with 510-foot pounds of torque at 2,800 rpm. I changed the bumper, and quarter panels, and put a new top on it. Repainted it with the original color." He opened up the door, unfastened the top, and had them all climb in. "I reupholstered the seats, I tried to add more speakers, but long story short, it didn't work, so I just settled on putting the original ones back in with this updated CD player stereo. Check out this CD." He put in The Byrds' Notorious Byrd Brothers CD.

Then Tom said "Fire it up, take it down the road. Show us how fast it goes."

"Okay," said Murmur. He pulled around to the road on the horseshoe-shaped driveway. "Sounds great," shouted Tom from the passenger seat. "Yeah, Flow Master mufflers. I like them better than Thrush Cherry Bombs." They turned right and then turned left on to the next road. The GSX turned around at Graphite Sales, and Murmur stopped momentarily to put in a new song, "Listen to this," he played Shakin' Street by the MC5. He drove back out to 224 and this time went west. He opened it up about as fast as he could go. The speedometer was buried beyond its limit of 160. Soon he came up to another vehicle, a semi-truck, and slowed down behind it. He signaled and turned left into a driveway, where he changed the music to Another Side of This Life, by The Youngbloods. He looked both ways and backed out onto 224 to go east. Again, he zoomed down the road at speeds above 160, slowing down for the railroad track and passing a couple of cars. He blasted his train air horn, which was about 160 decibels. He turned left into another driveway saying, "Check it out." He played the Heartsfield song House of Living. He headed back to the hideous house. Soon they turned back into the driveway. He said, "Check this out," and played The Remains song, Don't Look Back.

Now that the Buick was at the end of the line of vehicles, they could all start their engines and go about their merry way. "Look at all this land," Murmur exclaimed. "You know my dream is to live off the land, have a place of my own with a decent amount of property, 20 or more acres. Small farm. A smart home, but that for me means

fireproof, energy self-sufficient, everything I need right there, and a good woman to make the house a home." Deere mentioned that the idea sounded like the movie of Steinbeck's book, Of Mice and Men. "I like to invest in properties, I make all kinds of money out east," said Fred.

Murmur remembered something, "Another old farmhouse is at 1624 OH-4 between Bellevue and Attica Ohio, next to the burgh of Reedtown, with the Reedtown tavern. Also boarded up. 2112 square foot, with 3 bedrooms. I can't get in it though. It's out in the open, and it's not for sale. The farmer who built it was abusive to his new wife, and she hung herself in the basement after their baby unexpectedly died. He boarded it up immediately and left it vacant ever since then." Everyone had blank faces. "Yeah, try not to choose a house that's haunted like this one. That would be a good idea," one of them said. "Haunted?" Murmur gave a quizzical look. "Didn't notice anything strange here about this house?" Tom asked. "I don't know what you're talking about," Murmur sighed. He contemplated it and then told them, "I can't be haunted." At this Tom turned away saying, "See you around." Then Deere shrugged, "I guess I'll be on my way too." Then Fred hollered, "See you, bros! Take it easy. Later. I'm out." Murmur responded, "call me if you need anything. You got my card, Bye yo!"

Everybody got in their cars. Tom turned the key in his ignition, but nothing happened. "What the what?" Deere tried to crank up the bus's motor but was met with silence from the machinery. "Dag Nab it!" Fred tried to crank his van, but the starter did nothing. "Son of a mother." They got out

angrily and stared at Murmur who was waiting for them to move. "What's going on? Go!" "We can't go. Our batteries are dead, what did you do to our vehicles?" "I didn't do anything." Tom opened Murmur's door saying, "You wanna fight?" Fred came up saying, "yours is the only one that's not having any problems, why is that?" Deere ran up, "My bus has never had these problems until I brought it here! It's flawless." "Yeah, you fix it or else!" "Yeah!"

"Okay, dudes. I think I know what your problem is," Murmur said stepping out and holding his head high. He had a black Bible in his hand that had been given to him for free, from the glove compartment. "Follow me…" He walked slowly up to the front of the Cougar. "Place your hand on your car, bow your head and close your eyes. Evil spirits, be gone out of this car. Now! In the holy name of Jesus! Father, bless this car for the man." He did the same for the other two, and then told them to be on their way. He turned and hopped back in the GSX, and waited, staring back at them. "Well, what are you waiting for?" He motioned them to go. They each went back to their vehicles and tried them, one at a time. The Cougar started. The bus started. The van started. They drove them back out to the road. Tom turned left, he wanted to continue going north because he was from the South, but first he needed some gasoline. Deere turned right because he wanted to continue to go east, but he needed to find a gas station. Fred wanted to go further west so he turned left, hoping to find a gas station.

As Murmur drove away from the hideous house, he still had some gas and he wanted to go down to Florida, where Tom was from, but he

needed more money first. He went to Toledo, looking for houses to flip.

Finally, he found a house on 934 Rogers Street and came up with some money to buy it from friends nearby. He met a beautiful young stripper in a club named Summer Storm. They hung out and watched movies at the house, and she agreed to marry him. Then, he fixed it up in a few months and flipped it. He was about to buy another home there and flip it again, but she wanted to move closer to her parents in Bellevue, Ohio, part of the Firelands[3].

They got married in 2000 and rented an old farmhouse, on the corner of Knauss Road and 269. Murmur went ahead and got a CDL-A from Trainco Truck Driving School in Monroe, Michigan. While waiting to break into trucking without sufficient experience, he worked at menial jobs. He'd tell her jokingly, "I'm going to play you like I play my guitar." One day when he was working at a plastics factory, before break he texted Summer to tell her what he would like dropped off for lunch. "Pizza me," he suggested. Outside it was light rain. About 45 minutes later she texted back, "I Pizza'd you!" He went out to the car to get it. He devoured the pizza and listened to Rush's *The Camera Eye*. "They seemed oblivious to a soft spring rain. Like an English rain," as the intermittent wipers cleared the windshield.

He found a house on Freedom Street in Toledo he wanted to flip. He went to go look at it with the seller's real estate agents. It had an upper floor but when going to the basement, there was no

---

[3] https://lymevillage.org/history-of-the-firelands/

furnace. The agent lady explained it hadn't ever had a furnace installed when it was built. Former owners just used space heaters during the winter, one would presume. They needed to have one installed before closing. They wanted Murmur to get a cheap used furnace and install it himself ASAP. Meanwhile, she pressured him for "good faith money," to show his determination to buy it. And by the way, since it never had a furnace before, it would need a minimal number of vents and ductwork. Luckily, he had friends, R. Milner, who was a builder, and C. Tucker, who had been into real estate investing, who advised him not to do it. Needless to say, he never gave her any "good faith money."

The neighbors' house caught on fire while they were away on vacation, and the fire trucks came to put it out. They left afterward, but it caught on fire again the next evening. Summer cried like a river over it asking how bad things can happen to good people, and how a just God, if there is a God, could allow it to happen to them. Murmur tried to explain it, but she still didn't understand. Murmur read about a little girl who got run over while riding on a bicycle and died. He disagreed with some people who said, "Everything happens for a reason," telling them, "Sometimes just bad things happen." Later, when an annoying guy called Barley came over for a bonfire, he said about Summer being promiscuous, "You know, everything happens for a reason." Murmur punched him in the face, saying, "What about *that*, did *that* happen for a reason?"

Summer Storm was somewhat of a floozy, although Murmur did not know this for almost three

years. Later on, at the end of 2003, when Summer had left him to stay at her parents' house (exactly 3 years married), they kept acting like it was normal for her to be "carousing and perusing."

He found a used paperback copy of L. Frank Baum's The Wonderful Wizard of Oz. Several tornados were swirling around northern and central Ohio, as he read alone, in the upstairs of the farmhouse with his little dog, Felicity, who would hide under the bed.

Tom called on the phone one evening to check up on Murmur, they talked about how George Harrison had died at the young age of 58, on November 29th, 2001, shortly after the 9/11 terrorist attack. Then John Entwistle, bassist of the Who passed away of an apparent heart attack at the young age of 57, on June 27th, 2002. Murmur expressed his sadness, while Tom thought the remaining members of both groups should get together and form a new band called "The Whootles." Murmur agreed that would be a good idea, saying he'd pray for them.

"I thought a lot lately about getting the guys together and forming a band," said Murmur. "Have you heard anything from the other two guys? You know, Fred and Deere?" asked Tom. "Not at all," responded Murmur. "You're the first of the guys to call me. By the way, what made *you* call?" Tom replied to him, "Well, you know I've been going up to my cabin in Northern Michigan, and then the rest of the time I've been down in Tampa, and you're not going to believe it, buddy! I've found you a nice 1970 GSX like we talked about. The interior needs some work, but the body is clean. I've been trying to negotiate the price with the owner, but I don't

know what you can afford." "Cool! Sounds groovy, man! I'll talk to the guy and see what I can do. I need to come up with some more money. Maybe I can sell some stuff to the guys. I'll pray for them to call me." "Yeah, man! So, you're a born-again Christian?" Tom asked. "Yeah, man! You?" "Yep, I gave my heart to the Lord recently," exclaimed Tom. "Far out, brother, I can dig that," Murmur smiled through the phone. He was in a good mood. He had just drunk some peach moonshine.

Chapter Three, Cultic Studies:

The wind pushed inward through the cracks around the edges of the windows in the old farmhouse against the 3M plastic window insulator kits, making them stretch out almost like a clear convex bubble. The air escaping from the perimeter at the gap in the tape made a sound like air escaping from the mouth of a balloon, not unlike a 'whoopie cushion.' Murmur used a heating pad down by his feet to hibernate in the cold late fall weather.

He decided to return to college after the divorce. He had been majoring in Psychology. He signed up for admissions and started to attend Terra State College, in Fremont, Ohio. At this time, they only had one distance learning class over the internet, critical thinking. One day the class was discussing terrorism on the web portal. Either one of the students or the professor in the chatroom defended al-Qaeda as if it were a man named Al. "They ought to leave him alone! What has he done to anyone?"

He was able to go to some night classes on campus. Going through the corridors and upstairs hallways between classes in the evening, he viewed a painting of a windstorm as it was beginning to rain with dark clouds in the sky, as a man in the distance was trying to make his way against the wind in an amber field of grain. He got close to meeting some women at college, but they didn't care for him, with his long greasy hair and slightly ugly appearance. In the classroom for public speaking, he tried to sit next to a hot young lady who was seated all by herself, but the professor kept

asking him to move over a few seats. He said in case any "flailing of the arms," during tests and quizzes should warrant more elbow room. Murmur knew the professor was jealous. The professor asked about how he could get into truck driving, because he either didn't enjoy teaching anymore or didn't make enough money there. "It's not rocket science, but it's something I can do," Murmur explained humbly.

Times got rougher and Murmur sold his GSX, buying a yellowish 1978 Camaro and then sold it and bought a 1976 Buick Regal, and finally selling that to buy a blue 1986 Mustang. He had to sell that one because it kept breaking down, buying a newer car instead. He sold the stick-shift Mustang to a one-armed lady whose shifting arm had to be the left one, as it had always broken down just as he was arriving at school at The University of Toledo, ran across the parking lot, inside, up the stairs, out of breath into the classroom, late, after work, with everybody staring.

He was able to graduate with an associate degree in social and behavioral sciences. Then so that he didn't have to pay student loans back, he enrolled in Heidelberg University which is based in Tiffin, Ohio, but had an Arrowhead Parkway campus in Maumee, Ohio. Later at Arrowhead Parkway Maumee, one evening in the newer car, he walked out into the dark parking lot in the pouring rain. He had locked his keys in the car and was attempting to open it by himself with a coat hanger. It took about an hour and a half. They had him take as diverse of classes as Classical Music. He had taken Political Science, Philosophy, and Geology. He met a pretty, brown-eyed brunette named Bryn

Dimpleton in Tiffin Ohio at his graduation. Therefore, he had an in-school deferment. The location closed in 2015,[4] well after he already had his bachelor's degree in psychology.

He had finally started getting some experience in the trucking field, first with a straight truck, and later on with a semi-tractor-trailer, delivering agricultural products seasonally. Later there were more permanent jobs. In the meantime, his prayers for help were answered when Fred called and asked him what he'd been up to. Murmur told him about the divorce, jobs, career, and money troubles. "Well, I would be happy to help you out a bit financially. I've been wheeling and dealing. I made quite a lot of money in the stock market and got a lot of returns on my investments. Whatever you need, bro. I just remember how much you inspired me when I was out there. You seemed to have a good relationship with the Lord. You love Jesus, man. I'd like to draw closer myself. You have peace of mind. Confidence. I want that!" Fred laughed with a heartfelt sense of jolliness. Murmur chuckled joyously. "Yeah, come on out here. I'd like to get a band together if you can play any instruments. I heard from Tom too! You remember Tom, don't you? Here's my latest address..."

A few hours later that day, Deere texted and then called Murmur. "Hey Dude, you want to get together and smoke some pot? I got some hydroponics greenhouses set up."

---

[4] https://www.toledoblade.com/education/2013/12/11/Heidelberg-to-close-Maumee-campus-in-15/stories/

"Sure, you want to be in a band? Can you play any instruments?"

"Yeah, Dude. I can play the vibraphone, marimba, xylophone, hammered dulcimer, autoharp, piano keyboards, stuff like that."

"Can you play drums?"

Deere hesitated for a moment. "I don't know. Maybe you can show me."

It was sometime around the end of 2004, the day they were scheduled to arrive in town around 1:00 in the afternoon, Murmur was out in his car in the backyard drive. It was a fully restored 1968 aquamarine Dodge Polara with a mural of a polar bear sitting on an iceberg on each side. He did the work himself. It had lowrider rims from a shop in Detroit and an air suspension. Not bad for a car shaped like a cracker box. The three vehicles pulled into the gravel parking area to the left of him. Deere smiled as he got out and was followed by Tom and Fred.

"You guys hungry? Let's go get some lunch first," said Fred, "What's good around here?" "Food," said Murmur. "Food? I remember food," quipped Tom. "*Wish I* had some food," frowned Deere. "Hop in the car." Murmur drove the Polara into town to a sports bar. On the way, he turned on the radio.

A voice was saying, "104.7 WIOT."

[*Bed springs squeaking and the sounds of lovers*]

"Deeper"

"Harder"

"Faster"

"Stronger"

"MUSIC!"

Army people were heard marching and chanting (repeating what the drill sergeant called out), "I don't know but I've been told…Big leg woman ain't got no soul… sound off," a Led Zeppelin song snippet with the lyrics echoed their famous phrase.

"Toledo's Rock Station," the commercial concluded.

"Wow! You get that station way out here?" asked Tom.

"Yeah, I have a really good antenna," replied Murmur.

The radio played some modern rock. Candlebox. Jet. Velvet Revolver. Audioslave. Then they were there. The Polara slowly turned and purred like a fine-tuned kitten as it slunk into the parking spot of the busy parking lot.

In the sports bar, he had a bunch of friends there, and some sexy gals gathered around. One asked about what he did for a career. "I'm a big-truck driver, 53-foot trailers, which means I'm an expert at fitting long things into tight spaces. In my spare time, I like to make my porno films." Tom overheard and said, "That's not very Christian of you." Murmur explained, "Nobody watches them except me and the women." Later he talked to the guys a little more about the spirituality of driving. "Big Old John down in Tennessee warned me back in the day not to get into trucking, but I didn't listen. Driving a truck relaxes me so much as I get bored and start to doze off. I worked for the agriculture place and was heading back on Route 6 in western Ohio and saw a billboard, maybe on the other side of Ridgeville Corners, and the way I was driving I saw a billboard on the left, for a church

saying, 'God will send His angels to protect you wherever you may go.' It had a painting of a beautiful angel with wings and a horn, amid a blue backdrop. Just after that was an accident on the left side where a big truck went off-road striking a tree dead on in someone's front yard. The driver didn't see that sign yet, see? I've been protected ever since." Deere said, "*Must be nice*, to have God's protection."

Tom had a few drinks and said, "Hmm…Jesus drank wine, so I feel fine. It's okay to drink in moderation, he just didn't drink enough to get drunk. He set the example not to be a drunkard." The sports bar was closing so Fred paid the bill, and they went back to the house along the backroads. Murmur mixed some drinks back in the kitchen. "Murmur, I have been meaning to ask some questions you might have the answer to," Fred said. "Okay." "What is the meaning of life?" "To have a good time!" Tom quickly butted in, "It's supposed to be to serve and obey Jesus." Murmur reacted, "But Jesus' meaning, or purpose, is also to have a good time, is it not?" Tom rubbed his chin, "Yeah, God's good pleasure."

"Well, for the greater good of everyone, the Bible says many times things like 'Rejoice in the Lord always, again I say rejoice,' and the one ruler who would be like a philosopher King or a sun King would be Jesus. Jesus is the answer, He will fix everything. God is a happy God."

"Right," Tom said.

"Wish *I* could rejoice," said Deere. "*I* want peace, man."

"And you can," smiled Murmur. "We'll help you."

Fred said, "I've been so caught up in making more money, but there are things, you know, that money can't buy too."

Tom said, "yeah but it *can* buy like hookers… or lauding women with gifts can get their attention and later win their heart, in effect buying love, and that makes *me* happy."

"As long as they don't have V.D. man," added Deere.

"Yeah, of course!"

"I know, right?!? The happiest I ever was, was while I was married, and while we had the most money to pay off bills, I was happy that I didn't have to worry about money, being broke, or having a mountain of debt. Felt like the weight of the world was lifted off our shoulders," revealed Murmur.

Tom's eyes lit up like a Christmas tree. "Like in the Bible where Jesus talks about a mountain being cast into the sea if you have so much as a mustard seed size faith."

"Yeppers!" yelled Murmur.

"I got some pot here man," said Deere. "Like, you know, Cheech and Chong. You remember those dudes, right? They were funny comedians, but they knew how to keep it real, you know?"

"Exactly," laughed Murmur.

Tom said he thought it was okay to smoke weed, God made it. He just doesn't want you to get so high. It's not a 'gateway drug.'

"What you got: Indica or Sativa?"

"Yes"

"Never mind"

"Let's smoke it," said Fred. "How much do you want for it?"

"I grow my own, so… $150?" He held up the large freezer bag of marijuana buds.

"$100?"

"I could go 125, but that's super-cheap for weed, man, especially of this quality, but since you're my friends…"

"Deal." Fred whipped out a roll of cash from his pocket. "WOW, you're loaded, man." "Sure, I can teach you about how to make money. You know like Rich Dad, Poor Dad author Robert Kiyosaki. You can give a man a fish and feed him for a day or teach a man to fish and feed him a lifetime, just like Jesus."

"Or you know, a woman," added Tom.

"Yeah, he was fond of men," stated Murmur. "His creation, after all."

"And women," added Tom.

"Right," agreed Murmur.

"Yeah, you know *a hundred pounds of clay*[5] and *He made my life worth living*. And *I'm going to thank him every day*, that's a song you know," grinned Deere.

"What instruments can you play, Fred?"

"I can play kazoo, tambourine, triangle, maracas, castanets, cymbals, and the jaw harp."

Garden by the Groundhogs was playing on the stereo system in the other room, Murmur was showing them some of his guitars. "See what you can do with this candy-apple red Mexican Stratocaster." He gingerly handed the beautiful guitar over to Fred.

---

[5] McDaniels, Gene (2007). BGO Records. On *Hundred Pounds of Clay / Tower of Strength*

Twang, twang, twang, buzz… "wait…" *twankity, tewang, thwang, buzz…* "wait…"

"I thought all hippies were supposed to be good at playing rock music," Tom sighed.

"It's okay, I can teach you a few chords or you can learn to play something else," Murmur assured Fred. Murmur played some awesome guitar licks, chops, and riffs. When he was done, he very carefully took the strap off his neck, placing the guitar down on the stand near the other ones. "Would y'all like some more libations?" He poured out some wine from a bottle into his unique-looking crystal goblet, it had pewter-looking material molded into the stem.

"What's that on the stem of your glass?" asked Deere.

"I make artwork out of all my mistakes," replied Murmur. "It's a genuine crystal glass bought for our wedding, housewarming gift. It costs about $45 per piece. I was pouring a bunch of alcoholic drinks out on the counter, and the adult beverage poured out too fast knocking this over and breaking the stem. So, I could get another one from replacements.com but I saved this too and mended it with J.B. Weld." He sipped and looked at Tom, "Your turn, Tom."

Tom picked up a red Gibson SG and played House of the Rising Sun, Day Tripper, Paperback Writer, Don't Fear the Reaper and Godzilla, Working Man, Iron Man, Proud Mary, Communication Breakdown, Train Kept a Rollin' and California Sun. "Okay that's enough, you pass the audition," chuckled Murmur. "Let Deere have a go." Fred and Tom were standing too close and smelled something awful, that nearly made Fred

throw up. They were coughing. Tom was coughing enough to make a blood vessel burst in his eye. "Ugh! Was that an SBD?" Deere had been trying to hold gas in his intestines all night. "YOU!" Fred pointed. "Sorry."

He walked to the only bass guitar in the room and picked it up off the stand. "I can play this if you'd like," he said to quickly change the subject. He played a few hypnotic bass lines they'd never heard before. "Good, you're hired," stated Murmur.

"You mean I'm in the band?!?!? Awesome!"

"There you go, man! Now your whole countenance has changed! It's positive! That is what I like to see. I've never seen you smile before. Why are you always so glum?"

"Well, it's just…I don't know, I just wanted to be part of something larger than myself. Something big. Something epic. I want to be at one with the universe. I'm part of the universe but to be one with the universe, you know. I want world peace. I've tried to find the Grand Creator of the Universe, Prime Mover, God Almighty. I've looked into the various religions of the world, but especially Christianity. I've been in touch with Catholics and talked to Jehovah's Witnesses. Many denominations, Mormons, everything. I tried to see things from both sides, an Openminded approach."

"Very good," answered Murmur. "I too have had moments of oneness with God. I call them Wow-God moments, they're like epiphanies when God tells me something and it changes my life a little more, in a good way."

"Exactly!" Deere replied slowly. "And I want to be spiritual, not necessarily religious. Religion is like a man-made answer. Everyone has

their own idea about the origin of man or philosophy about life they develop anyway. So why listen to organized religion? It's like politics in the establishment. It's just someone's idea how everything else should be run. Mankind dominating over man to his injury. Factions and special interests are always trying to influence everything else and adopt their own ideas so that we're sheep following their leadership in an endless competition for power over others. We don't want to be followers of fashions, no, we would rather be leaders of gangs, trendsetters, celebrities, famous people, somebody special, not a simpleton, not a nobody, not a peasant, but rather a king or VIP."

"Right," injected Murmur, "we want recognition. We want everybody to notice us. Everyone should love us and if we're popular, everyone will love us. We'll be well-liked and well loved."

Fred and Tom were cozy by the space heater with fleece blankets wrapped around them each and covering their toes and keeping their feet warm. They appeared to be falling asleep. "So," Deere continued, "Catholicism is very well organized and is part of the establishment. They're the far right if anything is considered far right. People rebel against the strict authoritarian priests and nuns in the huge churches, catechism, catholic schools, and such that pervades and permeates throughout society, from the past history in which they pride themselves linking lineage with the first century of the church associated with Jesus and apostles. Giving us bad experiences with the Crusades, Spanish Inquisition, all the way up through 1500 when many thought the end of the world would

happen, but it still didn't, to the unholy molestation of altar boys by malevolent priests. Maybe they originally wanted to show they were in it for the right reasons, but because they had bad inclinations, bad motivations for working closer to the objects of their sinister desires, like bullies who turn into cops, which end up as the bad cops, people are able to generalize that most or even all priests, and cops, are bad."

"People develop a confirmation bias," added Murmur, using active listening.

"Anyway," continued Deere, "the religion is so rigid, full of rituals, rites, dogma, rules people have to follow to show they are followers of Christ; to show they are good people. People follow because they feel they have to, but not because they want to for the love of God. They need to feel the love for God, have a personal relationship with God, not do everything out of a sense of obligation, like in Islam for example. And as far as money…"

"Money's my bag, man!" Fred piped in suddenly.

"We noticed," said Tom, showing he was still paying attention.

"…goes, the obligatory tithes and offerings don't seem to buy their way to heaven or keep them out of hell, unless they are a cheerful giver and give from the heart. They have to do it willingly because they want to give it, not because they feel they have to pay it," continued Deere.

"Like Stairway to Heaven, man!"

"Yes, and when I was hanging out with those Jehovah's Witnesses, they were like, 'Naw, man, you ain't gotta give no tithes, that's a myth. We never ask for tithes during the service, you

know, the bible study, talks, Watchtower magazine study, or theocratic ministry school. Everyone simply gives whatever they want, whenever they want to, in the donation box in the lobby, without all the recognition or expecting eyes glaring at you to make a showy display of your obedience.' That seemed so much different from the Catholic church, and other…well they call everyone else in Christianity—Christendom, to differentiate themselves. So, I started noticing a lot of the things are opposite other religion's teaching, you know doctrine, so that they might differentiate themselves and separate themselves from others, who they call worldly. Um, words, even the word doctrine they never use for describing themselves, suggesting that all doctrine is false doctrine, but it just means church stance and teaching, like on the subject of predestination."

"Yeah, man," Murmur interjected, "I've come to the understanding we each should give according to what it's worth for us for the church to help us worship, help us learn, fellowship, pray for each other and together as a group, and for it to be a beacon of light for the community."

"That's another word," Deere chimed back in again. "Jehovah's Witnesses don't use the word church when describing their kingdom hall. I know Jesus so loved the church. He didn't say He loves the Kingdom Hall. They don't use the word hymn that's in most bibles to describe their pathetic, dreary, and dismal little songs. They just don't bring the glory to God in the same way the Bible says David used wonderful, glorious music with all kinds of beautiful instruments, making a joyous noise to the Lord! Positive and upbeat music! I used to feel

like I had to drag myself to go there every meeting, sitting through an arduous, tedious two hours on hard chairs, to be obedient to God, then afterwards I should feel better, but instead I felt the same, unfulfilled, empty, and cold inside."

"Because that is a performance-based religion," noted Murmur. "Their bibles are different too. The New World Translation, which I have referred to as NWT in my college essays. Made only for Witnesses, and only considered valid by the Witnesses or those who know them and approve of their ideas for the most part."

"Yeah, they don't use the word 'grace,' instead preferring 'loving kindness.' That is because they insist you need to do good works and not just have faith, to prove you are not a part of this world. But we are living in the world. Jesus so loved the world in John 3:16. The other denominations, which they don't consider themselves a denomination, they consider themselves 'the truth,' and the other branches of Christians by comparison must logically be telling a lie somewhere; you know, the truth, the whole truth, and nothing but the truth. True Religion. The Bible seems to contradict itself in many places so it's confusing to try to interpret."

"Now, hold on," Murmur ministered to him. "You have the more literal translations like the King James used by Baptists, to the more figurative or spiritual meaning like the Message Bible. Word for word, to thought for thought. Just because the Bible seems to contradict itself just means you have to try to understand the original intended meaning behind the word, considering the original language and context. Yes, we have to live within the world, but we don't have to be part of the world in another

sense because we aren't worldly. We have the Kingdom in our hearts for now until the Kingdom is indeed manifested throughout the entire earth like it is in heaven. Then you have God's perfect Kingdom, paradise on earth again, like Adam and Eve would've had, and many going to heaven too when they died to rule with Jesus. And if you didn't have anything on earth to rule over in a paradise-perfect condition, everyone would just be in heaven, on the other hand, you'd definitely need a wonderful place in heaven to go to, also. That's the restoration of God's original intention and perfect plan. People then will live forever in a perfect physical form, with spirit, and literally never die."

"Well, that's just it, isn't it? I've talked to Alexis VanDeVelde from the Catholic church each time I've had a question about Catholics. Also, Larry and others from the Jehovah's Witnesses' Hall don't believe in the cross, they believe it was a torture stake, they don't believe in holidays, they think they are all pagan, and they don't even really celebrate birthdays or Thanksgiving. I guess they think a national holiday to give thanks just one day out of the year is too worldly or something. Especially Christmas because they talk of its pagan origins, and they don't say the pledge of allegiance to the flag because it gives reverence to the country's government that they believe should be only reserved for God…and saluting someone. They think it's worldly to be patriotic."

"Yeah, and the Amish have a different idea of separating themselves from the world. They think cars, electricity, and more modern conveniences are too worldly," added Murmur. "Their buggies are only black because they wouldn't want others to

covet what they have, while Jehovah's Witnesses have nice shiny new Lincolns, Cadillacs, and other beautiful luxury automobiles. They wear suits and ties to look as neat for God as they can, yet usually your average businessman wears suit and tie. Aren't they worldly? Anyway, I've been looking on belief net comparing world religions and I read the Bible three times."

"That's what the Witnesses recommend doing anyway, but secondhand knowledge of course for the other religion, sometimes you just know better than to go into a cult, or a church of LDS, or Satanic Temple. That would be learning things the hard way. I have firsthand knowledge of Catholics and Jehovah's Witnesses taking them up on their invitations, sometimes. But, since they don't pester you for money, they draw you into involvement more and more expecting your every spare moment going door to door in ministry work, proselytizing others even when they are self-proclaimed Christians. They think you aren't going to make it at Judgement Day unless you are in the Jehovah's Witnesses, and even then, they are not totally sure they will make it unless they have enough zeal and follow all the rules! They quote scripture and say 'Broad and spacious is the road leading to destruction and many are the ones on it. Narrow and cramped is the road leading to salvation, and few are the ones finding it.' They point out that Catholics and others are on the broad and spacious road. They rarely if ever even crack open a Bible at church to make sure everything discussed is so."

"The Jehovah's Witnesses *are* broad and spacious," retorted Murmur. "They are increasing in popularity! I see their kingdom halls in about every

little town I drive through! If it were so easy, all they had to do was follow their directions and you'd be sure of salvation, it wouldn't be so difficult. You have to have a personal relationship with God through Jesus. That's why Jesus said many people who would come to Him on the last day would say, Lord, Lord, did we not cast out demons in your name etcetera? He would say something like, Get away from me you criminals! I never knew you. He has to know them personally; and have a personal relationship with you. He is a wonderful Counsellor and the Great Teacher. He set the great example of calling God, Father, Abba, or Daddy."

"They explain that God is a title, not His name, and many people don't know the tetragrammaton for YHWH which is Yahweh, and that is translated into English and other languages, which is why we say Jehovah. When you don't take the name of The Lord in vain, that's His name."

Murmur rubbed his chin as is the custom when somebody is thinking. "I read in the Bible Encyclopedia that originally Jewish people didn't want to say God's actual name for fear of blaspheming it, that is, the fear of displeasing Him, out of extreme awe and reverence for Him. It's highly disrespectful to call your mom or dad by their actual first name, or anything other than their title of mother or father. Jesus provides that closeness since the veil was torn. You never want to blaspheme the Holy Spirit either, Jesus said. That meaning was given by Jesus in the Bible when He explained the miracles that the Holy Spirit did; the Pharisees insulted God by attributing His power as coming from a demon."

"The Holy Spirit's just God's active force, they say, like God's finger. I suppose like EMF, electromotive force, or voltage. They don't use the words Trinity, or Rapture for that matter, and to be fair, they aren't biblical words, they're concepts developed by the Catholic Church or whatever, in later centuries based on interpretation of the texts," explained Deere. "They don't believe he died on a cross. They don't use that word; they believe it was a pole, a torture stake he was impaled on and that the cross is a pagan symbol for the false god Tammuz."

"But I've seen the actual crosses and nails they used in the Roman Empire to crucify people," Tom said. "If it was their custom, of course they would use a cross. The Bible doesn't make it clear if it was actually a cross or a stake or a tree."

"Cross or stake, whatever the case may be. Rapture or just an instance of select few like 144,000 Jewish remnant leaders, whatever the case may be, it's not worth arguing with others within the church, causing division or contention, causing public derision, but they think you have to go through the elite body of elders for all the decisions and answers. That's not having a relationship with God through Jesus, that's exactly what Catholics do wrong, thinking you have to go through a priest father." concluded Murmur.

"Actually, it seems Jehovah's Witnesses have made God's name a bad word. Like people might say, 'He became one of those Jehovahs.' Or 'what a bunch of Jehovahs,' which only shows their stupidity anyway. Whereas some music on Christian radio does use the name Jehovah occasionally, as well as many non-denominational

Christian churches mention it some too. They just don't understand because of the Trinity, and the terminology like Triune Godhead, that Jesus is the Son of God and not literally the same person as God. They are one in accord, opinion, and mindset just like man and woman becoming one flesh, and a married couple united in holy matrimony by God is a three-ply cord not easily undone."

Murmur's eyes lit up like a Christmas tree, as a smile slowly curved across his face. "Begins with a blessing, it ends with a curse. Making life easy by making it worse." He was referring to the song by Soft Machine[6]. "At first it seems to help you to understand the concept better, but then it makes it worse because of the many people, like Muslims who do not understand because they say God is One God, which is true. Then they shouldn't underestimate that Jesus is the only *begotten* son of God because everything else, spirit creatures and then the heavens and the earth is made by and for Him. The simplest explanation that makes the most sense is always the right--the correct one."

"So," continued Deere, "they don't believe in ghosts. They say they are demons."

"Of course!" said Murmur. "UFOs are demons. Except when there is an actual craft with an anti-gravity engine[7]. But the orbs of light are unclean spirits, and clearly not an actual craft. Anything dark and menacing that gives you a feeling or transmits thoughts telepathically, gives

---

[6] The Soft Machine. (1968). Why are we sleeping. On *Volumes One and Two*. Chas Chandler and Tom Wilson.

[7] Hoagland, R. C., & Bara, M. (2010). Dark mission. ; The secret history of NASA. Feral House.

you a foreboding sense of missing time, and generally bad vibes are like that. Cryptids. Cryptozoology is like that they originate with evil sources. God does not try to humiliate someone, corrupt them, or drive them mad with harassment until they want to kill themselves. That's the powers and principalities of darkness. You can tell the ones that seemingly defy physics and g-forces by zipping through the sky from a dead stop to incredible super-speeds and then diving right into the water. They never go out of our atmosphere and out into space."

"The Devil comes to steal kill and destroy, Jesus said," added Tom. "Jesus came so that we might have life more abundantly." He put his feet up closer to the heater to help keep them warm. Murmur put his socked feet up on a heating pad on the ottoman.

"I know that the Catholics cast out demons in Jesus' name and the name of the Father and the Holy Spirit. If there is something they don't understand about that, they just say that's a mystery we're not allowed to know yet," said Deere.

"I know there are people out there who would spend all the money they had to find out the answer to some of these mysteries," confided Fred, as he rubbed his hands together.

"Eh, well, a house divided upon itself cannot stand. If they are doing it for real and not just collaborating with the demons and they then come back and keep doing it, they're doing a good work," answered Murmur.

"I'm content not knowing everything there is to know. And seeing how it turns out. It's more of a pleasant surprise when it does work out. It

sometimes turns out even better than expected. But there are some things I just do *not* want to know. You know it? Like people can know too much," said Fred. "Like the 9/11 attacks we had in New York. That was so traumatic for me. At first, I was thinking, *this is it…The end of the world. Armageddon!* People were jumping. They were taking control of their destiny and dying in a different way than a fiery suffocating crushing and horrible death, something quicker and more spectacularly visible. The news reports are so negative, you just need to hear more positive stories. The terrorists are now fighting us within our own country. They infiltrate and get on our planes with simple tools like boxcutter knives and threaten and cause commotion and distraction to hijack and people are frightened because of the confusion. They don't know what is going to happen next. The fear of the unknown. I think that is what is so frightening about mental illness and troubles with wicked, evil people. The chaos. You just don't know what they are going to do next."

"Yeah man," said Deere, "I am so tired. But anyway, you can see the way the establishment wants this all to go. The CCP for example is learning to read our thoughts. The government wants everyone to go to a cashless worldwide currency. They are colluding with evil spirits, aliens, and dark forces, to get advanced technology to control the human race. They want us to have a subcutaneous chip implant to get people to pay for all goods and services. This might be included with the mark of the Beast. The Witnesses believe this Beast is government by man, the Harlot being false religion. They believe many of the people living

now can live forever because death with be eliminated literally in a literal worldwide Paradise on earth within the new Kingdom. Therefore, they believe in the immortality of people as originally intended in the Garden of Eden, but not the immortality of the soul. They think the soul is the same thing as the spirit in us as described by other religions, and that it's just the entire living being such as when animals are called souls. But then when people are dead, they are still conscious of nothing at all, which is consistent with sleep."

"Sure, they rest in peace," Murmur reacted. "Jesus said they were just sleeping. If they are resting in the grave, or heaven, they will be woken up and their spirit will go back to a living body again."

"If their body has completely decomposed after more than three days or longer, God has his Holy Spirit suddenly reassemble all the dirt basically into a brand new body again, like the dry bones in the valley." Deere yawned and stretched immensely. "But if there is no immortality of the spirit or soul, they cease to exist, and according to the Witnesses, they are snuffed out like a flame on a candle. That is not at all the same as sleeping as Jesus described." It would be a few years until Deere saw the movie 9, which was about as depressing as Watership Down. "The other Christian religions say you are still alive as spirit and go to heaven or hell, Catholics have a purgatory, but if you are alive only in God's memory, you come back as a cloned body, with all the memory, wisdom, and data reprogrammed into this new creature who lives on, like an identical son

who has learned all the same things, nature and nurture. That's not the same person."

"Wisdom is the practical application of knowledge," noted Murmur. "Witnesses believe that hell is just the common grave, not a place of perpetual torment. But a fiery hell, an abyss or lake of fire maybe, would be necessary for the evil spirit creatures and those who went against God, who seemingly live forever, despite having sin, which is just messing up and going against God, not something enticing and fun. God made everything originally needed for perfect bliss, so it has gotten very inaccurate connotations in pop culture. People were calling supposedly extremely good–bad, and bad–good. Like wicked or sick. But the Bible says that unclean spirits do sin. They do displease God, and rebel.

"But the other option is like the 'essential saltes' mentioned in The Case of Charles Dexter Ward, by H.P. Lovecraft, down in the catacombs searching for answers to secrets about life and death. The opposition tries to decipher clues to all life's problems by using alchemy and lost forgotten, archaic sciences, black magic (which presumes there is a white magic that is harmless and benign also), spiritism, and such. Clearly, there are secrets not divulged by God to Satan and the demons. They don't know how to build everything; they are still figuring it out. God is unlimited, evil spirits are limited. God is infinite."

"Cool." Murmur straightened up in his seat.

"But I've been depressed because some of the things seem correct. I'm not really sure if we have that hope for our future and our lost loved ones. I don't really want to be sitting up in a boring

cloud area for eternity, either. I want to live forever in paradise earth in a perfect body, but I don't want the Witnesses to be right about everything they are saying."

"The Witnesses are a cult, man! Just like the dang Mormons. Just like Scientology. True religion is one God gives you, through Jesus, a personal Lord and Savior," Tom explained.

"I don't follow your reasoning," Deere said.

"I've been on Wikipedia, read books and stuff, researching," said Tom, "as I am sure Murmur has." He extended his hand over toward him to gesture as Murmur nodded. "Cults have charismatic leaders, Jehovah's Witnesses had Charles Taze Russell, and then Rutherford. Then others according to the Catholics anyway, that I wasn't even aware of. The Mormons had Joseph Smith and then Brigham Young. Scientology had as its founder, inventor even, L. Ron Hubbard, then David Miscavige."

"Wait, I've got one," chimed Murmur. "The church of Scientology founder was originally named Moe. But he had to change it," he talked in a Southern hillbilly-type affect. "Everyone kept saying just lookit that thar Moe-ron Hubbard! Get it? Well, I thought it was funny…yeah, I know his name was Lafayette. HAHAHA! He always had that goony-lipped sneer. Looked so ugly as many evil people do. They often have bad breath, and don't take a shower because they love uncleanliness. Catholics don't believe in Armageddon, they excommunicate you, Mormons and Amish shun you, Witnesses disfellowship you, and with Scientology, you are blown."

"It's like Young Goodman Brown. They picture a community like the Lottery by Shirley Jackson. Or some negative utopia, which is someone else's idea of a utopia. We live in an oligarchy," figured Tom. "That's what both sides are rebelling against. If you rebel against organized religion as a part of the failure of mankind and the accepted establishment, then they see Christianity and in turn Jesus, as just another idea that keeps us all down. We want to rise above all that. Nobody has been able to do that yet. Except maybe a few Christians who really do have a personal relationship with God. That's what I saw in Murmur here. I saw the real deal. Not right away of course, but I examined life some more… an unexamined life is not worth living. Not that we should kill ourselves, but it takes some examining to give life meaning. I saw I needed more meaning in my life. Christians like us feel at one with the universe. Like we know something that hardly anyone else can understand. If a tree falls in the forest and no one else around hears it, does it make a sound?"

"Of course, it makes the same crashing sound it always makes with the sound waves going out," answered Murmur. "It doesn't say 'Oh! No one is around to hear me; I better not make a sound!' hahaha!" He hopped around exaggeratedly as animatedly as possible, waving his arms like tree limbs to make a special point. "And if there were ever a big clock in the sky, it would measure a thing we called time whether we observed it or not because this thing we call time is a measurement of conscious activity, physical action, or some sort of interaction with another entity. People have used it as a noun. It is a verb, an action you know.

Measuring an action is an action. We can't control time because it's not a *thing* you can control. Then you can't go back in time because doing so would require every little change, every single action to be *un*done. That's too much work for any machine or device. God doesn't want to go back in time. He once held everything else in place in the present so there would be a few more hours for a war on earth to be won. It's in the Bible; imagine some shadow similar to a sundial shadow staying in the same spot all afternoon. You can go forward in time. Its dimensions: length, width, and height, are three dimensions, and as far as measurement, time in which everything can undergo change. You can't really undo it because it's already been done. If you change it back to the original it takes even more time to change back because you've now progressed to the future, just for trying. The fifth dimension is the action of the mind. It's a mental measurement of some sort of mental activity."

"Yeah," Tom mused, "God instead turns the tables on whatever the wicked one does. He is turning everything for the better of those that love Him, for the good. The greater good. But sometimes it seems like there's another dimension, another astral plane God and spirits live in. Sort of like a parallel universe we can't see. We can't see wind, yet it moves the trees, and there is a force to it. The spirits might be made of smaller size particles we just do not see. Or if we do see, it's like fire, heat energy. Quantum physics is concerned with the very, very small, and the vast and huge out in space. The truth will set us free. Jesus is the way, the truth, and the light."

"Yeah, man! Groovy. Way to go. Far out!" Deere fancied, "I get the help from God-given drugs that help us find the dimensions in our mind! The Fifth Dimension is so cool. Timothy Leary was right. Tune into God, turn onto what's happening, drop out of big stupid and expensive, worthless colleges."

"Point taken," said Murmur.

"Money helps buy all the resources that we need, man. All you need is cash like the Rutles sang," was Fred's takeaway. "It can even help us buy drugs for your enlightenment," he pointed to Deere. "The Rutles remind me of the Beatles in an alternate universe or dimension."

"I love making love to all the beautiful women I can get my hands on, and if I could find the ultimate woman for me, who God made just for me, I'd marry her. She'd be my soulmate. We'd fit together like two pieces of a jigsaw puzzle. We'd be inseparable. We'd have been predestined for each other. Preordained. We'd have a holy union, a religious experience like a three-ply cord, God approves of. Not like the Kama Sutra or anything…He'd make a new life through us, and we'd have a baby." It seemed reminiscent of Flo and Eddie's Keep it Warm.

"Awesome…" Murmur was falling asleep.

"Hey what's your vice, man?" Murmur didn't open his eyes to see who said this.

"I have no vice."

"What's your motivation?"

"Hey, where we going to sleep, man? Hello? Yo!"

"Wherever you want, sleep right there for all I care. See you in the morning. Goodnight."

"Goodnight."

"Goodnight."

"Nitey-night."

Deere switched out the light. "We'll talk in the morning."

When the daylight started to peek through the windows, Murmur leaped into the air and said, "Hey! What are you creeps still doing here?" He ran down the steps. "What happened? I really can't remember! What is going on???"

"He's lost it, man," Tom shouted to Deere. "What did you give him?"

"I didn't give him anything other than you guys got, man! Just a little weed, I grew that myself, and he drank some alcohol and stuff. Not my fault, dude!"

Murmur was running around downstairs like a chicken with his head cut off, growling, shaking his limbs, he did a couple of summersaults and backflips. He jumped up and punched a hole in the ceiling. He crowed like a rooster and screamed, "WAKE UP! With God everything is possible. I can do all things through Christ who strengthens me. I will be an unstoppable force! Hallelujah! Praise the Lord! Carpe Diem!"

Murmur ran down to the Polara and drove away at a high rate of speed. "Is this place even his?" questioned Tom.

"We should probably leave," Deere said, lifting his arms upward and sweeping his hair back across his scalp. "That guy's not right. He's like a manic depressive without the depression."

"He's like an idiot savant without the savant," joked Fred.

"He's got all the assets of an autistic person without the deficits," remarked Tom.

"Well, he's got this dog here…" Fred pointed.

"What dog?" asked Tom. Then he looked down at the small black dog calmly staring up at them.

Deere scratched his chin. "Oh yeah…I think I saw him peeking out from underneath that bed last night. Why would he not live here if he has this dog?"

"I don't know," said Tom. "Maybe it's someone else's dog."

"What's your name, little friend? She looks like a girl," said Deere, "Are you a girl? Yes, you are! What's your name, little girl? What are we gonna call you?"

"I don't see a tag," said Tom, feeling around her collar.

"I'd call her Felicity," said Deere sitting cross-legged on the soft carpeted floor in front of her. Felicity was licking his face. Fred was petting her back, slowly stroking her fur with his fingertips. Tom went into the kitchen to look for a food bowl and a water bowl. "There are two bowls in here." He found a bag of dog food in the lower cupboard. "Hey guys bring her in here." They came into the kitchen and Felicity followed. He set the food bowl down with some Pedigree kibble and then set down the water bowl with fresh water. Felicity gobbled up the kibble and lapped up the water like she was hungry and thirsty.

"Either she is Murmur's dog, and he lives here, or …" Tom said as he rubbed the hair up from the back of his neck. "Someone else owns her and is

not around yet. We have to wait here until he comes back or someone else because we're not going to abandon her if she's been abandoned by others."

"Try to text Murmur and see what's going on with him," said Fred. "You got his number saved?"

"Sure," said Tom, "right here." He pulled his cell phone out of his back pocket and started texting Murmur.

Bling, bling…

Bling, bling…

"Anybody else hear that? Listen, I'm going to call him."

Tom pressed and then held the phone up to his ear while looking around. Fred and Deere were tilting and moving their heads around. "It's coming from the living room," pointed Deere. He headed back around to the living room, followed by Tom and Fred.

Bling, bling...

Bling, bling...

Bling, bling...

Bling, bling...

"Found it," Tom said, "It was right here behind this entertainment center." He looked at it for a way to unlock it. "Cheap phone, you think he'll be back for it?" He looked at it for ten seconds. "Uh-oh, this is a burner phone! We've been tricked again by this goon!"

Murmur was out tooling about in his car going very fast. A police car pulled him over. The cop was very menacing-looking. He got out and quickly walked to the driver's side door with his gun pointed at Murmur. He got to the window and tapped on it with the pistol. "Roll the window down

NOW!" Murmur slowly rolled the window down. He had sunglasses on. The cop shoved the pistol in Murmur's face and pressed it hard against his nose.

"I'm gonna blow your face off, punk! Get ready to die!"

"You know what you're going to do?" Murmur lowered his sunglasses. His eyes were bloodshot but immediately looked as if they were swirling into a hypnotizing pattern. He appeared to have psychokinetic powers. "You're going to turn that gun around and point it between your eyes, make it look like a suicide."

Without delay, the cop twisted his arm and wrist around, as if all his muscles were straining to stop himself. BLAM! His head had a huge hole in between his eyes and made a strange face before collapsing to the ground.

Twenty minutes later, Murmur was tooling around in his Dodge again as if nothing happened. He was heading to destinations unknown.

Back at the house, a couple of days went by, they had no word from anyone. They were still waiting for Murmur. It was sunny outside; it hadn't rained in days. The pleasant sounds of windchimes were lofting in the air. Tom walked all the way around the house to the back. There was wild ivy growing up two stories of the brick at the back northeast corner. The other two guys just kept sitting in kitchen chairs, upstairs. There were sunflowers on them with a green background. Even the curtains had the same sunflower pattern. Fred kept hearing a buzzing sound that would start out very quietly and then get louder. He followed the sound to the corner of the top cupboard. He opened the cupboard door and located a hole where a little

honeybee sound would get slightly louder until a honeybee appeared, then would pop out and fly off, and then another came to take its place, and then another. Tom knocked on the downstairs apartment door which he looked through the window of, and noticed it looked lived-in recently, but nobody was home at the time. He went back to the front and walked upstairs, he walked over to the table sat down, and ate the rest of the crackers, soup, and bread they had found in the cupboards to eat. The refrigerator was mostly empty.

"I'm going to leave and take the dog with me," said Tom. "Are you two okay with that?"

"Of course," said Fred. "If you weren't going to, I would take her."

"Yeah," said Deere, "if you don't want to hang around here anymore, and you're taking the dog, I'll head back home too. I have nothing better to do."

"You got nothing to do?" Tom asked. "You can come down to Florida and hang."

"Or you can come out to New York, and I'll show you ways I like to earn money," Fred said. "What else are you going to do, just sit around your house?"

"Grow some more marijuana," said Deere. "I got a blow-up doll in my crib. Wish I had a *real* woman right now. I might roam about the streets and find me a beautiful honey of a gal. But I can do that anywhere."

"Yeah, let's go out there to New York, make some money for a while, and then we'll go down to Florida, I'll show you guys around and then we'll go out to California, and Deere will show us around his neighborhood," figured Tom.

“No,” said Deere, “We should go to New York first, make money, then go out to California, buy some dope and stuff, then we can mosey on over to Florida and get some hot women down there. I hear they’re the hottest women in the world down there.” He smiled in Tom’s direction. Tom and Fred agreed, and they were off.

Murmur came back home, saw nobody was there, and looked around for his dog but couldn’t find her anywhere; the dog that helped him get through the separation and divorce.

Chapter Four, Forever Band:

It was January 1st, 2007, and Murmur wanted to get the band together. He met a pretty young lady named April December, bought a house with her, and moved down to Mansfield Ohio. Her parents had to help with the down payment in order to get it. They made plans to get married.

April had long straight honey blonde hair with lots of volume. She stood about 5'7" and was not too slim, nor too heavy. She was well built, with ample breasts. They met through C.J. also known as Christy Jane who was half Muslim, and half Christian but was going to the same college as April. C.J. was asked if she knew any good, godly, upstanding men. She said she did, as Murmur and C.J. had been chatting online somewhere, and had actually gone out on a date once in Bucyrus. C.J. had atrocious breath so it did not set a good first impression, and he was not interested in her after several unfavorable comments about religion.

He lined up a job with SOCI Petroleum, and K&D, for his trucking experience; and Foundations for Living for the use of his psychology degree and academic knowledge. He also looked into working at Silver Lining Group later, but he was putting in about eight days of work in a seven-day workweek. He combined the day shift full- and part-time with the night shift and weekends at FFL, trying to study the textbooks for college. While there, he had to do suicide watch all night, or prevent self-harming such as cutting, with contraband. He looked for a master's degree based online. He had only been able to find a fully online program in a couple of non-traditional colleges: Capella and a Master's in

MHC at Welden. He would have time to work and attend college online at the same time. However, Heidelberg wouldn't let him obtain official transcripts until he paid them off for the final elective required to graduate. Finally, he chose Welden University. Murmur and April rescued several dogs and settled them with good reputable new homes. They also rescued a number of cats.

However, he had a lot of red flags that April was considering continuing a promiscuous lifestyle, while he worked night and day, being gone long hours. She kept complaining that she was lonely, and she required a lot of sexual activity to satisfy her carnal cravings and desire. That was compounded by the fact that she couldn't keep even a part-time job for more than two months because of the drama between her and other female workers there. But besides that difficulty, April and Murmur seemed to have many interests and Christian values in common, so they stayed together as long as possible.

In the spring of 2010, April had now gone off to live with another man she met on the X-box multi-player chat, so he got a great paying LTL truck-driving job at Estes, which took him to many new places, but mostly local, home-daily route areas. He got ample raises along the way. He was well-liked, gregarious, and friendly at all his stops. But management had come up with numerous faults to consider letting him go. It lasted exactly seven years to the day, for him.

He called up Fred in the spring of 2015 and asked what he had been up to. He had gone with Tom and Deere to New York City and made a fortune in consulting and freelance work. Having

plenty of money, they went out to California, mainly San Francisco and San Diego. They manufactured and sold a lot of drugs, but also kept enough for themselves, especially marijuana and magic mushrooms. They got into hydroponics and later aquaponics for growing food. In fact, they became experts under the tutelage of Deere, who was a natural-born farmer. He had told them all about how his father used to take him out to help on the farm all day long and rode on the tractor he was named after through the fields, he helped with the animals and was also a great farm veterinarian. Following that they drove out to Florida to hang out with Tom. He told them he would find even sexier women for each of them. They spent most of their time in Miami and Tampa, where they found maybe over a hundred for each of them. Surprisingly, they never fathered any children though.

Murmur told Fred they would have to come up to North Central Ohio for now because he was too busy working, but eventually, they'd all meet up in Northern Michigan, the Upper Peninsula perhaps, and live off the land, build themselves a smart home for a clubhouse they can all hang out in. They planned to have tons of money saved up, a bevy of beautiful women, and all the drugs they could ever possibly use. The rest they could barter and trade for. Fred said that would be super awesome, and he would get a hold of Deere, and Tom, tell them about the plan, and get back with him. Murmur said goodbye and waited.

Murmur had a couple of Harley-Davidson Sportsters from Hale's in Mansfield and finally was able to use the motorcycle endorsement on his CDL license to go to work every day in the same town

the Music Explosion was from, and where the original Ohio Express, the touring band was from, not the recording band from New York fronted by Joey Levine under Kasenetz-Katz. Of course, he got to see these bands live up in Mansfield's theater, and later saw the Herman's Hermits with Peter Noone.

These idyllic summer months led up to the meeting of the guys to start playing some material so they could attempt to play live at very small venues. Mainly this was for a little extra spending cash and to try to get more hot women.

Murmur got back from his route for the weekend and when Deere arrived, he had his same VW microbus, Fred had a fully restored 1964½ medium blue Mustang, and Tom brought his 1953 red Corvette replica. They all looked like their hair hadn't been cut since the last time they'd met up.

Inside the house, Deere played the bass, Fred played drums, Tom played rhythm guitar and vocals, Murmur played lead guitar and occasionally vocals. Deere couldn't stop farting, the whole time they were playing cover songs. He kept playing loud notes to cover up the sound, but the rest of the guys noticed, so Tom and Murmur began to write a song for him, and in the process, they also came up with a name for the band:

Way down south in California
In a house among the redwood trees
There lived a rockin' rebel named Deere Muff
He used to let 'em fly without regret
An eye for an eye

With a knack for baking marijuana
Into butterscotch brownies
He liked to cook up muffins and pastries
He made them taste good
Like Eskimo pie

This is the song of Forgotten Band
Listen to the wind you can hear 'em, man
Tell me if you can...

Later, when someone mentioned the Song of Forgotten Band sounded a lot like Jimmy Buffet, they changed name to Forever Band. Murmur liked the name because it reminded him of Forever by Pete Drake and His Talking Steel Guitar.

"Just think of all the people who would pay good money to learn to live forever," said Fred.

"Wish *I* could live forever," pouted Deere.

"Forever is cool, man," added Tom.

"Forever it is!" said Murmur.

Murmur delved deeper into the Journal for Cultic Studies and read eBooks on Amazon Kindle like D**k Psychology, D**k NLP, and D**k CBT. It started to take on an air of Spy vs. Spy from Mad Magazine.

He passed all the classes for the curriculum at Welden, driving to residencies in Minneapolis, and Atlanta, during vacations.

Chapter Five, The Clubhouse:

In the spring of 2017, Murmur was fired from Estes. But he told the guys he was busy for now because he was trying to get unemployment, but after that, they could go up to The Clubhouse. They would be able to stay at Tom's cabin until Murmur found a place, or some acreage and built on it.

Meanwhile, Murmur was off for three weeks, getting his paperwork all together and checked out for a new job across Highway 30 from Estes' newer location. F&J Trucking would allow him to be regional. The main runs were driving down near Richmond Virginia to deliver bowling alley parts, getting a backhaul, up to the North coast, then back, which took 2 ½ days, the next leg of the tour was down to Nashville, and back up with a backhaul, then dropping it off somewhere in between. Estes continued to fight the unemployment payment, but Murmur won three times, finally getting over $1,100 for the three weeks. He worked through the summer for F&J; about three months.

It was during this time that he stopped in Front Royal Virginia and tried to observe the solar eclipse in the parking lot of a small truck stop. That's where he got a pretty good picture of the dimmed sun from outside the side window.

At the end of August, Fred brought out his Mustang, parked in Murmur's driveway, and waited. Tom showed up with his Corvette replica. They were waiting for Murmur and Deere. Tom noticed the tape player and played his Grass Roots

cassette. Wait A Million Years started its classic feel. "Yeah, I got a '58 powder blue Corvette also back home. It's pretty awesome." Fred said he would love to see that. And it would be worth a lot of money.

Deere showed up then with his 1967 Volkswagen Beetle, with a highly decorative flowery and love-themed paint job. "Did all the painting myself," he boasted. "You like it?"

"Yeah man, but you should have brought the van," replied Tom. "You still got it?"

"Yeah, Dude, I left it at home."

"If we all take a trip up to my cabin in Northern Michigan, we'd all like enough room," remarked Tom.

Murmur was just now pulling into the driveway. He had sold his Harleys to buy another cool car. He had a fully restored 1969 GTO Judge, in bright cheery orange. Of course, he had done most of the work himself. Tom asked him if he sold his last car. "No, I still have the Polara."

"Is it in the garage?"

"No."

"Then where is it?" asked Tom.

"Not here," stalled Murmur, acting like he didn't want to reveal its location. Finally, after some silence with everyone looking at him (he had obviously colored his hair) he continued, "It's on Boblo Island. They have got a bunch of stupid housing going up there, it's in the middle of a grassy yard. They said I could keep it there until I build my place."

"We'd have to take the biggest vehicle if we're all carpooling. That would be your GTO. You cool with that?"

"Yeah, man!"

"I know I have to get about ten hours of sleep first," Tom said. "Going cross country, you know."

"Me too," said Deere.

"Same here," said Fred.

"Y'all can crash here," said Murmur.

"We're gonna have to," said Tom. "Unless we go to a hotel."

"Or sleep in our cars," said Deere.

"No need to do that. Come on in," said Murmur leading the way. "There is one thing I'd like to resolve," as he unlocked the door. "Did you guys take my dog?"

"Oh! Yeah, of course." Said Tom, "I took her and gave her to a veteran."

"Oh," said Murmur. "That's good then."

"What happened to you that you ran off?"

"Ah, I had troubles with this chick I met named Bryn Dimpleton," said Murmur. "You know how it is." They all sat down on the comfortably upholstered sofas and chairs.

"B*****s!" said Fred.

"Now, don't insult female dogs," said Murmur. "I got another little dog here, Diva" She came over sniffing everyone as he leaned over and petted her.

"That other one we named Felicity," Deere remembered.

"How did you know her name?" asked Murmur, kind of surprised.

"I don't know," said Deere. "We guessed a name."

"Oh well," said Murmur. "No worries."

Murmur's cellphone started to vibrate. He picked it up off the end table. It was Bryn. "Hello?" She had been asking about getting a CDL class A license. She thought it wouldn't be very hard to do. He suspected she was asking for some guy she was seeing. She said she heard automatic transmissions were becoming increasingly available, so it should be easy to pass the test. She could do it no problem, all she had to do was find a truck driving school. Tom pulled out a bag of peanut M&Ms from his pocket and started eating them. Murmur was arguing with Bryn.

"Not everyone can just *do* whatever it is that I *do*! Many people have tried, many people have died," he said stoically.
He listened for a few more seconds. "She hung up," he said putting the phone down, then getting up gingerly.

"Yeah," he continued, "there's a few more snacks and stuff in the kitchen. I have three beds and a sofa. Take your pick."

"I can sleep in here and you can sleep in there? Fred can sleep there then, and Deere on the sofa," said Tom tiredly.

"I got gel pillows and some nice new My Pillows, and extra blankets and comforters in the hall closet. You know, I know how it is when you are so tired behind the wheel. Believe me! I'd sometimes fall asleep driving and hallucinate. Signs become lollipops. Groups of trees along the road become a tunnel, and the sky becomes a solid object. I would drive for some time as if on autopilot, and many countless times I would hear the rumble strip and jerk the wheel back into the

lane. Several times I would wake up more and not know where I was or where I was going."

Tom grabbed an extra pillow and opened up the covers on the one bed in the medium-sized bedroom. Fred went to lie down in the smaller bedroom. Murmur continued speaking, "I may or may not have sustained permanent irreversible brain damage from sleep deprivation. I'd be driving back from London Kentucky for example, and have to slap and hit myself, jump up and down in the seat, scream along to the loud music with the windows down, but the second I stopped doing anything I'd fall back asleep again. I wouldn't know it until I found myself waking up again. In the rest area where I would try to nap on the steering wheel, I'd wake up thinking I'd fallen asleep at the wheel, jerk my head up, and stomp the brakes. I'd drink 3 or more energy drinks in a day, but the one thing that kept me awake was eating. I can't fall asleep while I'm eating candy like Jelly Belly jellybeans, or peach gummy rings. I'd have to eat them until my mouth bled. Then ate some more. Sometimes my eyes would cross, and it was so hard to uncross my eyes." He heard them snoring. "Goodnight."

Murmur curled up in the big bedroom under the covers and picked up a book from the floor he found for free. Light a Last Candle by Vincent King. When his mind became fatigued, he struggled to stay awake, ran out of mental energy, and then reluctantly fell asleep.

The next day they got up and ate some breakfast from the kitchen, bacon, eggs, sausages, (except Deere, he's vegetarian) English muffins, rye toast and butter, orange juice, and cereal with milk, and left in Murmur's GTO, with Diva along for the

ride, going route 30 to 15 to 75 to 23. "75 had the exit sign for the ferry that left for Boblo until they closed it. I took a different ferry over of course from Ohio. I hang out on Middle Bass Island and Put-In-Bay a lot, barhopping and socializing. The whole Metro-Detroit area is my old stomping grounds, but we'll be going straight up 23 past Ann Arbor."

"Cool," said Deere. "Groovy," said Fred. They had never been. "Where is your cabin, Tom?"

"It's up by Sault Ste. Marie, in the wilderness," replied Tom. "If you want a place around Ironwood, or western Upper Peninsula Michigan, you could go through Chicago and up through Wisconsin but that might take even longer."

"I'd like to build a small home around Petosky," said Murmur.

"That's a good area. I think you'll like it. We can swing down 31 on the way back down," said Tom.

"What about that 1970 Buick GSX, man," asked Murmur, "you still have it?"

"Yeah, man! You'll get it, it's down in Florida. Just don't you worry! I got it in storage for you," said Tom.

They drove past the state line, toward the Michigan welcome center. "Man, I got to stop and use the bathroom! I don't know about you guys, but I drink so much coffee and energy drinks, that are diuretic in effect. Sometimes I held it in for so long on the road that I felt like I had done myself some damage to my bladder and kidneys," said Murmur.

"I know the feeling," Tom said.

"I know what you mean," agreed Deere,

"Me too," chimed Fred.

"Anyway, sometimes I peed in a Gatorade bottle while driving down the road, or a cat litter jug if I can pull over somewhere in the big truck, pee beside the truck, or out the passenger door if stopped somewhere acceptable."

Tom said, "I just unzip my pants and lean over, open the door, and aim out between the door and the rocker panel. And you don't have to be unusually large like me. If I were any longer, I'd just hose it out the window and go." They all laughed along.

Murmur noted, "once I was in a small town with literally nowhere to pull over or stop, and I just couldn't hold anymore, and I had to just open my pants and pee all over the floor. Later on, it dried up and didn't smell so bad, but I sprayed it down with disinfectant potpourri scent."

"Same here, I peed my pants before I could get out," admitted Tom. Murmur pulled into a parking space, and all got out to use the facilities, and Murmur clipped on a leash and led Diva for a walk around the grounds. When everybody was done, they got back in the car and back on the highway, driving north on 23 past 223. Murmur commented on this, the engine making a nice, satisfying, steady roar. He kept driving past where 23 and 75 merged back together again, and past Frankenmuth Michigan, past Saginaw, stopped again for a restroom break, then past Bay City, Grayling, Gaylord, Mackinaw City, crossed The Bridge, and went past St. Ignace. Finally, just past Dafter, they went west on 28, to north on 221 to Brimley. There was a very nice log cabin with a two car garage in the woods, with green doors. He

parked the GTO right in front of the front door and they all got out and looked.

"It's somewhat of a smart home, as you would describe it, Murmur, except not fireproof," told Tom. "Come on in y'all."

Tom waved his hand cordially for them to come with him. They all walked up, and Tom unlocked the front door with his key, while the cameras watched. "My smartphone disables the alarm with geofencing, but I can also disable it manually on the keypad." He invited everyone to sit down, have a beer, and watch television, a smart TV. There was an ocean show on with many different kinds of fish.

"I have solar panels, and little wind turbines, and generators and storage batteries, so I don't have an electric bill. I have good well water, with a filtering system, and septic tank, so there's not a water or sewer bill. I don't have trash pickup. I recycle, and burn in the burn-barrel, or haul it away. I do gardening, hunt, and fish for food. Barter and trade for the rest."

"You own it free and clear?" asked Murmur.

"Yes," answered Tom.

"But you have property tax...," said Murmur.

"It's 1.41%," said Tom.

"I don't really want to pay property taxes," said Murmur.

"Well," said Fred, "if you're looking for the best states to live well in the cheapest, South Dakota, Wyoming, Nevada, Florida, Texas and Tennessee, and Alaska don't have income tax. New Hampshire, and Washington state, have practically no income tax. Of these, Nevada and Wyoming

have the lowest property tax rate, followed by Tennessee, then Florida, then Washington, then Alaska, then South Dakota. Texas and New Hampshire's pretty high. New Hampshire has no state or local sales tax, as well as Montana, Oregon, and Delaware. Alaska has no statewide sales tax but may have local sales tax. Wyoming has a moderate sales tax. Florida has a bit higher. South Dakota has pretty high sales tax. Nevada and Texas have a high sales tax rate. Tennessee has a very high sales tax. So, with everything in consideration…"

"You have to take into consideration the sparsely populated areas as opposed to heavily populated areas," interrupted Murmur.

"New York City, New Jersey, and some areas of urban California are heavily populated," continued Fred, "Midwest states like Michigan down to Florida, and including Texas and Louisiana are medium, and most of the Western states, as well as Alaska and Maine are lightly populated."

Murmur sighed, "Nevada's probably too hot and dry. Northern states like Alaska are probably too cold. That's why Ohio's got the best balance of weather, hardly any tornadoes or earthquakes either. But I might like living up here or in Florida also." He sat Diva down and set down her food and water bowls.

"You'll love it," exclaimed Tom, "I love it down there, and I can show you around the best places!"

"Great! Let's do it," said Murmur, "Let's go there."

"Okay, you guys stay the night here and then we go back down," said Tom calmly. "We'll stop by Petosky on the way down."

"Cool," said Murmur, "where can I sleep?"

"Far out," said Fred.

"Groovy," said Deere.

"I got three beds," said Tom, "I can sleep on the couch, it folds out. Take your pick. Oh, and we'll stop by the national parks and attractions along the way, for sure!"

"Sounds great," said Murmur, "do you have anything to eat?"

"I got a lot of Jerky, and canned vegetables. There's also fruit in the refrigerator. Surplus apples, oranges, grapefruit. All organic. I brought most of it up from Florida, last time. I've been meaning to stop by Dearborn area and pick up some shawarma for us sometime."

"I had an authentic Mediterranean Baba Ghanoush and Chickpea wrap when I was down in Atlanta," said Murmur. "I always like Greek food like Gyros." He pronounced it the correct way, not the American way.

"I'm a vegetarian," remarked Deere.

They each got some food and ate, watching some shows about supercars before going to each bed to get plenty of sleep. He had some very warm and comfortable blankets and plenty of super comfortable pillows. They were soon out like a light.

The next morning, they awoke to the bird songs and chipmunks and squirrels chattering, outside the window that was cracked open at the bottom with the screens on. A fresh breeze was blowing on them, except Tom, because he was on the sofa bed.

Murmur had Diva sleeping on the blanket between his legs. They got up and looked outside. It was a wonderful sunny day.

"You got some guitars and stuff," said Deere. "I wrote a song, want to hear it?"

"Sure," said Tom.

"Here's the lyrics I have so far, ahem…"

Just an old gold blanket, my father died in

It's tattered and worn, smells funny too

Got some records and 8-tracks from 4 decades ago

Somebody might like them, somebody like you

Mister Salvation Army man give me a helping hand

Please. I'm down on my knees

Mister Goodwill Ambassador hold all your laughter for

Me. Take my stuff from me before I die

"Then you have this Celtic, Gaelic, Irish style guitaring. Chords and then this melody in it." He played about as well as he could for demonstration purposes.

"Pretty morose," said Murmur, "don't ya think?"

"It's for the homeless! I'm empathic," responded Deere. "I want to give so much of the proceeds to charitable organizations."

"Oh yeah," said Murmur, "I can dig it."

"Do it yourself, then," said Tom. "You won't need us for that. Do a solo record."

"Okay," said Deere.

"I don't think it'd be very profitable," said Fred, "It won't be lucrative for us, if it sells at all."

"I need all y'all's help for all the guitaring," replied Deere. "There's like three guitar parts or something."

"We'll see," said Tom. "I got this cool song I've been working on called Equinox." He started playing the funky up-tempo guitar chords on rhythm guitar. "Then you play this on bass." He played a funky bass line. "This is sung by a woman singer;"

Can you tell me where to begin
Someplace I'm free from sin...
Oh, it's Equinox
Oh-h-h Equinox,
Darlin'
Lead me to the fountain of youth
Or perhaps the garden of truth
Is it in the Equinox
Woah, Equinox
Honey
Someplace I can be sure of
Whereas I can stay strong
Take me to the eternal
The shore of evermore

"And so on…," Tom finished up. "It doesn't sound like any other song I might have forgotten about, does it?"

"I don't think so," said Tom.

"Not that I know of," said Deere.

"Probably not," said Fred.

When they were done relaxing, making music, and eating delicious food, they got back on the road and headed south. They stopped at federal and state parks and attractions, checked out Petosky, and went back to Mansfield to get their

cars. On the way back they talked about radio stations.

"I've been listening to K-Love, Radio-U, and other Christian stations," said Murmur. "I remember CKLW, and I used to listen to Willie Wilson on WDET, and NPR was so eclectic and had a huge variety, but not anymore, they have become too politically charged."

"Yeah, too leftist on its agenda," said Tom. "And I hate those pledge drives, almost as bad as commercials sometimes. They act like they're different because they let you vote with your money to hear something no one else plays and to hear more of it, but don't other Christian stations do the same thing because they can't get sponsors for the different music?"

"Yeah, just like public television. But for alternative music there is 89X, Windsor, Detroit," Murmur said. "And you can listen to Sirius-XM all over the place. You just subscribe and have no ads. Much better variety."

"Yeah," said Fred, "that makes it nice for cross country driving."

"Don't forget about indie music," said Deere. "Sort of a college station type music."

"Oh, like Findlay's Indie," said Murmur. "They play a lot of different songs too."

"I also explore a lot of different music on Amazon, YouTube, and random searches or just buying stuff that looks interesting," said Tom.

Murmur got another text from Bryn. "She's asking me for money again, but every time I try to see her, she makes up an excuse. And every time I try to share information with her, have a conversation, she contradicts everything I say,

seemingly. She's a leftist, and I wouldn't be surprised if she's become a Satan-worshipper. She might have cast a demonic spell on me."

"Dude," said Tom, "why do you even put up with that stuff. What happened to that chick you had before, Summer?"

"Oh, her boyfriend has had her brainwashed for the longest time, like he was using cult tactics, maligning me with nonsense about lot lizards. You know I have nothing to do with any lot lizards. She came back and everyone tried to deprogram her, but nothing worked because she ran back, thinking I was going to get back with Bryn, but I was just going to fix her toilet like I had promised. Sometimes it just doesn't pay to be honest or keep your word."

"Sorry to hear that, man." Tom said, "Never ever give a chick money, no matter what kind of sob story she laid on you. Never again unless you marry her. I don't care if she says she's boiling in hot oil and getting ready to be eaten by cannibals unless you can pay a ransom by a certain time through cash app. Don't respond, cut off all contact: it's what you should have done a long time ago, after the last time you got with her. That's my advice to you. You'll follow it if you know what's good for you."

"Yeah, man! It's like he can't get anyone else, or fool anyone else unless she was actually that dumb," lamented Murmur. "It's like he has a cult for one going on there."

"We can find you another woman, right guys?"

"Yuh," said Deere. "I can help lure them with better drugs!"

“Yeap,” said Fred. “I can help buy them with the money!”

“And then we’ll find better chicks for ourselves I’m sure in the process,” added Tom.

Chapter Six, A Cult for One:

"*That was absolutely, positively, without a doubt, thee worst* experience, *I have ever* had *in my entire* LIFE!"

Tom walked in as Murmur was saying these words over the phone. "What's up?"

"Just trying to make arrangements for this stupid asinine practicum and internship," replied Murmur. "And to top it all off, while having to walk across the side of the yard during the road construction, with Diva, she ran over to me and was motioning over to her butt, where the ground hornets were stinging her fiercely. Did you know the skunk family likes to dig up their nests and eat them? However, many of them were also hit by cars. I ran her inside and stomped the ground hornets into oblivion. True story."

Later at the prospective practicum site, the phone rang. Murmur fatefully answered it. The pathetic guy on the phone was moaning and groaning, talking his ear off for like fifteen minutes; "…Nobody ever helps me, my old therapist, the one before that, and the one before that, and the one before that, and the one before that, my psychologist, my psychiatrist, my counselor, the doctors and nurses, my family, my support group is nonexistent. I can't do anything right, nobody likes me, I always have the worst of luck, in fact, if it weren't for bad luck, I'd have no luck at all. I know it sounds cliché, but I was born under a bad sign. God and the Devil both hate me. Women think I'm disgusting, and even my blow-up doll can't stand to be around me. I think this time I'm really going to do it, man. I swear if you don't help me out this

time, I'm going to blow my brains out! Nobody cares about me. I've taken about every drug known to man. Every time I try to overdose some do-gooder comes along and saves my life. It's just prolonging my agony. My dog ran away, and I thought it was just an ordinary thing, but then I got another stray, and it ran away so fast it got hit by a car, then I got a cat and then another…"

"Stop! Stop! Stop! You know what I'm hearing?" Murmur remarked. He was met by stunned silence. "Uh-WAH, Uh-WAH, Uh-WAH. Sounds like a dang crybaby, dude! You know what? I don't blame all those people. I can't stand to listen to you either, with your namby-pamby whining, you have more whine coming out of your mouth than I have in my basement wine rack. You gotta pull yourself together man, You gotta…" BLAM! Bump-bump.

"Uh…hello???" He encountered only silence. "Yeeshhh…"

He slowly hung up the phone, staring at the wall. He couldn't believe nothing was going right anymore. All the doors that had opened leading, beckoning, and welcoming into his bright future were diabolically, and suddenly slamming shut. Just like the Welden professor suggested, they were going to be the "gatekeepers." They were closing the gate, keeping him, one of the undesirables, out of the profession, leaving him to pay back the near $200,000 looming student loan debt that was ballooning with the interest everybody in the financial services offices had warned about to no avail. All on the wages of a meager dead-end job and inadequate career, instead of the high-paying one that would've put him in a position to pay back

the ludicrously monumental debt load. He had to do something. It was all on him to figure something out. He always had before. If you want something done, you have to do it yourself. You have to make it happen. It wasn't happening.

This prevented him from continuing with the trip down to Florida with the guys at the time. The rest of them weren't ready to go then either. Deere said, "Yeah, man. Not only do I not really want to put more miles on my car, or waste more gas and time, but since I don't really have much to do in California then I would be coming right back out here again to do stuff with you guys."

"Same here," said Fred.

"Well," said Tom, "I don't suppose you'll mind if we all stay here with you for a while, since you have enough rooms for all of us. If we have any women as guests, we'll keep it quiet and stay to ourselves, right guys?"

"Uhm, sure," said Fred.

"Agreed," said Deere.

"That'll work," said Murmur. "Thanks for understanding. Maybe if you want to, you all can help me in my psychological research."

"Haha! Like what?" asked Tom.

"Careerwise, working so much, I eventually forgot how to sleep. I became so good at staying awake. I used to be able to wake up exactly when I wanted to. Then as things got worse, I overslept, I would be late to work almost all the time. I still never had enough money, though, working for someone else. I wanted to be more self-employed, so I fell for the allure of college being the ultimate panacea, but which turned into the Pandora's Box. I always believed what Timothy Leary was saying

when in high school, and then when I started having success in college, I thought that college was for me. But when I went to residency in Minneapolis, back in the hotel room alone, I had another epiphany. I came around full circle and understood what he was saying, college is not the answer everyone is looking for. I had to tune in. I had to tune into my Creator, into feeling as one with the Universe and having perfect peace. I had to turn on. Turn on to all the groovy positive vibes that create a good feeling all around me. I had to drop out because even successful psychologists and psychiatrists are not fully happy themselves, nor do they ever make enough money. They are in it for the process of achieving their objective, but if they do achieve it, they're still not living fulfilled. Many rely on illicit drugs or gurus to feel real, but they most often take artificial, prescribed drugs which are pharmacists' and drug companies' attempts to simulate what can be had from nature and nature's God naturally, for true happiness. And it would be free, and relatively easy to obtain.

"The people like Dr. Syndee who had a man's voice, but up there in front of an audience, dressed and adorned as a female, alluded to the source of his trouble. One of his earliest memories as a child, being pursued and pestered by bullies on his bicycle, labeled as queer, homosexual, and more derogatory names they were calling him. Pelting him with sticks and hitting him with stones. He became 'Other.' You become what you're labeled. He had to cope as a victim of some outside force for the rest of his life, Over-compensating for lack of self-pride with gay pride rallies, activism, and promotion of acceptance. He went to Drum Circle

Therapy there. Not really being happy but constantly proving to himself that if it weren't for the opposition and oppression, he would have total, true happiness. Being who he thought he wanted to be, instead of having a higher purpose of being who he was made to be by the Creator. I have sympathy. I don't hate him. It would be just a disservice to act like I'm supporting him with my agreement. See, I don't fear, I don't have a homophobia, I'm not scared of it in any way. I just don't approve or condone of his lifestyle. Big difference. It's contrary to nature, so it's unnatural.

"But being forced to use preferred pronouns is believing a lie. It is a sin to *believe* a lie. People know it's a sin to *tell* a lie, but willingly *believing* a lie is a sin too. Just think, what did Adam and Eve do in the Garden of Eden? God was like; Just *trust* me. I may not always have the time to explain why, but you'll have to trust me on this and do what I say, and don't do what I say *not to do*. But instead, when the Devil came along as a talking Serpent, what they didn't do was hesitate, and confer with God about the discrepancies in what they were told. They in essence, had faith in the Devil instead of God.

"See, I had faith in college. I believed a lie."

"Fear is showing faith in the Devil and the demons. Fear, depression, and hate are what they feed off of. You have to let go and let God, man," Tom reasoned. "It doesn't mean you don't do your part. Lord knows we have to do good works. We all need to do our best and take action against evil. Someone once said; The only thing that's needed for evil to prosper is for good men to do nothing. God grant me the serenity to change the things I

can, courage to accept the things I cannot change and wisdom to know the difference. Or something like that."

"But the Serenity Prayer has one automatic presumption," said Murmur, "Do you know what that is?"

"What?" asked Tom.

"That everything needs to be changed," said Murmur. "I suppose you're one of those people that believes everything happens for a reason. Like, nothing just happens by happenstance or freak accident."

"In a way, that could be true," said Tom. "It could be God's reason, or it could be Satan's reason. It could be evil done by the Adversary, and then it could be God turning the table after that and working all things together for the good of those who love Him. But whatever the matter, it involves human participation."

"So," said Fred, "what are these things you need help from us to research?"

"Selective attention is just one thing you can try," said Murmur. "Let's say we turn on this cool music over here…" He ran over to the stereo system and put on the Chocolate Watchband. Then he went over to the stand-alone radio on a side table, turned it on, and world-famous gay recording artist, Dalton Dean, was playing.

"AHHH! That sucks," yelled Deere, "I hate that crap!"

"Sounds horrible," shouted Fred.

"Audio torture! Isn't that what the FBI uses on criminals to drive them out when they're in a standoff?" Tom asked.

"Hmm. During the Waco siege, I remember they played Nancy Sinatra's These Boots Are Made for Walkin' but they also played some Alice Cooper songs, the power and water supplies were cut, and they played sounds of rabbits being slaughtered at high decibels, not only to torture them but to deprive them of sleep. If you asked me, I would have recommended playing the Kirby Stone Four's Baubles, Bangles, and Beads over and over repetitively for hours on end at high volume, but then that's what you get when you cut corners and save money with amateur agents instead of experts like me. Apparently, fires were started from within. With selective attention, you just understood which song you preferred," (The Chocolate Watchband), "and which one sucks," (Dalton Dean), He turned off the radio with Dalton on it.

"THANK YOU!" screamed Tom.

"Imagine tuning out whoever is cussing and talking nonsense, but at the same time tuning in to what you really wanted to hear. Okay? Now imagine listening to two very important conversations and comprehending them both fully, at the same time. Most professionals theorize that you can't do it. You alternate your full attention back and forth at perhaps a higher rate if you're good. But I think I've been able to do it for short times and get better with practice."

"What else you got?" asked Tom.

Murmur sighed for a second looking up and to the left as if thinking. "Lucid dreaming therapy. I don't know if anyone is doing it yet, but I've been able to train my mind to dream lucidly."

"Uh," said Deere, "I've had recurring dreams of going out to feed the farm animals I used

to have, but in my dream, I realized I forgot to feed them for years and water them. So, I go back out with gallons of water anticipating they might not have made it, but still being hopeful, you know? The last couple of ones had a more positive outcome, and I felt happy and relieved."

"Probably you're supposed to feed the Lord's sheep," said Murmur.

"The recurring dream I have," said Tom, "is that I'm trying to get through this passageway, where I need to make it through this stairway, or doorway, or basement crawlspace, in which the opening is very small. I have barely enough room to stick my head into the opening and feel like I'm going to get stuck, but I have to make it through. It's the only way back out. I know I've done it before; I made it through, but this time it just seems tougher because I'm bigger or something. I guess I've grown, maybe?"

"Maybe you feel there are some troubled times ahead, they're getting more challenging," said Murmur. "You have to exert yourself vigorously to make it. You're a little anxious because your best efforts might not be good enough, and you might get stuck. Then you won't make it out to the other side, but ultimately you know you can make it again, because you've done it before, and it must be possible."

Fred said, "I've had recurring dreams of being on a ledge. I'm sitting up there and it's nice and serene and peaceful. I'm enjoying the view and not at all scared. I am aware that I could fall, but I know I'm not going to. One time it was behind this church I've seen. I'm glad because I knew it was ahead, so I didn't run off and die."

"Hmm," Murmur said, "the feelings that you feel during these vivid dreams seem to be important in the interpretation of them, almost being self-explanatory. I used to have night terrors growing up, but I have since read that most children do. They get tired of being afraid of the dark and they just start ignoring their fears. Like, I found the connection to my voice and would wake myself up from a bad dream with a siren-like sound. If you train your subconscious, good stuff in, good stuff out, instead of garbage in, garbage out. You do it when you practice your instrument. Through repetition, the subconscious brain learns to do it without having to think about it, cognitively. Muscle memory. You may not be able to stop the garbage in, but if you ignore it, and keep thinking good things. Keep overcoming evil with good. Return evil for evil to no man, says the Bible."

"You know about that book and documentary The Secret, that uses the law of attraction, thinking positively, believing you will have whatever you want and need, and maintaining good emotions about it all?" asked Fred. "That's a lot like showing faith."

"It's really like the agnostic view of Alcoholics Anonymous. They admit there might be a higher power and you can appeal to it if you like, but they present it that way to appeal to everyone, a wider audience. However, they might do better in specifically addressing the Master Grand Creator of the Universe, God Almighty," said Tom.

"Alcoholics Anonymous," said Murmur, "assumes you're always sick, your identity is continually an alcoholic. It's like the sick-care system; it's not the healthcare system. They want to

keep you coming back, so they don't really want to have a permanent cure for cancer, it would put a whole lot of oncologists out of business. They want job security. They want continual pathology. They don't want a world where there's nothing wrong with you because they might be out of a job. Similarly, some Christians think we're perpetual sinners when our first identity as Christians is followers of Christ. We *were* sinners. When we're born again, Christ says to go and sin no more!"

"What else are you working on?"

"I found this book about drawing on both sides of your brain," said Murmur. "Check it out!"

"Cool," said Tom.

He took out a giant drawing tablet and started drawing with both hands at the same time. He drew a vase with the impression of two faces facing each other on the sides. "I'm going to try to make an actual pottery vase like this next."

"What else are you working on?"

"Well," said Murmur, "considering the theta and delta brain waves that can be monitored during sleep, I'd like to try the biofeedback or neurofeedback like they were doing at Foundations for Living with the gamma, beta, alpha, theta, and delta brain waves. Also, I have some Marley Mellow Mood relaxation drinks for you guys, and you can take up to five melatonin pills while listening to binaural beats before you fall asleep for the night. You have to use both ears." They took the pills and drinks and drank them, then listened to the music, felt groggy, and fell asleep.

Then in the morning, they woke up and started making music again with the instruments. "I'm glad we didn't call our band something stupid

like Squirrel Nut Zippers, or Toad the Wet Sprocket! Hahahahaha!" said Deere.

"See," said Murmur, "I originally thought of all those stupid names like So and So the Thingamajig, or What's-his-face the Whatchamacallit, and the idiotic likes of that, and was going to call my band Somethin' Tha Somethin' in which case I would be calling those ridiculous bands out on their silly names without being one of them, because of the *Tha* in the middle. I remember the first band I auditioned for. It was at a member's house in Petersburg. I wasn't good enough for them yet. I failed the audition, but their name was Public Access, more like Public Success. I was told they prob'ly don't know what they're looking for."

"Public Success?" asked Deere.

"Yeah," said Murmur, "you know, Public Suck-cess, because they suck!"

Deere said, "Here's a groovy song I made up;"

Banker man
Do what you can to raise my interest rate
Banker man
See what you can do to raise my penalties too
Banker man
Please stop and see just one more time for me
Banker man
Can you raise my charges and fees until I can't see straight?
Hey, where do ya think you're going with all my money?
All my money

It ain't funny
That's all my money
Banker man…

"I made up another hypnotic song in my sleep, and I was able to play the melody on the guitar, here it goes like this," Deere played the pattern in the open position. "It goes on for about nine minutes, somehow, and the vocalist is mumbling some stuff like; 'I *feel pretty good* when nothing's alright,' before finally singing the last verse; 'the carnal dogs, and the b*****s that use us.'" He played a grand majestic guitar ending.

"I want to try to record as many of these songs as possible in my home recording studio," said Murmur, "on the computer. I learned MIDI and have this big keyboard that helps." He showed the guys some loop-based music, and multi-tracks on the screen.

Bryn called Murmur again. Tom tried to tell him not to answer but it was too late.

Murmur told her, "Next time you try to outsmart someone, make sure they are not actually *SMARTER THAN YOU!*" He then hung up on her.

He was also getting weird texts and crank phone calls, from an unlisted number, but he eventually researched and found it was from the phone of some elderly couple, by the name of Adams in New Washington. At first, it was some crack-sounding guy who said, "I don't think you know what I'm capable of…" Many times, it came up as unavailable too, whether or not it was always the same person was unclear, but they had similar characteristics. Often the mysterious person would disguise their voice, like one time, he thought he heard a little girl calling from a number he hadn't

recognized at one particular location. Then, as the disguised voice started harassing him, saying something disgusting about his girlfriend last night, Murmur shouted back, "I don't have a girlfriend right now, Goon!" Ultimately Murmur prevailed against the crank call harassers, sending the police to their house repeatedly, after being interrogated by them himself a few times.

"You guys staying here again tonight?" Murmur asked.

"We could," said Tom. Deere and Fred agreed, nodding their heads as Tom looked around.

"Tell us about your meditation," Tom said toward Murmur. "It's not like Deepak Chopra, Sadhguru, Meher Baba, or Maharishi Mahesh Yogi?"

"No," answered Murmur, "You know to be at one with the Universe, psychologically you're supposed to have an internal locus of control, but then spiritually speaking you need to recognize an external locus of control as well. If anything, clearing and opening your mind up to demonic dark forces only exacerbate any mental health propensities for problems, which is why you'll need to be more specific in the mental suggestions utilized in meditating on the Word of God. Originally in the Garden of Eden, Eve and Adam were not at all too self-conscious, even though they would commune with God in the nude and think nothing of it, just like in classical paintings and sculptures. After they ate the forbidden fruit, they were overly self-conscious and noticed their bodies were imperfect. So, as I will show you, we'll relax and know who you are in Christ. Not worrying about being a perfectionist. Christ lived a perfect

life in the world, so we don't have to scrutinize ourselves. You need agency, you need autonomy, being aware of the outside forces, being introverted, yet extroverted, too. Close your eyes and scan your body to ensure each part is comfortable."

The lights were dim. Tom was lying on the bigger sofa, and Fred was lying on the smaller one. Deere was lying on top of the inflatable air mattress. "Relax your eyes… Relax your forehead… Relax your jaw…" He went through the body parts one by one. "Now imagine the view of floating above your body, looking down at your body, seeing how relaxed you are. If it's not super easy you're doing it wrong. You are floating up to the ceiling. Effortlessly passing through the ceiling. Now, through the roof. You're floating up into the atmosphere, out into space, past the moon… past Mars… past all the planets…" Murmur continued very softly, slowly, and calmly as the fragrant candles flickered with a light flame. "Jupiter, or Big Jupe, as we affectionately call it… Saturn… Uranus… Neptune… the dwarf planets; Ceres, Pluto, Haumea, Makemake, and Eris. Thirteen in all. Maybe more, those are just the ones that have been discovered. I have them up on these wall posters. Now, you're floating out of the solar system…"

"It's not working," interrupted Deere, "just like the binaural beats. I can't make it happen."

"Yeah," said Tom, "all that stupid psychological garbage sucks!"

"Yeah, Stupid psychology!" complained Fred.

"Don't try so hard," Murmur said, "Remember, Jesus said 'My yoke is easy. My

burden is light. Although you will have troubles in this world, take heart, for I have overcome the world.'"

"Tell us what else you've learned," requested Tom, "there must be something useful."

"Well," said Murmur, "Maslow's Hierarchy of Needs shows a pyramid with a base of physical needs our bodies need to survive like clean air, fresh pure water, and good nutritious food. Originally sex, but that isn't really necessary for every individual, just for the perpetuation of the human race. Next up is the need to feel safe and secure, like locks on our doors, and firearms. Next is the relationship needs, to feel love, belonging, and being a part of something. Then we need to feel good about ourselves. Esteem needs. Lower esteem from others, and higher esteem for yourself, which is great self-esteem. Those needs we are aware of when they are not being met. The next higher needs are the needs we become aware of when seeking to grow. We need to find meaning. We need to find beauty, and finally, we need to find self-actualization and spiritual fulfillment. Being and becoming, I call it. For example, your dream is to be the best soccer player that you can be, so you play soccer every day. It makes you happy. Therefore, you are a soccer player, while striving to be the best and attain your goal. You don't just *one day decide* you are good enough to call yourself an actual soccer player. Carl Rogers started the Rogerian school of thought, of having 'unconditional positive regard' for clients. He gave people the benefit of the doubt. You don't necessarily have to think the best of people all the time but don't overestimate or underestimate

people. Treat them as you would want them to treat you. The golden rule. But don't idolize a mortal human, don't put them on a pedestal. Albert Ellis taught us not to say 'I must do this,' 'I must do that,' and he said it's called 'Musterbation,' in his own words."

"Cool," said Tom.

"Your preferences, your favorites, things you like that make you happy, those are what determine your identity and who you are," said Murmur. "So, let's get these recordings done so we can play our rock and roll instruments down in Florida."

The next day, they were cruising around town in the sunshine. They went past the Ohio State Reformatory where Shawshank Redemption was filmed. "Have you ever been on the tour there?" asked Tom. "Of course," said Murmur. "What was it like?" asked Tom. "Boring," said Murmur. "Oh," said Tom. "Up here is the Harley dealer where they have some cool events going on sometimes. They had a band called Felt, who played some country-folky acoustic new Alternative type songs. Not the Felt from Huntsville, Alabama who did the song *Look at the Sun*, then got back together forty years later to release Felt II in 2012," said Murmur. "I like Indian motorcycles," said Tom. They went back to downtown, where Murmur pointed out a bare lot. "Here is where T&N Automotive was at. I had a car that the tires were about to blow out. I needed some used tires, which were all that I could afford. They were about to close for the night, but I was so tired. The Holy Spirit urged me to get up and go and have the tires done. When they were all done, they needed some more cash for the valve stems and tire

disposal, so I asked if they would wait, and I would run to the bank really quick and get it and get them the cash before they went home. They were so gracious and patient, and I stayed true to my word. Then the next day I was driving around in the big truck and noticed some firetrucks blocking the road. It didn't click at first. When I went past in a different direction, I noticed it was T&N that had burnt down! Somebody had accidentally set some paper near the tire repair station on fire. I hoped they took the cash out in time before it all went up in flames!"

They went past Weiner King on Lexington Avenue. "April told me that was probably a cover operation owned by the Russian Mafia," said Murmur. "Anyway, it always had these two ritzy cars sitting in the parking lot and not many other customers. Call me racist, but I believed her and couldn't get much more information out of her, so I assumed if I walked in there to check it out, there'd be this Russian guy at the counter, I'd ask for their hot-dog wieners. He'd say, 'Veener-r-r-s? Come in back, I show you Veener-r-r!' Then I'd be like, 'Uh… No.' But later, after April left me when I got up the nerve to check it out myself, I went in to find this little old gray-haired man, he said he couldn't take cards, he would only take cash. So, I bought a couple of nice chili dogs and some root beer. The décor was antiquated, but then the younger generation of kids took over and they started to take credit, debit cards."

"Far out, man!" exclaimed Fred. "I'm hungry, let's stop and get some hotdogs. I'm a foodie!" They stopped in and had a few chilidogs and had a great experience, except Deere. He's a

vegetarian. Everyone was so nice there. Then they hopped back in the GTO. Deere said, “Hey, listen to this song on my MP3, I love the bass line. It’s Friend & Lover, Reach Out of The Darkness. Listen closely to the bass. I love how bouncy it sounds.” They listened to it and liked it. Then he played some other bass lines he liked to play on bass guitar, Ultimate Spinach’s Ballad of the Hip Death Goddess, The C.A. Quintet’s A Trip Thru Hell, and so forth. “That sounds like an excellent song to drive at night to,” said Murmur. “Yeah, man,” Tom smiled with his sunglasses on. He started up the car. They continued to drive south on Lexington Avenue.

“And there’s this nice Chinese food place. A Wok, in this plaza. They have really good dumplings. But I imagined going in to order a two-for-one deal on an eggroll, from this cranky Chinese guy. I’d say, ‘The sign says buy one, get one, I want that.’ Then he’d say, ‘Here you go,’ hand me the bag with one eggroll in it. I’d say, ‘But there’s only one eggroll in here.’ He’d say, ‘Yes. That is correct,’ to which I’d say, ‘but it’s buy-one-get-one free.’ He’d say, ‘Not free! You buy wan, you get WAAHN!’ Hahaha!”

“You should be a stand-up comedian, Murmur,” said Fred. “There’s a lot of money in it, like up in New York City, not here of course. I mean you’d have to work very hard and hustle, but it might be worth it for you.”

“Yeah,” said Murmur. “You know, there’s one race,” Tom said, “The human race.”

“Right,” said Deere. “We need to celebrate and enjoy our differences. There are good white people and good black people. There are bad white

people and bad black people. They just have different levels of pigment in their skin. We should be able to be proud to be white, just as they have the right to be proud of being black. Or Asian, or Native American, or whatever."

"I met them. They're pretty nice people," said Murmur.

"Hey," said Fred. "Let's stop in and have some grub! I'm so hungry again! I'm a foodie you know." So, they stopped in and had some dumplings and other Chinese food. It was very good. The people were nice. Deere had some nice vegetarian food, "Yummy!"

Murmur took Diva and some musical instruments. The men got in their cars and took off down to Florida. They would race each other along the way, on I-75. Tom's house was a nice little place at Indian Rocks Beach, near St. Pete's Beach and not too far from Clearwater and Tampa. They played in coffee shops and small theater venues. They found a pretty decent singer for Equinox, named Cardamom Flowers. She was attractive. She came to audition at Tom's house. Then they recorded it in his high-tech studio. It was very professional sounding. They would hand out these CDs at their little concerts. That evening Tom found a bed for everyone to sleep in. Murmur invited Cardamom to share a bed with him. Surprisingly, she agreed. Murmur changed into some freaky pajamas, and they started to cozy down for the night. As he knelt for the prayer at the bedside, he also said, "And thank you God for this sex we are about to receive." Cardamom heard this and leaped out of bed and ran from the room, saying, "Oh, *hail* no!"

As she ran out, the guys heard and were laughing. "Leave her alone, you jerk!" Tom reached for her arm and consoled her. "Please don't leave, we need you! Here, you can sleep over here." Fred booked the gigs and worked as the Forever Band's manager. They played around Orlando: House of Blues Restaurant and Bar, Tanqueray's, Bullitt Bar, The Woods, The Haven, Velvet Sessions, and Will's Pub. They had some really good eats along the way. They needed one more song to round out the set, one night, so they asked Murmur to think up a song really quick. He said, "This here's a song I wasn't going to use, in fact, I just used it to practice back in the day. It's about a band you've never heard called Public Access:

The dummies come around every night
The dummies really think they're out of sight
The dummies bother me every day
The dummies wouldn't have it any other way
The dummies...
The dummies who think they're cool...
Dummies who think they're cool..."

His guitar parts sounded like an Offspring song. It was mediocre at best, but it gave them a chance to make it to a half hour of their original material. Then they asked for requests to play covers.

After they were done, Tom said he had a surprise for Murmur, and took him to an undisclosed location, as he opened a huge barn door, they saw it! The '70 GSX. It was yellow with a black stripe. "You like it? I could paint it the GM white with the black stripe," said Tom jokingly. "No, yeah, I like it if it's the original color, which it seems to be." Tom told them about finding it with

the help of Buick GSCA.[8] They spent a couple of hours sitting in it and then drove it around. Murmur put Diva in the yellow GSX. He said he wanted to drive it to Mansfield. Tom said he couldn't, not until he got paid for it. Fred said he was going back to New York City to take care of more business, make some more money, and call the rest of them to come on out there. Deere was going to drive back to California, park the car, and fly out to New York.

Murmur was heading back one evening from a concert at the Crofoot, Pontiac Michigan when he was pulled over by Fenton police. The cop strolled up to the car. He started commanding Murmur to roll down his window, and immediately he claimed he sensed the presence of alcohol and was harassing him.

"Take off those shades, so I can see your bloodshot eyes! Get out of the car now," said the obnoxious officer. He was pointing his gun at Murmur. Murmur lowered his sunglasses. His eyes were mesmerizing.

"You know what to do with that gun," shouted Murmur.

The annoying cop couldn't help but turn the gun around. His expression was one of shock because he couldn't stop his hand. BLAM! Suddenly the cop wasn't there anymore, and Murmur was on his way.

Murmur kept finding creeps and jerks seemingly coming out of the woodwork from all different directions to battle. People with ulterior motives, like the one who kept April in captivity in

---

[8] https://buickgsca.org/

his parents' basement, not letting her think or speak for herself, or respond to anyone that he did not approve of, above all not Murmur. Many of the guys were not charming enough, clever enough, or particularly even smart enough to have a larger following, so they kidnapped and hid away whoever they could control, in an abusive dysfunctional relationship. Suffice it to say; that they only had enough influential power to trick and keep one person.

Murmur had been trying to get the house in Mansfield sold, which entailed getting April to sign off from the house. At the same time, he had been working on remedial writing assignments concerning the conflict of interest red flags from Welden University. They did not like the fact that he was associated with Christian counseling. They did not like the fact that he voted for Trump. They did not like the fact that he was conservative. They did not like that he was pro-life. They wanted him to be pro-abortion. They hated him because he refused to support gay pride issues. They did not like his paper exposing the LGBTQIA+ community, showing how one man, George Weinberg, coined the term homophobia, based on personal reasoning, not science. Murmur stated how he tracked the original terminology for the acronyms to stand for lesbian gay, bisexual, and transsexual, of course, but then he contended they added Q for queer. They tried to then say it was Q for questioning. He claimed a fringe group was thinking about adding F for faggot, to which Murmur responded that if he had decided he wanted to identify as faggot, who was there to stop him or question it? They changed that part to 'figuring it out' and handily erased the

website championing it, adding I for intersex, and A for asexual, aromantic, or agender, or else A for ally or allied with someone who does identify that way. The acronyms then included 2S for two-spirits and continued on and on, prompting the plus sign. He refused to compromise his values on these issues.

In 2018 Dalton Dean said, "F_ your freedom of speech." It was heard on a particular radio show. Media changed the print wording quote to "Well, sod your freedom of speech." None of the former wording was to be found.

It didn't help that Murmur was getting almost zero clients or supervision and got involved with some unsavory characters who he had hoped would help him in his quest for counseling sessions. They tried to con him instead, taking advantage of his kindness and generosity. He did three gigantically long remedial papers, and his best was not good enough. He was informed that he was dismissed from the program. By the spring of 2020, he had all his things packed and ready to go.

Chapter Seven, Revenge:

Doctor Reginald Bluhm was in charge of approving or denying Murmur's remedial writing assignments over the year-long ordeal, where Murmur's future lay in limbo. Ultimately, after three rewrites of each three papers, he got the phone call with the decision, "You've been *dismissed* from the program," the voice said haughtily. "But wait, I…" Murmur started but noticed they had hung up.

He tried calling back the number, and several other numbers related to Welden, but couldn't reach Dr. Bluhm. A few times he got a hold of another person on the line, but they said he had the wrong department and would transfer him over, which took an endless rabbit trail, and often the connection was lost. Murmur tried from different numbers, but when he tried to get Dr. Bluhm, they asked him what it was about, and he had to make up a plausible story. Finally, Murmur's phone was ringing through to the desk of Dr. Bluhm.

"Hello, Doctor Bluhm here."

"Doctor Bum?"

He paused. "This is Doctor Bluhm, how may I help you."

"Doctor Bum, you say?"

"No, it's pronounced Bloom, not Bum. Okay?"

"Oh good, I'm so glad to be able to get you on the line, Doctor Bum. How are you doing, Mister Bum?"

"Listen, I don't have time for this. Either you address me in a respectable manner, or I am going to end this telephonic call."

"Certainly, Mister Bum!" [*click.*]

Murmur tried a few more times and then hopped in a car and drove out to Welden University to get Dr. Bluhm's attention. It took several hours to get there, but it was well worth it.

His research showed that Reginald would be at the administrative building that day, so he disguised himself as part of the faculty and went in to use the bathroom. He had brought a burlap bag to capture the man with. He flung it up over the adjacent toilet stall and began to relieve himself in the urinal. "Ah, what a relief," he said to himself as a man opened the bathroom door and walked in to use the urinal to his right. He suddenly recognized the man as Doctor Bluhm. Ever so nonchalantly he started singing a little nursery rhyme, minding his own business. "I'm a little teapot short and stout," Doctor Bluhm quickly looked to the left and gave him a dirty look, but Murmur did not look up or away from his urine stream. He continued, "Here is my handle here is my spout." Just then as Doctor Bluhm was ready to flee, a stream of urine leaped into his eyes blinding him. Then in one fluid motion, Murmur zipped up and swung around grabbing the burlap bag, and back around full circle, encasing Reginald in it. He tied the ends with rope. Then he pretended to be a janitor taking out the trash. Yes, Reggie did attempt to scream a bit, but a few knocks on the head with his masonry hammer from his tool belt silenced him.

The body was rolling back and forth in the trunk of Murmur's vehicle with every twist and turn of the road. It took several long hours to get to another undisclosed location.

When Dr. Bluhm awoke, he noticed his hands and feet were tied, and his mouth was gagged. His head was pounding in pain, and he could barely move. He looked around himself. It looked like it was a haunted old shack, way out in the middle of nowhere. He had chains restricting his mobility, and what looked like locks on the chains. Hours went by. His head was spinning with vertigo.

As Reggie's eyes slowly opened and came into focus, an ugly face appeared. "AAAAAAH!" It was Murmur. "Do you know what time it is?!?!?" screeched Murmur. "It's time for WOW! WOW! WUBBZIE!"

Murmur dragged the whole assembly with the engine block and weights to the little TV hooked to a VCR run on battery power. Then he pressed play and made him watch it. "Oh no you don't! no closing your eyes." He propped open the guy's eyelids with sharp toothpicks. Reggie tried desperately to look away and plug his ears. The torture went on for hours. Murmur was looking on with an extremely exaggerated happy look on his face.

"Do you know what would make this even better?" Reginald did not answer. "If…I…pooped…on…your face! Ha-ha-ha-ha-ha-ha-ha-ha-ha-ha-ha!" In an unequivocal and unbridled showing of malice, Murmur dropped his shorts and put his butt cheeks on top of the man's nose, straddling it. Then he let loose a river of diarrhea that almost drowned him. Murmur ran to a pot of boiling water amid his camping equipment and splashed it on the man's head. "You can't die yet, Creepozoid… Awe, are you burned? Here's

some peanut butter and jelly to spread on your skin!"

Since Reginald was near death's doorstep, Murmur decided to perform a little bit of bee sting therapy on his arms and legs, and everywhere else. "I don't want to harm the little honeybees; it pulls their poor little stingers out and then they die." He set the decorated box down carefully on Reginald's skin. "Therefore, I came up with this wonderful little alternative. Meet your new best friends, the ground hornets! They just sting and sting forever, until, well…forever, man! Have fun! Mua-ha-ha-ha-ha-ha!" Murmur triggered a little trap door on the box as he exited the place.

Another time, when Murmur came back, he noticed the man had found a sharp scissors and tried to stab him with it, but Murmur wrestled it out of his hands a replaced it with safety scissors instead, scooting the sharp one down in a crack in the floorboards.

Then yet another time, Murmur came up to him and said, "Your breath smells like mothballs. That means you're gonna die soon!"

Murmur got a call from Fred, "Hey, man! Can you fly out to New York? I got you some stand-up comedy gigs. Plus, I'm calling all the other dudes from the band, we got a lot of things to do out here."

"Sounds groovy, man. You just tell me where to go."

"I'm sending you an email with a plane pass, just get your little dog in a kennel somewhere and then go. You don't have to pack anything with you," said Fred.

"Okay!" When Murmur hung up the cell phone, he printed the tickets out. He got Diva ready and brushed her teeth. Then he brushed his own teeth and took a nice shower.

Murmur drove Diva over to Mohican kennels and got her set up to stay for the few weeks that he'd be gone to New York. On the way back that evening, there appeared a cop's lights pulling him over. He looked in the side-view mirror and noticed some pointy black boots walking over to his vehicle amid sepia-tinged mist, as he was hungrily eating a Butterfinger candy bar. The driver's window was open. The cop swung and knocked Murmur's candy to the ground. "YOU LIKE CANDY DO YA, PUNK??? I'M GONNA GIVE YOU SOME CANDY YOU'RE NOT GONNA LIKE, AND YOU'RE GONNA LIKE IT! DO YOU HEAR ME? YOU BETTER SPEAK TO ME WHEN YOU'RE SPOKEN TO, PUNK. I'M NOT YOUR AVERAGE RUN-OF-THE-MILL COP. YOU BETTER BOW DOWN NOW! GET OUT OF THE CAR AND PUT YOUR HANDS UP! I SAID NOW!"

Murmur calmly and slowly but gently pulled his shades down his nose, until his eyes appeared with a swirling effect, which halted the officer's aggression. The cop swished his head back and forth and squinted his eyes shut, "Nih," he started, unable to make out another complete word. He took a step back and whipped out his pistol, pointing it between Murmur's eyes, but then shutting his again.

"Look at me!" Several seconds went by. The officer relented and opened his eyes, but couldn't pull the trigger, it was stuck. Like a giant piece of iron, shaped like a gun, it was molded in one piece,

with no moving parts. “I’m telling you what you’ve got to do now. I’m telling you that you’ve got to turn that thing around and point it at your own head, right between the eyes.” The officer’s arm freakishly rotated beyond all control to aim the pistol between his own eyes. “And tell me now,” Murmur continued, “do you think that is the position that someone who kills themselves gets a bullet?”

“NO…YES!” BLAM! The pistol dropped to the ground. The person who was standing there turned into a pile of powder. The wind picked up soon and blew the powder away, out into the wooded area across the road. Several cars passed by with the drivers not paying any attention. Murmur drove on. He went to the airport in Columbus and flew out to New York.

Fred met him at the airport. “What’s going on, man?” Murmur smiled and replied, “Oh you know, same old-same old.” They both laughed heartily.

Once in New York City, he did stand-up comedy at places like Gotham Comedy Club, Comedy Cellar, St. Mark’s Comedy Club, West Side Comedy Club, Stand Up NY, Comedy Shop, The PIT, The Stand NYC, and New York Comedy Club.

The other guys from the band came out and played at rock clubs like Rockbar NYC, The Bitter End, The Red Lion, The Bowery Ballroom, Mercury Lounge, Rockwood Music Hall, and Café Wha? Believe it or not, they had quite a following of groupies, fans, and followers. Women were hitting on them, not just the band, but also waiting for Murmur after his comedy shows.

"I like big breasts," said Deere.

"Who doesn't," said Tom. "Reminds me of the Boobs A Lot song."

"I love breasts, and I love a woman's hot long sexy legs coiled around me, holding me inside," said Murmur. "Those childbearing hips, rocking back and forth. Gyrating. Gyrations. Rotating. Moving. Rather than itty bitty titty committee, we have the best-blessed breasts in the Midwest contest."

"Oh, and sexy women's big butts," said Fred. "Believe me boys, you're gonna find a whole lot more than you bargained for here in New York City, and then some! Hey, speaking of which, Cardamom is here! I flew her out and she's gonna sing with us. Hi, my darling!"

"Hey, what's shaken, hot stuff?" greeted Cardy. She brightened up the whole room, as she strutted and strolled in.

"Oh, I got some groovy new tunes that I wrote," said Fred. "Let's get set up in the studio over here and I can play and sing them for y'all. Meanwhile here's an old demo I made back in the day. Check it out!" He turned over to the control panel and flicked a switch. Different voices sang the different parts:

We come from France
To save our souls
We come from Germany to save our country
We come from England
We're gonna make you a bargain
One heck of a price to lose control
We Come from Spain
Can you stand the pain
We come from Portugal

We're gonna fly like a seagull
Kinda mangy like a beagle
Peck you just like an eagle
We're all a bunch of vultures
Can you stand our tortures?
I don't know what I'm gonna do
Or if we'll ever meet at all...

It was a pastiche of late-60s and beyond, rock music styles.

"What do you think?" said Fred.

"Wow! Sounds like the Who," said Deere. "And Bowie!"

"Sounds a little like Zeppelin, in the bar chords in the instrumental break," said Tom.

"Yeah, I stole those chords," said Fred. "Kind of hard not to. They own them!"

"Nice chord progression," said Murmur. "Nice flowing feeling to it."

"Well, I kind of liked it," said Cardamom. "You got a lot of nice voices, and some of the Byrds' harmonies, especially at the end."

"Why, thank you! We get a lot of musicians around here and they like to help me out and I help them out on their various projects, but it's like, you know." Everybody was laughing and eating some chips and dips. Deere was especially hungry, looking in the well-stocked refrigerator for beer. "Yeah, help yourself," said Fred. Deere pulled out a brown bottle of Amstel Light. "Wow, now Light's spelled the *right* way! You guys want anything?"

"What all you got in there?"

"Beggars can't be choosers."

"I'll have one of those."

"Wow, you have Sam Adams."

"Let's have a party, man!"

"Yeah, let's party, dude!"

"That's sounds awesome!"

"Check out my stereo system, guys, I also got all this."

"Nice…"

"Cool…"

"Far out, man…"

"I like it. I like it a lot"

"New York's the place to be. Come on I'll show you around…"

Fred showed everyone his wonderful place. "We got a lot of things to do today. But first, we are going to party! Let me call a bunch of friends on the phone." He called them on the phone as the All Tomorrow's Parties video was playing on the stereo and flat screen, by Velvet Underground and Nico.

"Check out Poohbah, from Youngstown," He played I'm Crazy You're Crazy from 1972's Let Me In, and then Crazy from U.S. Rock, and We're All Crazy from 2014's Cosmic Rock.

"I can dig it!" declared Deere.

"Far out, man!" stated Murmur.

"Groovy, dude!" contributed Tom.

Just then there was a knock on the door, and a party platter had been delivered, it was full of charcuterie items, snacks, and hors d'oeuvres. It was too much to be delivered via drone. Then Martha, Aimee, Dorothea, Tony, Richard, Martin, Tonya, Janet, Todd, and Beth showed up, dressed in casual and party clothes. Fred introduced all his friends to the bandmates. Fred had a bar in the basement to serve drinks and have everyone stay out of trouble by spending the night if they had too

much to drink. He didn't want them to drink and drive.

"Wow," said Murmur, "I notice you have a lot of food all over the place, all the time."

"You have a refrigerator in almost every room," said Deere.

"Yes," said Fred. "I always found stockpiling an abundance of food comforting. I don't like to chance running out."

"See, I don't get the concept of comfort food," replied Murmur. "That phrase always seems foreign to me. Food is neither comforting nor discomforting. It's just food. You just eat it."

"I guess," said Fred, "when I was younger, and my father left on his drinking binges, and we found out later to live with his surrogate family, my mama was left to try to scrounge up enough money to put food on our table. We went from having a hundred bucks to spend on a couple of carts full of groceries each week to having to put so many things back that we couldn't afford at the checkout. I had this little green Incredible Hulk bank that is one of the few things he got me for Christmas. Although I kept emptying it so often, I just cut a large hole in the bottom and kept taping it back closed with a piece of masking tape. I also had this little Cashbook. I documented every penny I ever made or lost. Every amount I'd been cheated or won. Mama used to be a stay-at-home mom before but after that, she had to work slaving laborious jobs like on the tomato harvester or picking strawberries. So, it reminds me of the song, *Handbags and Glad Rags*.

"She tried to go up to the community college, and at the financial aid office, they were

talking down about her, saying something about everyone wanting a free ride to college, they want something for nothing. Trying to make her ashamed of trying to get a leg up. I used to get so depressed on Mondays. Halfway through Sunday, I'd get depressed too, thinking that the weekend was almost over and anticipating the Monday coming. If I had a weekend off, I'd spend it trying to figure out a solution to fix my life. To get out of the rat race. It's like trying to get off of Gilligan's Island. Every hour of those long hours spent trying to put food on the family table cuts into quality time that is so precious. You trade your time for money, and money is scarce. So, every time they charged a bank fee and got further into the negative, or got a traffic ticket, I call it crisis mode, it's like taking food off of the family table, taking food out of the kids' mouths."

"I worked at a factory a few times. I made good money there… just not enough of it."

"That had to be extremely boring," empathized Fred.

"I had suffered from sensory deprivation from the boredom and sensory overload from the stress at the same time. There every minute felt like an hour, every hour felt like a year."

Murmur opened one of the refrigerators stocked full in every space and scanned with his eyes for food he liked. His stomach angrily rumbled. He was 'hangry.' "You know, it's funny," Murmur said. "I like to run on empty with food. I have one or two things in the refrigerator or the cupboards, and I just trust that I'm going to be able to find more. But we come from similar backgrounds. Different reaction results."

"It's not money that's important in the end," said Fred. "It's the quality time with people. Money is just a resource that enables us to exchange stuff we need or want. In the end, we won't use money. We'll just have personal relationships and barter, trade, and deal with each other."

"Yeah, man!"

"Check out my prepper pantry, downstairs!"

For his comedy show, Murmur came on stage and said,

"Look for it wherever you get your podcasts.

"I get my podcasts from a GARBAGE CAN.

"I get my podcasts from the TOILET! How about THAT HUH? I'll ask Alexa to package herself back up and send herself back for a full refund. *I can't do that*! Hey, I got to watch the time, or I'll be late for my brain transplant tonight.

"What about the way they changed the design logo of the Pepsi bottle cap? It was just a red, white, and blue wave on the top of the bottle cap. Patriotic, yes. Pretty cool. Then it became a Pepsi Globe on the front. Then in 2009, they paid over a million bucks to this worthless design firm, Arnell Group, calling it the Pepsi Eye. I say, if it's an actual eye, it looks like a wavy drunken stupor eye, or someone got poked with a stick in the eye. Very stupid! They're gonna have to revert back to the classic, just like the flavor of the 'new Coke,' which everyone in a blind taste test liked better, but it wasn't 'classic.' [laughter] *Retro* Pepsi was the Throwback with real sugar!

"Just like the wonderful classic logo for the Red Roof Inn. When a weary traveler was peering through the rainy car window in the distance, they

saw these letters in the shape of a hand with a red glove on with the index finger pointed up and thumb sticking out and the other fingers folded down halfway. Pretty nifty. You can't improve upon that, so don't try! Now that they've done this stupid redesign to try to look modern, it looks like a bloody hand that got caught in the blades of a lawnmower. Nothing to do with a hotel! They paid this jerk, David Canaan (one of the Canaanites, obviously…) of Laurel Group, they paid this clown a lot of money to ruin a classic logo. Uncalled for! [applause]

"Chevys got the bowtie, very classy! Started in 1914, World War 1, the Great War. Audi had the Auto Union rings. Ford has a big blue goose egg! [Laughter] Back at the auto shop, do you know what we call a Ford wrench? A sledgehammer! You all know the acronym; Found on Road Dead, Fix or Repair Daily, Funked up old Rebuilt Dumpster. We'd freak Greenhorns out by calling for some blinker fluid. Why does my left blinker not work? Oh, you just need some more blinker fluid. Other competing shops would tell them they needed all-new muffler bearings. Do you mean muffler clamps? No, they're fine, I just had them inspected two days ago at the shop down the road. [Whoops and Hollers]

"I have to call out this clown, Mike Brown almost single-handedly had Pluto declassified as a planet in 2006. Now all the searches are going to come up with this big stupid organization of self-appointed so-called experts, the globalist organization IAU, and a chief proponent of reclassification of Pluto, that idiotic Ethan Siegal creep. NASA said it is still a planet, and scientists

are going to add it back where it belongs as our 9th planet. Also, Pluto has 5 moons and is not part of the Asteroid belt or the Keyper belt, so there's that. Free Pluto! [applause as Murmur raised his fist in the air, defying the global establishment]

"A few months ago, I walked into a bar and ordered a beer and was looking around the room, I saw this guy sitting a few yards away and had his back turned. I thought to myself, is this my friend Gorton? But when I saw his face turn, it was just the uglier, older version of Gorton. Then I had a scary thought, am *I* the uglier older version of… *me*? Same thing with doppelgangers. Or an evil twin... wait am *I* the evil twin? Oh *no*! Well, people are talking about spirit animals. My spirit animal is a *gargoyle*. [laughter and applause] Anyway, I mixed up way too many different drinks and I projectile vomited my way on out of there. Now, I better scoot on out of here before I get into too much trouble. You all have a great night and I'll see you next time! 10-4, over and out!"

He dropped the mic but then caught it before it hit the ground and placed it back up on the mic stand, then ran off the stage right.

They all had such a great night each time they went to the comedy clubs. They ended up staying up all night long, until daybreak with Cardamom, and all the groupies. They had a blast! At the bars, Fred usually ordered an Old Fashioned. But since he had his own bar at home, that was just for occasional socializing. The rest of Forever enjoyed Scotch and Soda, Gin and Tonic, Whiskey Sours, Screwdrivers, and craft beers.

One of the guys who joined them at the bar was a Black guy named Chuck, who was great at

singing karaoke. Tom started writing a great funky song when he got back to the dressing room and picked up a guitar. He thought Chuck would be great at the vocals. He was playing a lively rhythm. Deere played a hot popping bass part. Fred grabbed a couple of pencils for use as drumsticks. Chuck was invited back to sing with them. Tom told him the lyrics were as follows.

Put a little love in your heart
Put a little love in your soul, soul, soul
It starts a little spark, and it grows
You'll be feeling good from your head to your toes

Your love takes me across the mountains
Your love takes me beyond the seas
We've got to get this thing together, just wait and see...

Chuck sang the song and asked if he could continue touring with them. "We're going out to California next," Tom said. "Right Deere?"

"Yeah, man!"

"Is that okay with you?"

"Sure, man that's cool. Real cool. I always wanted to go out west, but never had a good reason to," answered Chuck. "Which area are we going to, Los Angeles? San Diego? San Francisco?"

"Yes," answered Murmur.

"My place is near San Francisco," answered Deere. "But I do have some other hideouts… all around the state.

"That sounds great," said Chuck. "Yeah, Dudes, whenever you all are ready, I'm game."

“Well, we got a lot to do in New York first, of course,” said Fred. “We’re making a lot of money right now.”

Friends like Martha, Aimee, Dorothea, Tony, Richard, Martin, Tonya, Janet, Todd, Beth, and the groupies wanted to go too. Most of them could sing backup vocals. Or at least look good dancing up on stage. So, they decided to drive cross country on an old school bus, painted up with Hippie slogans, logos, and designs. “Can I ring up my buddy Marvin, too?” asked Chuck. “What instruments can he play?” asked Fred. “Saxophone, trumpet, flute, trombone, stuff like that,” answered Chuck. “Sure,” said the guys in the band.

They played the rest of the scheduled dates, as Tom and Murmur finished fixing up the old bus. They had plenty of cash on hand for gasoline.

Deere helped them hook up the CD and MP3 surround sound system. Fred made sure they had plenty of music curated to get them thousands of miles down the road. They played songs from bands like the Eyes, The Flies, The Azteks, The Undertakers, The Knickerbockers, Richard and The Young Lions, The Rascals, The United States of America, Fifty Foot Hose, The Sonics, The Castaways, Sweetwater, Donovan, and The Ventures. Of course, they had a lot of newer music between them, too, such as Eleanor Friedberger. They talked a lot.

They had a television installed and could even play their instruments. They had all kinds of camping gear, a little sink and shower, and a toilet, too. They had some beds they could take turns sleeping in.

Tom drove the first 500 miles; Murmur drove 700 more miles. Deere drove about 500 miles. Fred drove 700 miles, and they all stopped and rested for a while at the Grand Canyon National Park, Arizona. Deere drove them the rest of the way to San Francisco, California.

Chapter Eight, Gurus Galore:

Once they got nearer to San Francisco, the group of 17 friends and groupies got out and stretched their legs again at a truck stop. They used the bathroom and then got back in. Deer drove them up to his huge underground garage where all his other vehicles were stored. The garage door opened automatically with the remote. He drove the bus in, then shut the door behind him.

"Wow, do you have an underground house too?"

"I do," smiled Deere.

"Way cool!"

They played in places like Boom Boom Room, and Bottom of the Hill.

Murmur did stand-up comedy at The Punch Line, Polite Chuckle Comedy, Cobb's Comedy Club, Kung Pao Kosher Comedy, Cheaper Than Therapy, and Best of San Francisco Stand-up Comedy. The Milk Bar was a place where the band also played, so they hung around to watch Murmur's comedy.

"There are so many gurus around today. Tai Lopez, Tony Jeary, Preston Ely, and Tony Robbins, to name a few. They live such lavish extravagant lifestyles. Tai, in fact, said he bought a Lamborghini, or test drove it I suspect, *very fun to drive through the Hollywood hills*, back to his garage, or neighbor's garage, maybe. Get this. I don't know if you all, or any of you here watched the video, but it's like a one-room building, with a small man-door on the side, and a little one-car garage door in it. A black Lamborghini inside, and behind him his *seven new black bookshelves*, filled

with *2000 new books*, he *had* installed. He didn't have the fortitude to make them and install them himself! Though, isn't that the idea of self-help? He's got these special black plastic glasses specially designed to make him look approachable, down-to-earth, and studious. And what's a full collection of books doing in the garage? Call me crazy, but shouldn't they be in, oh, maybe… **A LIBRARY?!?!?** That's why I believe it might be a one-room rented building. You'll notice he doesn't pan the camera around enough to see the rest of the room. Maybe that's all there is to his house. Besides, if you did have a few books in your garage, I would guess they would be Chilton's manuals, Haynes repair books, or even historical books on Ferrari, Lamborghini, Corvettes, or Porches. Unless…I don't know, you wanted to pull into your garage, close the garage door, and suddenly want to read a book on cars, so you get back into the car with the motor running and just read yourself to sleep. And never wake up!"

[chuckles from audience]

"Of course, you might expect him to be reading Chaucer, Whitman, Shakespeare, or some other inspirational authors and it might be a bit smarter to go to that special place we call a PUBLIC LIBRARY! You can socialize and meet some hot chicks, or even a hot librarian there! You can't do that in your—*garage library!*"

[some more laughter from the audience]

"Knowledge can be gotten through reading a book a day, but wisdom is the practical application of knowledge. That means saving your money for something more valuable than paying to some dumb guru who's using you to get rich, just because *you*

want to be rich! Isn't that what you really want? Save it! Okay, so you've had many millionaire mentors, and you want to help us by condensing all the best advice. So just put it in one book, we might buy it, instead of 2000 books! Besides, get out and live life, not spend it indoors all day with your nose in a book! Unless it's a comedy book; I love a good comedy book, by a comedian. I hope you buy *my* book! I just have to write it first."

[light laughter, noise, and chattering from the audience]

"If one of these doofuses tells you to pay big money for a seminar, and you'll be going to a sweat lodge for a couple of weeks in the desert, don't go there! *Don't doo* dat! If someone tells you everyone in their special sect is referred to as *The Family*, run the other way! Jesus said you're not supposed to have sects. Hey, I said sects, not sex! Get your mind out of the gutter! If someone has some new leftist church called the People's Church and they say they are going to Guyana because the folks here in America just don't understand us. Get the heck out of there! Leave immediately!

If someone tells you they're part of a group that wants to leave their material bodies behind and go drink a poisonous concoction of phenobarbital and vodka, lay down and die so they can join up with a spacecraft from heaven that's coming for us hidden behind a comet, GO! Skedaddle on out of there, as fast as possible!

"If you fall for those scams, you'll likely believe lies such as chemtrails are just contrails. I know. I have seen them both in the same sky at the same exact time, with the same exact atmospheric conditions. I know how much you good folks out

here in California care about your health, Mother Earth, and the environment, but never trust the establishment. Don't trust fake news CNN, don't trust fake news of The Weather Channel, don't trust fake news NPR. They got blood on their hands, having their hoodlums, those paid goons they got going out setting the…*mailbox fire. The MAILBOX FIRE. The lunchbox fire. The LUNCHBOX FIRE! The briefcase fire. The BRIEFCASE FIRE!* They'll blame it on global warming and climate change. It perpetuates their globalist agenda and enables them to exert more control.

"I come from Michigan and Ohio, where we have our cows and horses grazing so we don't have acres of overgrown grass. You'd think the place for that would be out in the great plains like Iowa, Minnesota, and Wisconsin. Happening all over the world. It's global, right? I was going east on Route 30 and saw this billboard that said, "What's happening to our sky? Geoengineering watch dot org." They're loading up aluminum, which causes Alzheimer's, and dementia; they're loading barium and biohazards. Part of the dumbing down of America, so they can manipulate the feeble-minded voters and common citizens, against their will. One elderly Native American reported that a plane came down low over the community and he was outside sitting when he felt the spray drift down upon his head and shoulders, he started getting sick and within a few days his health deteriorated, and he died. What a coincidence right?

"You'd think NPR, with all its caring and obscure references to indigenous peoples, would report on that. Instead, they're like, here you alleged Native people, we'll give you this free meal if you

will talk about how the dangerous climate conditions caused by pollution, particularly carbon emissions from automobiles running on fossil fuels, leading to the impending climate catastrophes killing the earth, are impacting your communities and life, and impoverishing your reservations."
[chatter and noise from the audience]

Murmur had a date with a young woman, who had become a fan. She had pretty blue eyes and long blonde hair. She was very sexy and flirtatious. He took her out to dinner. They went to Epic Steak. She was a liberal and asked him why he talked about liberals and conservatives. "What's wrong with being liberal? I'm liberal with my love. I give love freely. I want more fairness, peace, justice, goodness, and harmony among all people."

"Want some pepper for your steak?"

"Oh, sure, thanks!"

Murmur handed the pepper shaker to Maya, saying, "People on the Right are right, remember Jesus went back to heaven to sit at the right hand of the Father, so it is very meaningful. Those who are on the Left are not right. If you take away everything that is right, the Left is all that's left."

"Oh," said Maya, looking deep into Murmur's eyes. She looked down and shook the pepper. The top flew off and pepper dumped onto her steak. "Dang Freakin' pepper!"

"Hahaha! Politically speaking, the government, with taxing and spending, and getting involved and mucking things up, is a lot like them convincing you pepper is the solution to everything and dumping it out on your steak," said Murmur.

"I don't understand," said Maya.

"May I?" Murmur gently picked up Maya's plate and brushed off the excess pepper into a napkin. "If you were conservative with your pepper, you would use it sparingly, traditionally, and only as much as needed."

"Oh," said Maya, "I get it. But people on the Right…Republicans, only care about money. They're the rich people and supposed to be racist, like the KKK? Or something."

"Who? The Northern anti-slavery party, or the Southern Democrats who were the slave owners? Yeah…Democrats are some of the richest people with extravagant mansions all around Pennsylvania and stuff. Also, RINOs and lying career politicians."

"Well, I think the government should tax people more so they can pay for more government programs and provide free stuff for people who need it!"

"Seriously? You sound like a chick I knew, Bryn Dimpleton. She was a true leftist. To be honest, I started out being a moderate. I like cannabis, we smoked a bit of weed, together and apart. Willie Nelson smoked pot a lot, and he was a great guy and still is. And I hate to say it but I…wasn't a pro-lifer. I told people abortion was needed for cases of rape and incest, very disgusting things indeed. But in effect, I was a pro-abortionist. She liked Ladonna, and also Enenen, two of the worst people to ever disgrace the face of planet Earth, as I later found out. When she asked me if I would ever go to a Ladonna concert with her, I said maybe. I got her a Ladonna calendar for her birthday. But ultimately, I did get her to go to a Kansas concert together with me and she kind of

liked it. I am also for student loan forgiveness in a way. Not having taxpayers fund the payback to the banks but charging it back to the big leftist universities that failed us and bankrupting them so that they go out of business. Look at it this way, indefinitely doing deferments, forbearance, or having it excused upon death or moving to other nearby possibly slightly hospitable planets is merely placating their payback until later or never, or they can charge back these greedy universities that keep raising the costs per semester or quarter that don't actually deserve the money because their buttload of useless information and indoctrination for future generations, and forcing the professors to repay all their wages for failing on our students."

"Amen to that," said Maya.

Later in Los Angeles, they drove up to Laurel Canyon to see another place where Deere often crashed at a friend's house. They saw the places where many '60s rock stars lived. Deere explained how expensive housing had gotten. That night, Tom went out on a date with Cardamom. Deere went out with a beautiful slender brunette girl, with huge ample breasts, named Cindy Gossamer. Fred dated a nice, gorgeous redhead named Marcie Belasco. They came along for the trip with the entourage on the bus. They drove to San Diego and stopped at the farmland Deere inherited from his parents. They stopped and took naps and showers. Then they drove off to Vegas for several of them to get married.

"Yeah, man," said Deere, "I'm going to stop in Vegas and get married to Cindy by an Elvis impersonator if you all don't mind." Cindy was

wearing an engagement ring, held up her hand, and smiled with all her teeth.

"Sounds good, dude," declared Tom. "I'm happy for you!"

"Well in that case," said Murmur, "Will you marry me, Maya?" Murmur got on his knee and held out a giant diamond engagement ring. Maya said, "Sure!" She beamed radiantly.

Not wanting to be outdone, Fred glanced over to Marcie and popped the question, searching his pockets in vain. "I'll get you a ring, I promise when we get back to New York." Marcie happily said, "Yes!" They kissed passionately.

The twenty, plus groupies drove back to Ohio to drop off Murmur. "I need to get Diva out of the kennel," he said. "Then I'll drive out to New York to hang out with everyone when you're ready."

"Oh," replied Fred. "Cool." Everyone was making out with someone. Martha, Aimee, and Dorothea were making out with Tony, Richard, and Martin. Tonya, and Janet, were making out with Todd, and Beth, while Chuck and Marvin were making out with Cardamom. Tom was making it with several groupies. The bus stereo was playing *Making Time* by the Creation, and they took their time getting back.

Chapter Nine, When God Bought Me a Coke:

Maya and Murmur had sold the house in Mansfield and were hiding out in a secret hideout, not too far north from the sign that "Jesus is Lord over Castalia." Occasionally they would hang out at Pat Dailey's favorite hangout spot, The Boathouse Bar and Grill. They seemed to be soulmates and twin flames; made for each other and sent from heaven above. The old raggedy but cleaned sofa from a garage sale was where they were snuggling at the moment, other times they cuddled on the bed in the dim, quiet light. "You see," Murmur was saying as he sighed, "these days I drink a lot of water. I always drink a lot of beverages with a meal, at the dinner table, or even just sitting around. I used to drink a lot of sodas, well, up north we call them pops. At first, you know you grow up drinking a lot of milk, or chocolate milk, you can make it with one teaspoon of cocoa powder, two teaspoons of sugar, or tablespoons for a larger glass, putting in about a quarter cup of hot water, stirring it up and then pouring in the milk to the top. Or you can make it with Hershey's syrup, or Ovaltine. Or Tiger's milk as my momma called it. You mix up some molasses in the milk. She used to make a Boston Cooler with a glass of Pepsi and stir in a tablespoon or more of powdered milk. The phosphoric acid used for the citrus taste would react to the calcium and make a foamy head just like with a root beer float. Dad and I would go to an A&W root beer stand, or Stewart's to get a few chili cheese coney dogs, footlongs even. But now we got them Skyline chili places from outside of

Cincinnati. You've been there? Well then later on when I was a teenager, Dad used to fix me a hot toddy. Everything that ails you can be fixed by a hot toddy. You just use a little instant tea, lemon, and hot water and then pour a little shot bottle of whiskey into the cup. Got a fever? Have a *hot toddy!* Got the flu? *Hot Toddy!* Did you get strep throat? *Hot TODDY!* Overdose? The Clap? Alcoholism? *HOT TODDY! HOT TODDY! HOT TODDY!* But anyhow, according to William Poundstone in Big Secrets, cola flavors typically have three components, vanilla flavoring, citrus approximation from the corrosive acid, and cinnamon-like flavor. In Coke, you find more of the cassia bark for fake cinnamon. Phosphoric acid rots your teeth out and kneecaps off if you drink too much and can't compensate for the lost calcium. Or in the body shop, we can dissolve some rust with it. Usually, if you drink a little now and then, your saliva rinses it off, unless you are constantly drinking a 2-liter. They make it addictive by adding the drug, caffeine, which is a white chemical powder form from decaffeinating coffee or tea. However, I've yet to turn down a free Coca-Cola, especially when I went down to Atlanta for the residency. They had it free in the hotel rooms and conference center, and at the World of Coca-Cola."

Maya stretched out to reach her tall cold glass of Arnold Palmer, half lemonade and half iced tea, which she sometimes added alcohol such as bourbon. "Things taste even better to me when they're free," continued Murmur. "It's magical when The Lord provides. I am so thankful, grateful even. It's a spiritual moment in an ordinary day.

Did I tell you about the time God bought me a Coke?"

"No," Maya cooed.

"Actually, I have to tell it in context. I loved to drive up to the rest areas, with the big truck, hop out, go to the bathroom, and check the vending machines for spare change people forgot to take. So, I would get a quarter, dime, or a few pennies here or there. A penny saved is a penny earned, you know. Sometimes a snack or a beverage would fall. Upstairs in K&D's locker room, there was a pop machine, and a can of Coke was already dispensed. I wasn't about to let it go to waste, so I drank it. The next night after a long day at work, there I found another can of Coke again!"

"Wow!"

"Yeah, so later that week, you know I was always praying for intuition, I got out of the truck at the rest area on 30 westbound, I looked far off at the vending machines in a row, and when I saw the Coca-Cola machine, I envisioned myself walking up to the machine and finding a nice cold 20-ounce bottle of Coke, picking it up and holding it out in my hand, and saying "Thank you, God! I got it!" before drinking it up. So, guess what happened, I slowly strolled up there, and there at the bottom of the machine, behind the dispenser door, was…an…ice…cold… 20-ounce bottle of Coca-Cola, not diet Coke or anything yucky! It was just as I had imagined it. I held it up high toward the sky and in a loud voice, said 'Thank you, God! I got it!' I drank it all right away. You know I never waste anything. I think you can't show appreciation and then just throw away what's been given to you. Anyway, that wasn't the end of it; later on in that

machine I had found the free cans of Coke in, there was $2 worth of quarters in the change compartment, I used it to buy 4 more cans of Coke for a total of 7 drinks."

"Ohhhh, you talk too much, Babe," Maya softly purred as she began to gently kiss him, caressing his neck, hair, and shoulders.

"Mmmm, true dat," Murmur replied in a calm, peaceful deep voice, passionately kissing her soft, sweet, rosy lips back.

"Being a conservative that means you conserve on stuff, doesn't it?" asked Maya.

"I just don't like to waste things," replied Murmur, "since I had an epiphany in the lunchroom. I would occasionally get a stewed tomato on my tray, and I didn't really like them. So, I would save it for last and if I felt kind of full I would throw it away. I knew my brother just loved stewed tomatoes. My Momma worked so hard to put food on the table after Dad left. So…that day I just looked at it for a couple of minutes. I went ahead and ate it. I actually liked it! Everything changed in my outlook after that. You know, we have Milliron recycling, I'll show you, we'll go recycling, nothing gets wasted here. It's not just weirdos who want to save the Earth, a lot of sensible people do too. Besides, I worked at a lot of places involved in recycling firsthand. I've seen the trend of zero-waste facilities. I don't believe in global warming or climate change; carbon is a normal part of life. It doesn't hurt anything. Trees breathe it in and breathe out oxygen."

"I see," Maya said as she slid the tip of her right index finger playfully down his nose.

"We don't need more government interference or intervention in our lives, don't need a Nanny state. We don't love the establishment. All the hippies should agree with that. They view organized religion as part of the establishment, and false religion is, but not true religion. True religion is personal. Jesus said we should be no part of this world. The Kingdom of God is the future, not mankind's government. That'll be a thing of the past. You don't want your boss peering over your shoulder and micromanaging you at work. Big Brother watching. Big government, the Deep State, and the old New World Order want to micromanage you and get inside your brain. If you think these days that you're always on camera, you are. Some devices of ours are listening. It's really easy to be paranoid. Reagan said government is not the solution to problems, it is the problem. We just need enough law and order to have protection from crime, from others, but the anarchists want chaos because they think all that drama is fun. That's why we're conservative. Politics is all about control over other people. Persuasion, convincing, and advertising is all about trying to make other people see your way is best. Just how ethical is that when it's done on a massive scale? Remember Ronald Regan said governments can't control things, a government can't control the economy without controlling people…"

"God doesn't micromanage people???" asked Maya.

"No," answered Murmur. "Everyone has always been endowed with free will. We are given grace. Grace is enough. We're no longer under the Law. As saints, which are believers, we just have to

trust and follow. Take God's word for it, and love God."

"Mmmm-hmm," sighed Maya as she sexily smiled, arms outstretched around his neck, forearms resting on his shoulders, "that sounds lovely." It was as if she had a British accent.

"You're free to be you," added Murmur, "a character with an individual personality, although if you ask me, I'll tell you my definition is first and foremost a Christian. It's what I think of first about myself. That's the meaning of being the salt of the Earth. We season the Earth by being real people made in the image of God. If our salt became flavorless and bland it would be like the rock salt that we throw out on the ground in the winter to trample over. Not like Gourmet Pink Himalayan Salt, Celtic Sea Salt, or French Grey Salt."

"You're delicious, Darling," flirted Maya. "You can season my pot of stew anytime!"

Later, the two of them gathered the bins of glass bottles, plastic, flattened aluminum cans, tin and steel cans, shredded paper, cardboard, clean or stripped copper, and such into the car and drove it up to Milliron on 39 toward Shelby. They pulled up along the front of the building and turned to face one of the sets of overhead garage doors. It opened and Murmur drove in. In the other lane was a white pickup truck with the top chopped off and no windshield, a couple of guys were unloading while a couple of workers asked what all Murmur and Maya had collected, and which would they like to unload first. After getting the gross weight, they unloaded each category at a time and got another reading, until they were done and got an empty, tare weight. One of the workers handed Murmur a

printout sheet of paper, and the other side door opened into the back. Their car went around to the parking lot and Murmur and Maya got out, walked inside, stood in line, and got paid a few bucks and some coins.

The glass bottles, though, had to go over to Richland County Solid Waste Recycling and Electronics disposal. They wouldn't pay anything for glass, but you get the chance to properly dispose of it there. Most people don't care enough to do so.

"Styrofoam," explained Murmur, "can be compressed in a compactor into a bale and trucked off when the trailer is full of bales to a special recycling facility. There are not many of those around yet, and everybody just throws it away. Same deal with TerraCycle where you send things through the mail like Febrese cans to Tennessee. Individuals need to take initiative to get it done. Not many people want to bother to make the effort. But they'll act like they care about the harm done to the earth by carbon footprints, and big polluting corporations, namely some elusive enigmatic problem we can all unite behind called global warming and climate change. People automatically think they are experts about that because of all the propaganda they've heard about it in the media. Mainly they'll view it as someone else's fault. The minuscule things they tell us to do don't make a significant difference, anyway, compared to how bad the CCP is. If they talk about renewable energy, that is primarily government-funded and developed to hand over to the big power companies from which we have to buy high-priced electricity. Every home should be energy and food self-sufficient, as well as fireproof."

"And we need a generator, storage batteries, and an EMP shield," added Maya knowingly. She used to read Mother Earth News.

"Yep," yawned Murmur. They were almost back to the hideout. "I realized something when my friend stopped in from out of town. We didn't have much money, so we were cruising around looking for something to do. I showed him where the Norwalk Raceway Park, now called Summit Motorsports Speedway, was and he wanted to check it out, so I parked in the parking lot and was going to approach and ask at the ticket booth how much the event was for admission. I had no expectation, you know, it's a want, not a need. Much to our pleasant surprise, they were very friendly. They just beckoned us and said not to worry about it, come on in! Then for the quarter mile races, we didn't have any earplugs, we just put our fingers in our ears when it got loud and had a great time. God was seemingly providing for our wants and not just our needs. That sort of thing happens a lot! More than you know! Look at it this way, God could have made us see in just black and white, but he made all the colors for our enjoyment."

"God is amazing, baby," she said rubbing his right shoulder.

"Yeah, God is everything to me, because He made everything. Especially everything we love. Who would not love God?!?!"

"Everyone *should*," stated Maya, "Maybe they just need it *explained* the right way."

A couple of months went by, and Tom had not heard a thing from Murmur or Maya. It was as if they had dropped off of the map into oblivion. He did reach Deere, and then Fred, asking them to

come on down to Tampa, Florida. When they both drove up, they saw Tom surrounded by a bevy of women, almost like a harem.

"Wish *I* had a group of beautiful women surrounding me," lamented Deere. His wife didn't hear, she was waiting patiently for him, back home.

"How are you guys on money," asked Fred, "you got enough money?" He was flashing his stacks of cash around.

"Thanks, man!" Tom grabbed a stack. "I really appreciate it."

"Thank you, dude!" Deere took a stack. "You want some pot?" "You know I do, buddy," Fred said. "Yeah, man," Tom said. "I'll have a bag too, you know I would give you a couple of my ladies, but you both are married now, and I'm sure your new wives wouldn't like that very much."

"Oh well," said Deere sadly.

"It's cool. I understand," chimed Fred.

"So, let's go to park your cars and we'll go cruising around," Tom suggested, "find something to do."

"Groovy grapes," said Deere.

"Awesome possum," said Fred.

They hopped into their cars. Tom told the ladies where to meet up, since he didn't have room for all of them in the LTD that he was driving, a few of them did hop in though, and also in Fred's red Chevy Nomad, and Deere's powder blue '57 Chevy. As soon as the garage door opened, Tom knew there was something wrong. Something was missing. The others hopped out and left their doors open.

"Wait just a minute…" He glanced around. "Hmmm…"

“What’s wrong?”

“Uh-oh…”

“THE ’70 BUICK GSX IS GONE!” Tom screamed at the top of his lungs. “THIS PLACE WAS LOCKED and has a SECURITY SYSTEM!”

“What’s this little piece of paper?” Deere bent down and picked up a tattered dirty scrap of paper with some words scribbled on it. No sooner than he started to read it. Tom snatched it away and read it out loud. “IOU, sorry I don’t know how much you want me to pay you, but I need to use it now. See you around. Your pal, MURMUR!”

“Ugh!”

“That doortee, mutha hunchin’ pile of…seaweed! AAAAAAAHHHHHHHHHGGGGGGGGGGGG!”

“What will we do now?” asked Deere.

“Find him,” shouted Tom, “Of course.”

“Oh,” said Deere.

“Okay,” said Fred. “Let me try calling and texting his phone. Do you guys want to do a gig tonight, while we’re down here?”

“Without Murmur?” Deer asked.

“Yuh!” said Fred. “Chuck and Cardy are on their way down now. They can more than make up for his talent.”

“What’ll we call the band, Forever Endeavor? Endeavor Forever and Ever?” said Deere.

“No! He doesn’t own the name! He’s one person. He’s outnumbered. We stick with Forever,” said Tom. “Besides what is he going to do, replace all of us and use the name? Good luck with *that*.”

"And so-what if he does," contended Fred. "They'll suck and get booed off the stage by our many loyal fans. Then the fans and Tom's groupies will come looking for *us*!"

"They won't leave us to begin with," said Tom, "they know who's legit and who's fake. They're smart. Especially my groupies!"

"We need Cardy especially to sing our most favored song, Equinox," explained Fred.

"You bet!" declared Tom. "It's a hit!"

"I know," added Deere, "we should open every show with it."

"We shall," opined Fred. "Undoubtedly."

"Without fail," prophesied Tom.

A few days later they set out on the road in the jade-green Ford LTD four-door to look for Murmur. The three of the guys were in the front seat, the favorite groupies were in the back seat.

They made it to Ohio, only to find new owners were in the house. Deere went in to ask them if they knew where Murmur was. They said they really had no idea. A pedestrian was walking along the new sidewalk. He stopped and told Deere he knew where the previous occupant had gone. He gave an address and very brief verbal directions according to some local landmarks. Deere caught Fred and Tom's attention, "Hey I know where he is…"

"Who told you this?"

"This guy," Deere whirled around to look, "well, he was here. He just walked off down the road to wherever he was headed."

"I didn't see anyone," said Tom, "last I saw, you were out by the mailbox, and you appeared to be talking to yourself. Were you on dope?"

"No," said Deere, "just some marijuana. Let's go to the place. I'll show you. I ain't lying."

They drove to the address at 1943 Park Avenue West.[9] It was an abandoned half-built church. A for-sale sign was out front. Nobody was there. "This would be an excellent place to live or worship," said Deere. "I could do different drugs, and nobody would bother me here." They listened intently to the atmosphere. The birds were chirping. They cleared out of the car and went inside.

"No sign of Murmur," declared Tom. The place had a strange echo. There was a card table with folding chairs by the door. On it was a plate of Greek chicken souvlaki with tzatziki. Still warm.

There was a cozy living space room in the far corner of the interior, perhaps meant for a sanctuary. Tom had a flashlight from the trunk of the LTD. They all walked in to see a loveseat, coffee table, and end tables. A cot was set up against the side wall with a blanket and pillows. It looked lived in recently. "Hey there's a lamp set up," said Tom. It was a Cabo arc floor lamp. "Wow, that's like a $300 lamp," remarked Fred, "let there be light!" He went to turn it on. There was no power. "Hey, dude, go check out back for a generator, if you find it, turn it on…wait, what's this?" There was an opened letter addressed to Mortimer Murray sent to a post office box. "Yes! He was here…Looks like a bill…a storage bill."

"Let me see that," Tom grabbed the letter while Fred held the flashlight for him. "It's from

---

[9] https://www.mansfieldnewsjournal.com/story/news/2023/06/07/zoning-change-requested-for-site-of-half-built-church-on-park-avenue-west/70282811007/

that island in the lake, formerly known as Boblo, Bois Blanc Canada. Probably where he has that polar bear car, the Polara."

"Should we wait here for Murmur and Maya or go there now?"

"I'm going to eat his souvlaki," exclaimed Fred, "I'm a foodie! I'm not going to let that good food go to waste, just in case."

"Wish *I* had some souvlaki," complained Deere softly, "but *I'm* a *vegetarian*!" Tom glanced at him with a disgusted look.

"Just ignore him," said Fred.

They hung around for a few hours and rested. Until someone pulled up with a huge pickup truck. It was a 2019 orange Ford F650 winch truck. The driver's door flipped open. A weird guy with cowboy boots, a cowboy hat, and a brown handlebar mustache slid out and stomped onto the ground. He ran over to the back of the building. "What in the world are you folks a doin' out heyeah?" he said in a Southern Country style affect.

Tom had gone out to the trunk of the LTD and retrieved his acoustic guitar and was strumming it gently and singing just inside the area where the window should be.

"Who the heck are you?!?!?" shouted Tom as he ran out the door toward the man, aggressively.

"Who are *yew*?" said the man.

"I asked first," said Tom.

"No, I asked yew a question first," said the man.

"I don't have to tell you nothing," Tom shot back.

"I guess then I will have to call the po-lice and tell them someone is here trespassing on private property. I happen to own this place."

"No you don't," said Tom.

"Yes ahh dooo," said the man.

Tom stuck out his chest and took two steps closer and got up in the older man's face. "You're a liar. I can tell when someone's lying to me, so stop that fake accent."

"I'm not afraid of you!"

"You think I'm afraid of you???"

The man paused for what seemed to be a long time. "Truth be told, it's owned by the Berean Baptist Church. I'm a member. We meet in another location until the Lord provides us with enough money to finish this building. The contractor refuses to complete his work until we pay up."

"Fair enough," shared Tom, "my friend…our friend, Mortimer, lives, or lived here…it looks like."

"Yeah," offered Deere. "I got a tip from his last known address to come and check it out."

"We don't take too kindly to trespassers or squatters, I have my trusty shotgun to run them off," said the man.

"Would he happen to be a member of your congregation?" asked Fred.

"Could be, I don't know," said the man pensively. "We have so many people at any given time, hard to keep track of them."

"Because we found this bill with his name on it," Deere showed the man the name and post office box address on the letter and envelope. He looked at it, and said, "What's he look like?"

"He looks like a psycho weirdo, pretty ugly. He really looks ridiculous," said Tom.

"Well, that could be almost anybody," said the man.

Deere offered more detail, "He has frizzy but straight hair. It's yellow, and the same with his eyelashes and bushy eyebrows. He's about five feet, eleven and three-quarters inches tall. Usually wears an "Ask Me About Jesus" T-shirt. Jumps all over the place, like a flea, Mexican jumping bean, or Bugs Bunny. He's kind of slim but has super-human strength."

"Oh," said the man, "yeah, I might have seen him a time or two. I guess he helped us move some church pews and stuff."

"Any idea where he might have gone? Or when he might be back?" questioned Fred. The man looked over the bill.

"My guess would be he maybe went to get this car. I think it's the aquamarine Dodge Polara I've seen around with a polar bear mural painted on the sides of it, sitting on a glacier or iceberg. I'd bet it's on that island. As for when he'll be back, your guess is as good as mine."

"Do me a favor, will you?" said Tom. "I'm going to write down my number, just call me if you see him back around these parts. It's real urgent I get a hold of him. We have a lot of questions for him, okay?" Tom wrote the number of his cellphone down on a piece of paper and handed it to the man.

"Will do," said the man and turned to be on his way. "So," said Fred "what do you want to do at this point?" Tom said, "I'd rather just get going up to that island and see what we can find. You all cool with that, guys?"

"No use hanging around here," said Deere.

"I agree," said Fred, "I've never been to this place. Might be a nice adventure." The ladies were down with that too. Once they all got their stuff and piled in, they were zooming. They got on route 30 West from W. 4th Street.

"And don't go to Bois Blanc Island in Michigan, that's the wrong island," noted Fred.

"I'm not stupid," said Tom. "You do know that we're essentially going from Ontario Ohio to Ontario Canada, right?"

"I have to pee," said Deere.

"Already? We just left the place," shouted Tom. "Couldn't you have gone before we went? There is an empty kitty litter jug back there you can use. I'm not stopping."

"Maybe I can use this empty Gatorade bottle," suggested Deere.

"To each his own," replied Tom in a derogatory tone, squinting an angry face in the rearview mirror toward Deere. "But remember to screw the lid back on tight and chuck it out the window when no one is looking."

"A trucker bomb? Those are bad for the environment," called out Deere.

"Listen punk," screamed Tom, "urine is slightly corrosive, and I don't want anything messing up my original paint job!" Deere finished peeing into the Gatorade bottle and rolled down the window hurriedly stretching his arm out and pouring the urine out as far from the car as possible. A new car behind them started flashing its lights rapidly, and the wipers immediately turned on as if the urine only hit the windshield.

“**WHAT DID YOU DO???**” Tom scolded Deere as if he were the parent of a rebellious child. Deere blushed. Tom floored it and practically blew the new car’s doors off. They didn’t see that car again, though.

Woodhaven Exit 32 of I-75, West Road, has The Detroiter truck stop, so they decided to stop in and get showers, but they were deterred from getting anything else because of the high prices. Tom drove over to Canada on the Ambassador Bridge and then ON-3 and along 20 and Boblo Island Boulevard and took the Boblo Island Ferry in Amherstberg.

They drove around the simple streets until they saw a house with a nice pole barn behind it. There appeared to be some cars that were being worked on. Tom hopped out, saw something, and began walking back to it. It was a teal or maybe aquamarine automobile. It was a Dodge Polara, *The* Dodge Polara, with a polar bear and ice mural. An older guy came walking out of the pole barn. “What can I help you fellers with today? Like the car?”

“We know this car,” greeted Tom. “How’d it get here”?”

“Friend of Mine, Morty, he brung it out…to work on it with my garage and tools,” replied the older guy. “I sent him a bill, heh heh heh. I’d let you have it, but…”

Tom saw from the road it had a likeness of Murmur in the Driver’s seat. Tom opened its front car door. There was a straw-filled dummy with yellow-blonde kind-of-frizzy hair, slightly ugly in appearance. The radical eyes were pointed in two different directions, just like the real Murmur. And there…in the dummy’s lap was a folded-up piece of

paper. Tom picked it up and looked. It was on stationery paper, just the words Ha ha!

"Well we're all looking for him," explained Tom. "He has a car of mine, somewhere. He needs to pay me for it. A '70 GSX."

"Like I was saying," continued the old guy, "I'd let you have it if there was an *engine* in it. Someone out here stole it during the night." He popped the hood release and they all looked into the bare engine compartment, the motor, both engine and transmission were gone."

"How'd that happen?" questioned Tom.

"If I knew," answered the old guy, "we probably wouldn't all be standing out here having this conversation righ'-now."

"WOW," exclaimed Deere, "is that a 1977 Cobra II Mustang?"

"Yes sir," said the older guy. "That one's mine." It was white with the wide red stripes, probably repainted many times. "The salt in the water gets to them bodies and they tend to rust here by the lakes. Down South, you know interiors fade with decades of bright sunlight and heat. But you know get a clean, not rat-infested interior up North and a clean body down South. Put 'em together. That's what we like to do."

"Wish *I* had a nice Cobra II Mustang," lamented Deere.

"For the right price I'd sell her you know," said the older guy.

"Never mind we ain't got no money," said Tom, annoyed.

"Just out of curiosity," pried Fred. "How much would you take for her?"

"Needs a new paint job, but if you can deal with these here rust bombs, I'd let her go for $800. It's a steal if you know how rare they are."

"First off," argued Tom, "if it was a steal, I'd just steal it."

"Here," Fred peeled off eight big hundreds and flashed the cash stash in the guy's face.

"Well, well," the older guy delightedly chirped. "I thought you guys didn't have no money."

"*They* don't, *I* do. That's why I'm buying it for me," Fred boasted.

"Let me get you the title," said the older guy excitedly.

He returned to the guys a little while later from his workshop with a little green paper. "This is the same as a title in Canada. Hey, by the way, do you like history? Check out the blockhouse from the War of 1812. Morty always loved history. He in fact wanted to revamp the island to be a nostalgic theme park filled with old cars and memorabilia. Developers instead started building a bunch of boring houses, which is how I got this one." He waved his hand over to the house like a Vanna White impersonator.

"Do you have any idea," enquired Tom, "where he is now?"

"Sure," said the old guy who started puffing a cigar without offering them one. "His favorite place is probably the Hatfield-McCoy trail. There are over a thousand miles of trail but I believe he'd be taking his four-wheeler, and his new wife, uh, Tierra or whatever her name is, on the most difficult of the trails. Here I got the number and address on this brochure." He handed over the brochure to Tom

and the keys to Fred. "Great," Tom said with a sigh of relief, "there will be more room in my car now, you drive that." They stopped by the blockhouse first before leaving on the ferry.

The Mustang Cobra II and LTD drove from Michigan to 180 Appalachian Outpost Trail, Man, West Virginia. They spent a little over a week driving around looking for any of his cars and asking people if they had heard or seen anything of Mortimer Murray and Maya, to no avail. They stopped at a little makeshift outpost used as a laundromat, and mess hall. It was a Quonset hut with an exterior covered in moss and lichen. There was a lost and found table with the recent visitors' laundry and personal items. Tom, exhausted and tired, spotted a cleaned and dried shirt saying I heart Jesus. He sat in the chair looking at it and saw the name Mortimer penned on the tag on the inside of the collar. "Hey, Lady! When did you find this shirt?"

"Oh, that was left in the dryer a few days ago," she said with a soft, kind, gentle smile.

"Thank you," said Tom.

"You're welcome, sweety." She was tall and thin and had short dirty blonde hair, likely a couple years older than the crew.

"You didn't see him?" asked Fred.

"Oh, no. I just come by to clean up after everyone who comes in late at night. Sorry."

"That's okay," comforted Deere.

"Let's go guys," said Tom thoroughly defeated. "I'm going to head back to Florida and regroup."

Tom drove them back to Florida.

Tom hung out with his ladies for a few weeks and the other guys were socializing around Tampa. They wanted to go sightseeing. Fred surprised the group and organized a cruise, so they went.

Later, the Forever band members and crew were returning to Florida from Nassau Bahamas where they enjoyed a tropical vacation. Murmur and Maya were setting out on a yacht to Aruba, to visit Murmur's old friend, "Bob." They were literally two ships passing in the night.

Unfortunately, Tom's anger and frustration issues were increasing to alarming new levels. "I can't get those stupid Dalton Dean songs out of my head now," explained Tom. "Ever since that jerk Murmur had us do those ridiculous meditations, binaural beats, and look into that New Age mysticism with the Secret. He messed with my head! I forgot how to think!"

"He's just another crackpot," said Deere.

"Don't let him get to you," said Fred.

"How can I not? He broke in unexpectedly and got my car! He didn't pay me for it! I need the money! We can't get a hold of him. Fred, did he ever text you back?"

"Nope," said Fred.

"Great! Just great!" said Tom sarcastically. "I keep seeing his ugly face in my mind, laughing at me. It's like PTSD. You know, he kills people! He's a murderer! A murderer and his wife, if she's still alive, are driving around in my car partying and cruising and doing God-knows-what."

"Calm down, Dude," said Deere. "You want some drugs?"

"I'll give you some money if you want," offered Fred.

"I need something," said Tom, "something to calm me down, so I can relax and sleep. I can't even have fun anymore, I'm too worried."

"Let's start with some St. John's Wort and chamomile tea," suggested Deere.

"Thanks, buddy," said Tom. "I need all the help I can get." Tom also smoked marijuana and ate full-spectrum CBD gummies and blue raspberry magic mushroom gummies. "I'll get by with a little help from my friends," said Tom.

They also visited an oxygen bar where the speakers were playing *Love Is Like Oxygen* by Sweet. Tom met some more sweet ladies there. He invited them back to his pad to hear him play that song on guitar while singing it into the microphone until he fell asleep and slept for many hours.

Fred and Deere went up to Tom's suite and one of the girls, Millie, let him in. They pulled out the Marshall and Orange amplifiers and plugged in the Ibanez and Stratocaster guitars to wake him up. They turned the volumes to eleven and blasted out a jam similar to In-A-Gadda-Da-Vida. Tom woke up, clasped a pillow over his ears, looked at them, and started to laugh.

"Feel better? You were asleep for about eighteen hours, Dude," said Deere.

"So, we made a little Marshall alarm clock," said Fred. "Hey, that would be a good name for a band, man! Marshall Alarm clock, or Orange Alarm clock."

"No," said Deere, "there's already a Strawberry Alarm Clock. It would be too close to that name."

"We'll stick to Forever," agreed Tom.

Chapter Ten, Miracles:

Murmur was driving the 1970 Buick Skylark GSX west to California. Maya started waking up in the passenger seat.

She yawned and asked, “Where are we going now, love?”

“Oh, good morning, my love,” cooed Murmur. “I felt a calling from God to go to Hollywood, somebody there must need my help.”

Diva was in the back seat, so they had to stop often for her to have a little walk, usually at rest areas.

“Go potty outside, Good girl, Diva,” said Murmur. “You’re so good…yeah…wow!”

Diva would wiggle her entire body and wag her tail. She would run in little circles to show she was delighted. Through positive reinforcement, Murmur trained Diva, since she was a puppy, encouraging the reverse wheelbarrow pose, dragging her hind legs on the ground behind her, and ducking down in a praying pose when she was happily wagging her tail. She had a few tricks, such as ‘sit,’ ‘lay-down,’ and ‘roll-over.’ It seemed she was a person, because, in essence, she was. For one thing, she had hair, not fur, that kept growing. It had to be cut regularly into a puppy-cut. The water bowl sat on the back floorboard. They poured in bottled water. The food bowl sat next to it. They put in a serving of Caesar soft food with a little Royal Canin dry food.

Whenever they saw roadkill, say a dead armadillo, Murmur would softly say “poor critter,” and as soon as they were out of sight, the little animal would be healed and come back to life,

scampering safely off the roadside to the path to the wilderness and its habitat.

The GSX traveled the original Route 66 as much as possible, gliding through Illinois, Missouri, Kansas, Oklahoma, Texas, New Mexico, Arizona, and California, all the way to its end of trail sign at Santa Monica pier, just before it was a Bubba Gump Shrimp Company location.[10] "I feel a calling to go in there," said Murmur, "somebody needs help."

"Okay, honey," purred Maya. They hopped out and raced inside the restaurant. There was a man sprawled out on the floor, all life support efforts had ceased. The middle-aged waitress looked them in the eyes, "We don't know what happened. It was a noisy atmosphere, and someone walked by and saw this guy slumped over. We checked his vital signs, but he had none."

"Let me help, I'm a professional," Murmur got down on his knees beside the man. "Everybody, stand back," said the woman, "give him plenty of room." Murmur placed his hands, fingers locked together on top of the man's solar plexus as if to give him chest compressions. He looked up toward the heavens as if seeing through the ceiling. Everyone around stood silently expectingly, as Murmur cleared his throat. "What's 'is name?" As more people were shuffling in, someone in the back of the crowd said, "Dan. His name is Dan. I know him." Silence ensued as Murmur looked around into different people's faces, locking eyes momentarily. "What are you waiting for?" said an obscure voice.

---

[10] https://www.bubbagump.com/location/bubba-gump-santa-monica-ca/

"Get on up, Dan," shouted Murmur, "in the name of Jesus!"

As he got up and started to leave, someone in the crowd said, "Is he serious right now?" Then the man who had been dead suddenly started coughing violently as if he were trying to dispel smoke or water from his lungs, and opened his eyes, trying to get up on his feet. "Hey, what happened?" asked the resurrected man. "I work miracles every day," said Murmur confidently in the direction of his detractor. Clapping and then cheering erupted in the place. "Hallelujah, Praise the Lord!" people were saying.

"Wow," exclaimed Maya, excitedly. "Ready to go, love?" Murmur smiled to Maya, taking her gently by her hand.

Tom was driving the LTD entourage west on I-70 through Glenwood Canyon, one of the most beautifully crafted and fairly new, high-tech highways, incorporating a heart for nature, local peoples, and all the stakeholders. It's an expensive and important highway. Deere was studying to be a personal fitness trainer, interested in possibly starting his own gym or chain of gyms. He told everyone how much trainers are supposed to make and also, he was studying to be a certified nutritionist.

Once back at Deere's home in California, Fred and Tom discovered just how much of a following Deere had among health-conscious individuals. He also started community gardens throughout several cities, using hydroponics and aquaponics, teaching folks to be self-sufficient and food secure. "I like what you've done here," remarked Fred. "Being a foodie like me, huh?"

"Certainly," replied Deere, "teach a man to fish, you know, feed him forever."

"Chicks dig it," said Tom. Everybody laughed at the garden pun. Everyone was having a great summer day in the sunshine. It was the first Juneteenth, 2021. Wind chimes were chiming, and colorful pinwheels softly spun with the gentle breeze. The pretty gals were sipping their wine coolers and Arnold Palmers. Fred was tending the barbeque grille out on the balcony. There were Impossible burgers, Beyond Meat, Quorn products, Morningstar, Boca burgers, and Loma Linda meatballs from Deere's freezer. Fred and Tom obtained organic grass-fed beef, pork chops, and free-range locally sourced chicken for everyone else. People brought their pets out to enjoy the day too.

Deere wanted to show his fans how easy bodybuilding as a vegetarian could be. He was all for healthy clean living.

The very next day, a little girl out riding her bicycle got run over by a speeding car and mangled beyond recognition. Her mother ran out crying and screaming. Murmur and Maya were nearby and heard the commotion. They both ran over to the scene of the accident. Murmur knelt beside her on the ground touching the girl softly with great care and said, "Be completely healed and wake up, in the name of Jesus." Wounds closed. Mangled limbs straightened. Dislocated and broken bones went back into place. She came alive as spectacularly as the dry bones of the soldiers in the valley. Even the blood disappeared. People all around shouted, cheered, and jumped all around.

"It's a miracle!"

"She's alive!"

"Oh...My...God!"

"What?!?!?!" her mother said and then embraced her daughter. She clung tightly as if never letting go. Everyone was so amazed at what God could do. "Thank you so, so much," the mother said. "Don't thank me, thank God," said Murmur. They continued walking Diva down the sidewalk. It was a long time, that evening, before the bystanders calmed down.

Murmur began coaching other comedians at the comedy clubs before they went on. He became known as their comedy consultant. He went ahead and had some business cards printed. It proved to be very lucrative. They were in Los Angeles. "You know, my love, they don't just call it Angeles, they call it Los--Angeles because people that go there from other areas get *Lost*! It's so big, you know."

"Ha-ha, my love," cheered Maya.

"My brother told me that one," added Murmur.

Murmur had a concealed carry holster with a Taurus 1911. They were casually walking Diva down a residential street when Murmur heard some muffled cries and immediately ran into a house to investigate. Maya did not have as sensitive of hearing but followed along. Soft sobs of a child were coming from the bedroom. Maya waited just outside with Diva so she wouldn't bark. An older girl came out of the room down the hall. She looked at Murmur, who held an index finger to his lips, "Shhhh..." She nodded. He turned around and opened the door to the little girl's room. A naked grown man was trying to force himself on the nude little girl on the small bed and there was a tripod set

up with a camera to take video. "God's perfect timing," declared Murmur. "That's my dad and his stepdaughter," stated the older girl who walked in behind. "Has he done stuff like that to you?" Murmur asked the older girl. "Yeah…" admitted his older daughter.

"Why don't you get the hell out and mind your own flipping business?" said the pervert sadistically, with a gruff, revolting voice as he strutted forward toward Murmur. "This is how I make money for us and support our family. It pays the bills since the wife left."

"I got a better idea, how 'bout we make this into a snuff film?" Murmur boldly said as the naked man got up into his face.

"Fine with me. Should I snuff you now, or should I *hesitate*?" The possessed man sang with a growl.

"**Ah-Ah-Ah…. AHHHH CHOOOOOOO!**" Murmur sneezed powerfully into the disgustingly smelly man's extremely ugly face. **BLAM!!!** The demonized old perv stumbled back with a giant hole in the middle of his chest, from Murmur's gun. He tumbled back a few more paces, collapsing on the floor as the blood ran out, evacuating his body.

"Yay!!!" said the two girls as they cheered and celebrated. The older one helped the younger one get dressed. "You're not sad that I killed your dad?" Murmur asked.

"No, we hate… hated him," said the girls. "We're glad he's dead, he used to be an abortion doc… performer before he drove Mom away, but what about the body?"

"I will disappear it," said Murmur kindly, "don't you worry about a thing. I'm just sorry I didn't get here sooner before the other trauma occurred." Maya walked in with Diva. Murmur introduced them and told Maya what happened. "Do you have any place else to stay now?" They shook their heads. "We will take care of you," promised Maya. "No one will ever hurt you again."

Tom had heard Murmur was spotted in the comedy clubs and was livid. He wandered the streets around the club looking for Murmur, yelling and rampaging when he was strolling near an alleyway with a Sansui boombox playing a Dalton Dean track. He ran up and swiftly smashed the boombox to bits. Springs and plastic pieces were flying all over the place. Tom screamed "I HATE DALTON DEAN! WHO IS RESPONSIBLE FOR THIS HORRENDOUS ATTROCITY?" No one came forward to speak for the boombox pieces which had been silenced.

The friends who had been with him were concerned. "The Who is not responsible, Tom," said Fred. "Calm it down," said Deere. "Here, have a Sqwincher," said Chuck soothingly, putting a Sqwincher bottle in his hand. "I DON'T WANT NO FREAKING SQWINCHER!" Tom threw the bottle as hard as he could against the dumpster. It bounced off, hit the outside brick wall, and splattered out immediately with extreme force. The friends paused, looking around at each other. "You wasted a perfectly good Sqwincher, Tom… jerk!" Fred said. They all turned and walked away. "I'm done," Tom said and went to take a nap. He was exhausted.

Murmur coached clean comedy, for the most part. The goal is to get a favorable reaction from the audience.

"I thought I'd become a stand-up comedian," said the funny man Murmur was helping. "I was used to working at the auto factory, standing up all day so I'm already halfway there. How hard can it be?" [chuckles and light laughter]

"Fourth of July is approaching soon; time to celebrate being an American. Be patriotic. Of course, when we look at the map of America, it seems fairly symbolic. Michigan is a big blue mitten. It's a right hand on the palm side. Or it's a left hand on the back of the hand if you want to be backhanded. It's your choice, you can be slapped silly with the palm or be backhanded. Nevertheless, I show the geography with my hand.

"Ohio is the heart of it all, it looks like the back of your hand folded into a fist. I usually use that when showing the geographic location of something in Ohio.

"Following that pattern, Maine looks like the head of the country, a little tiny head, comparatively speaking. But America has its head up in the clouds. Doesn't it? If Canada is the cloud. It's almost indistinguishable if we don't know where the border is. New England looks like a proud chest sticking out into the ocean. So, Florida is the, um, you know. And behind that, Louisiana is the uh, well, you know what is hanging behind a large… Florida." [laughs]

"California is the butt of the United States, the butt of our jokes. Mexico must be… what comes out of a butt?" [some laughter]

"And Bob Evan's restaurant, I don't know if any of you good folks are familiar with the sign in the front wall, but there's been a hole in the roof they have not fixed since inception in 1968, right at the top in the middle, it's obvious. It's a huge circular hole you can see way out from the road. Are they inviting an eagle to build a nest up there, or are they such old cheapskates that they won't use the exorbitant price of your meals to make the necessary repairs to their buildings? Such an eyesore, so annoying!" (They didn't know anything about Bob Evan's of course).

"What is with those anthropomorphic cartoon characters that have only four fingers on each hand, three fingers, and a thumb? Like Mickey Mouse and the Simpsons? *They claim* it's to save the animation studios time and money by having to draw fewer fingers…over the years…Well, guess what? I can quickly and easily draw five fingers on any character, and I am not a professional cartoonist. So, Walt Disney and Matt Groening needed to go back to art school and learn the basics of simple drawings. No. You don't draw bunches of circles for hands and fingers, Walt. Are you dumber than a kid in kindergarten? For punishment, any drawer or inventor of said anthropomorphic character caught red-handed needs to have a finger amputated, which is one reason they don't do that nonsense in Japan, and the fear of mentioning the number four because it sounds like the word for death. Harry the Bunny has man-hands, and the man has to place his last two fingers in the same glove hole. How about we remedy that situation for any unnecessary unwanted fingers, eh? Matt Groening came out saying his worst mistake was the episode

with Principal Skinner that offended China which was his worst mistake they should never mention again. Except they claimed it was the fan's most hated episode. Namely, the fans in communist China. Namely, the CCP leaders who control everybody there. Easy Peasy Japanesey. Not Lemon Squeezy; that's offensive! HEY! Japanese are our allies. They are our friends! They're smart! NOT THE COMMUNISTS! If they want to be easy and peasy, what the heck is wrong with that? Would you deny them the honor of being easy and peasy? Hong Kong people are our friends; they're very much like us. They love America and freedom. I love Chinese food. I don't like Communism. Get rid of the CCP and save the Chinese people. South Koreans are our friends and allies. North Korea is Communist, and very oppressive of its people. Capitalism has worked, at least. Communism hasn't worked for anybody for over a hundred years. It's like beating a dead horse that's been beaten for over a hundred years, expecting different results; expecting it to come back to life, work better, and be a utopia for humanity. It's like; *Oh, we can rebuild it, build back better, this time it will really work and be great because it's democratic socialism, we have the know-how, we're smarter than those other versions.* **Forget about it!**

"I think we need to re-examine what people are told or sold they should be offended over, and what's really offensive. It's okay to offend us. They employ feigned incredulity. Oh! I'm offended. Hey! Aunt Jemima, Uncle Ben, great American people. Nothing is wrong with how they're portrayed. They give people pride and dignity. They have good moral family values. Abraham Lincoln; Republican,

Anti-Slavery party; would not be disagreeable with President Trump or have endorsed anything like today's Lincoln project. He was at odds with Southern Democrat KKK slaveowners, not even speaking of the Confederates, or the Confederate flag that Leftists found offensive, with their feigned incredulity. History, learn it. (Not available on fake news CNN, MSNBC, CBS, ABC, NBC, New York Times, Michael Moore, Meathead Rob Reiner, or CSN, and sometimes Y)."

Forever band played various concerts around Los Angeles that summer. They formed a coalition to get Steve Earle booed off the stage and played there instead. When they hit the stage the crowd would go wild. They would have standing ovations. They were still not playing much of any cover songs unless folks requested them. They were trying to write their own original songs without Murmur. Playing bigger and bigger venues until they sold out arenas, they began to employ a feedback-laden, sustained false ending, complete with flashing psychedelic light and smoke show, that would allow them to disappear and break out the back into their limousine and be halfway to the hotel before the crowd noticed they had finished the show and left.

Tom was messing around on the guitar with some double-stop bends that sounded bluesy. Over the course of a few days, he worked it up into a song, adding more layers and many instruments. Fred contributed lyrics that matched the rhythm and melody. However, Deere discovered the original riff sounded too similar to a Guess Who song, so he went on eBay and bought Tom a 4-string G/B-

bender and gave it to him to put on his telecaster. It cost about $290.

"My body, my choice," shouted the young lady with the short rainbow hair in front of the abortion clinic. "It's not your body that's in question," Murmur responded boldly. "It's the baby's body that gets destroyed." Maya nodded. "I was just like you before I met my husband. He taught me that life is sacred. Nobody has the right to take it away besides the Lord, especially from the weakest and most helpless among us. God judges us by how we treat the least of these; we're in charge of our animals, the elderly and disabled, and of course, developing infants. If we can't treat them with love, then how would you expect God to want to treat us? If you will only believe in a mother's pure love, then maybe you can believe in God's perfect love for you, also."

"Well spoken, my love," cheered Murmur.

"Thank you, my love," sang Maya.

"Bark, Bark, Bark," barked Diva.

Just then the abortion performer shot out to the sidewalk on a rampage almost like the Tasmanian Devil in an unreal cartoon. He was red-eyed, unshaven, dirty, had a foul odor, and was unkempt. He probably hadn't slept in forty days and forty nights due to being so busy doing thousands of abortions, and he immediately said with multiple voice tones at once,

"ARRRGHELAAARRRRDEFFFFFZZZEE ASSSSAAAM GET OUT OF HERE YOU LOVERS OF GOD, YOU HAVE NO RIGHT TO BE HERE. YOU'RE TRESPASSING. YOU'RE ON THE WRONG SIDE OF HISTORY."

“We are on the right side, you are on the wrong side, sir,” declared Maya.

“Get out of him, Leave now! In the powerful name of Jesus,” stared Murmur holding his smoothly sanded wooden cross, “NOW!” The abortion provider fell limp. Later he became conscious.

“Huh?” said the bewildered person who was possessed. “Where am I, and who are *you*?”

“Go and sin no more,” hollered Murmur. “Make sure this place gets shut down,” he said, turning to the young lady. Maya took her under her wing and befriended her, as they talked and went for boba tea together. She gave her heart to Jesus and when they said goodbye, she promised to keep in touch.

Maya and Murmur went to the nearest hospital and helped pray for a cancer patient named Nancy. She eventually made a full recovery and was a believer. They also helped pray for a drug addict who almost died from an overdose. His name was Doug. He turned his life over to Jesus and was no longer an addict.

Forever was booked to play in Los Angeles at Lyric Hyperion Theater and Bar on 2106 Hyperion Avenue. Murmur saw the little promo sign on a telephone pole. There was also one on the bulletin board at the laundromat and one taped up on the glass door at the library. Murmur saw another flyer for the band’s next show and tried calling them at the number, which just rang and rang, so he saved the number and told Maya to get ready for the show. They would get a dog sitter and meet up.

It was a hot, sunny, very windy day, in late August. Deere had his military headphones on, listening to the song Hookah by Tintern Abbey. He ducked into a little music shop ahead of Tom and Fred. He saw Murmur's comedy consultant card just inside the double doors to the foyer. He put up a flyer for the band's next show, which would be even grander. He didn't want to alarm Tom. He gave the number a call on his cell phone. It just rang and rang, so he saved the number for later use.

That evening Murmur walked into the dressing room suddenly holding a show flyer and surprised the band. "What's up with this? Singing and playing without me now?"

"Jerk!" shouted Tom.

"Creep!" shouted Murmur.

"You took my car without paying me," shouted Tom.

"Oh," said Murmur handing Tom a stack of cash which he briskly snatched and started counting, "here you go. I had to become a comedy consultant to make that much cash to pay you, dude."

Tom said, "*We* had to follow you on a wild goose chase even to find you and get it from you. What happened? You formed a dangerous cult, didn't you? How many people did you kill so far?"

Murmur raised his eyebrows and said, "A cult? The only cult I would start is an anti-cult cult, but then it wouldn't be a cult because I would be against myself starting a cult. What about you? You have this huge following of pretty women following you everywhere you go, they're in the dressing room with you now, your group of groupies. Fred, you've always had a big following of friends, as

you call them. You dole out cash to constantly keep them around and like you. Deere, you have this new-found bunch of people who use you for the drugs…and whatever else. God knows!"

"We don't have time for this! We got to get on stage in like ten minutes, you gonna be with us? If so, we got to rehearse quickly," bellowed Tom loudly. So, they went over their set list and Murmur got the idea of what to play from the printed pages he was handed. The show was great, and the crowd went wild! Then they went to the bar and had mimosas and wine coolers with the women.

Deere talked about how he and Cindy were trying to have a baby of their own and missing his mother who had been dead for 12 years. He said, "Check out this song I discovered by Flo and Eddy of the Turtles. It's Keep It Warm." He played it for them on his phone, although it was pretty loud in the place. "I found this song, *Green Power* by Archie Bell and the Drells to be very inspiring when I started making big money," said Fred, "and *We're Gonna Make It,* by Little Milton." Murmur spoke up and said, "You know how people butt-dial someone with their cell phone in their back pocket? I accidentally bought a Country song and downloaded it while trying to fuel the big truck. I don't remember what song it was."

The next day the four guys and wives, Cindy, Marcie, and Maya were motoring around, and Murmur asked where Deere's mother was buried. Deere directed Tom to drive to Evergreen Cemetery. Deere got out and was walking the path as the LTD slowly idled. "Up over here," he pointed. They formed a circle holding hands around, closed their eyes, and Murmur said a little

prayer, “What’s her name?” Deere said, “Sarah.” Murmur continued, “Sarah…GET ON UP, COME BACK TO LIFE RIGHT NOW, and COME OUT OF THERE in the NAME OF JESUS! Uh, everyone, get back and give plenty of room.” They spread out as the ground started to rumble. Dirt flew up in the air and they saw a hand reaching out, climbing through the rubble. “M-mom?” said Deere, “you look so young again.” His mom, Sarah said, “ Hi Deere dear! I feel like I could use a shower, how are you doing?” “I’m great!” They hugged. “I missed you.” “Awe,” said Sarah, “It’s good to be back. I had a good nap. It’s like I flew forward instantly in time!” “Let me introduce you to my friends…”

Later Fred asked Murmur about resurrecting his mom. She had been cremated. “I don’t know,” said Murmur, “that one might have to wait until Jesus gets back.”

“Why don’t you go get your Dodge Polara?” Tom asked Murmur.

“I don’t have time right now,” answered Murmur.

“What do you mean you don’t have time right now?” asked Tom.

“I have other things to do,” said Murmur.

“What are you talking about? You don’t have anything that needs doing,” said Fred.

“We had to practice time management in college. It’s like in the factory, everything has to be done a certain way, and in the right order. I need a good reason,” said Murmur.

Fred, Murmur, Deere, and Tom bought motorcycles and did a lot of riding the rest of that year. Soon, Tom was able to buy a 2023 Dodge

Challenger SRT Demon 170. It has a 6.2L V8 supercharged engine with 1025HP, added a Rocket performance chip, and the optional parachute for additional stopping power. He was able to outrun the police or anyone tailing him with high maneuverability and strategic evasive skills. But they didn't get into any trouble on the road.

Chapter Eleven, The Argument:

Deere asked his friend Jay, whom he thought he knew well, to get some Kratom for them to try. He gave Jay money and sent him out to look for a place to buy it since it was legal. It turned out he couldn't be trusted.

Jay returned that evening with a small paper bag with the top rolled down in his hand, "Here, try some of this stuff," he said as everyone was getting ready to party. The attendees were feeling jovial, so they obliged. There were a couple of different things in the bag, though. Some hand-rolled joints, some leaves, buds, and some tea. None of it was labeled.

Some alcohol was available from crystal decanters. Murmur volunteered to be the bartender because he knew how to mix all the drinks. Deere passed out hors d'oeuvres and special gummies. Tom helped deejay the music on the expensive, high-tech Marantz stereo system. He played songs like *I Just Want to Celebrate* by Rare Earth, *Celebrate* by Three Dog Night, and *Celebration* by Kool & The Gang. Visualizations appeared on the big-screen Sony television. Fred was teaching everyone some awesome dance moves and socializing.

"Why are you acting so bizarre?" a hot chick asked Murmur.

"Because Bryn Dimpleton is a witch and she cast an evil spell on my brain," was his simple reply. He started walking into Deere's kitchen, possibly to get some bartending supplies.

"Where are you going, Murmur?" asked Tom, thirsty from lighting and deejaying work.

"Farther than you'll ever know," said Murmur, quoting Syd Barrett.

Fortunately, he came back after just five minutes. "I want some Kahlua," ordered Tom, "and some mudslides for my two ladies." He had it narrowed down to two, now.

"I like this job," reflected Murmur. He made himself some spiked Arnold Palmers, using caffeinated tea. He rubbed his face with his hand as *New Direction* from The Black Lips played on the audio equipment—next, *Energy* from The Apples in Stereo played. "…much better than working at the factory. I had bad dreams about it. All night, I'd be toiling away at one such factory I had been at before, sent from the temporary service. However, this time I wouldn't be paid. I failed to report to the supervisor, so it was a total waste of my time, wandering around trying to look busy…trying to look important. It was almost noon there. Then when I woke up, I realized I had never worked at such a place. I even remembered other places I worked at exclusively over the years in dreams. It was like an altered reality."

"Bummer, Man!" Tom sympathized.

Murmur broke out in a cold sweat, his hands started shaking. "Even at the body armor factory, the electronic ignition factory, the seating manufacturer, and the plastic automotive supplier. Same thing, do the same thing…over and over and

over and over and.”

“MURMUR!” Tom stood up holding his drink, irritated and ornery. “ENOUGH!”

“Wait, I’m not done yet. Over and over and over and over and over and over and over and over and over and over and over and over and over and

over and over and over and over and over and over and over and over and over and over and over and over and over and over and over and over and over and over and over and over and.”

“SHUT UP!” screamed Tom.

“Stop!” shouted Maya. “Why are you acting this way, my love?”

“…because Bryn Dimpleton is a witch and she cast an evil spell on my brain! You see, the thoughts won’t stop. They go on over and over an.”

“You’re annoying!” shouted Tom.

“Am not,” said Murmur.

“Are too,” shouted Tom.

“Am not,” said Murmur.

“Are too,” shouted Tom.

“Am not,” said Murmur.

“Are too,” shouted Tom.

“Am not,” said Murmur.

“Are too,” shouted Tom.

“Am not,” said Murmur.

“Are too,” shouted Tom.

“Am not,” said Murmur.

Tom was having none of it. He punched Murmur instantly like Bruce Lee in the jawbone and knocked him out cold. “Thanks for ruining our party, you idiot,” muttered Tom.

“You are ruining it too,” claimed Maya. “Just ignore him.”

Fred helped Deere prop Murmur up on the sofa and had him sleep it off. But Murmur awoke in

a few minutes and said, "…because Bryn Dimpleton is a witch and she cast an evil spell on my brain," and then went back to sleep for the rest of the night. Maya added pillows around Murmur to muffle the sound and soothed him with sheets, a blanket, and a quilt. "Zzzzzzz-zzzzzzz-zzzzzzz-zzzzzzz-zzzzzzz-zzzzzzzz-zzzzzzzz-zzz." Tom remained angry the rest of the evening, complaining of a terrible headache that wouldn't go away. "Right behind my eyes, and the back of my head feels like it's been hit by a steel baseball bat."

Fred had trouble keeping everyone dancing in formation. People were hallucinating, trying to jump off the back balcony and roof, and harming themselves. Many were banging their heads while *Metal Health* was playing. A friend of Fred's charged the wall and rammed a hole in it with his head. Deere was crying, pouting, sighing, moaning, and groaning. He had excruciating stomach aches, lethargy, and heartburn that felt like a possible heart attack. He also saw the holes in the wall that would need fixing.

The next morning, Jay stopped in to see if Deere needed anything else, asking how it went last night. Deere asked, "What did you get us?"

"Uh," Jay said, caught off guard, "Oh, they…didn't have Kratom where I went, so I just got you some Jimsonweed, some nice Crack, Meth, and PCP, assorted junk like that. Figured you wouldn't mind; just as good. It's all good!"

Deere grabbed the nearest thing in his kitchen, a skillet, and knocked Jay over the head with it. "Tom, please take out the trash for me, will you?" Tom hoisted Jay's limp body over his

shoulder and disposed of him properly. Fred held the door open for him.

"What do you guys want to watch tonight in my luxury movie theater? I got DVDs; The Good the Bad and the Ugly, The Mothman Prophecies, The Fourth Kind, A Clockwork Orange, Saving Private Ryan, Full-Metal Jacket, Monty Python's Meaning of Life; I love the part with Mister Creosote."

"I guess I could stick around," said Murmur.

Maya whispered to Tom, "He doesn't remember a thing about last night."

"How's Diva, today?" Deere asked. Diva came running in wagging her tail.

Tom came back in noisily through the screen door.

"Wanna go potty outside?" Maya asked this time. Murmur went to the door to open it.

"Be careful," said Deere, "I don't have a fence around the yard."

"She won't go far," said Murmur, "my Shih-tzus have always been good at not wandering off.

That afternoon Murmur talked with Tom, "You're pretty cool, Tom. I must admit that's one good thing I like about you."

They were seated in Deere's den on some comfortable wicker chairs with handmade pads sewn together with love. The oscillating fan was softly blowing their minds. The air freshener was Jasmine.

"I appreciate that, Morty. Could you elaborate?" said Tom.

Murmur contemplated for a long time. "You know what's cool. You're a Christian; if you get upset, you cool down rather quickly. A lot of people

say they're cool, but they're not. You are the genuine authentic cool guy."

"I guess you're cool, too…in a strange sort of way," reciprocated Tom.

"God is the epitome of cool. He invented the standards by which we discern coolness. That means Satan is uncool. Jesus is the ultimate hippie."

"Yeah, Man, you know, God wants us not to go to bed angry. He hates violence. He has righteous indignation, but it's like, look at how His anger blazed against Moses because he didn't want to go out and talk to the people like God told him to. Yet instead of lashing out at Moses, though, He simply allowed him to use Aaron to do the speaking because *he* had better public speaking skills," Tom acknowledged. "But I'm still working on my anger issues, day by day."

"I discovered getting angry, complaining, and being negative, pessimistic, or throwing a fit and breaking your stuff doesn't make you feel any better. It makes you feel worse," said Murmur.

Maya entered the room and brought a tray with teacups of Earl Grey, said "Hello," and sat down on the rattan armchair. Deere and Fred sauntered in and sat down on the 84-inch long settee.

"Let me regale you with one of my anecdotes," commented Murmur, "I've always liked to fix things, work on stuff, and tinker around in workshops. I had a Samsung boombox when I was much younger, and I had a malfunction with something about the tape player. Maybe the capstan, pinch roller, and some wires? But I took the screws out and pulled the case apart. Springs and spacers and various mysterious parts were

flying out all over the place, getting lost on the floor and under furniture. It was simple to do the initial repair, but it took me hours to compress and hold everything back into place at the same time, remembering how it all went in there, screwing the little miniature screws through the long holes in the back and other fasteners in the front. Now of course I could have just said the heck with this, I'll just smash it all up with a sledgehammer like a watermelon at a Gallagher show. At least that would be fun for a minute to take my frustrations out, but then I will have failed to skillfully fix the challenging broken boombox."

Fred and Deere looked at Tom. Tom looked at Fred and Deere. "Maybe I shouldn't have lost my composure and busted up that boombox." Fred, Deere, and then Tom cracked up laughing. "No, that was righteous indignation," called Fred.

Murmur smiled. "You know, that's the way of the world. They don't have enough skill to fix things, so instead they revel in destroying things. Like…" He looked back and forth into each of their sets of eyes. "The Enemy, he's come to steal, kill, and destroy. He's not able to fix all the world's problems, although they'll pretend they can. He and his followers will act like they can do all God can do themselves; that they don't need God to set things right. They're sorely mistaken. God is omnipotent, omniscient, omnipresent, unlimited, from time indefinite to time indefinite. God can control or change the laws of physics. Satan the Devil, fallen angels and demons were created. They are creatures. Limited. They don't know everything God knows, certainly not as mighty. God knows everything!"

Fred, Deere, Tom, and Maya nodded while sipping their tea. Murmur added stevia. The others added organic local honey to theirs.

"You have some good insight, Love," complimented Maya.

"Nothing special about me, that I should brag, but my knowledge of God and the Kingdom," admitted Murmur. "You know how I pray for intuition. I also prayed for wisdom, the practical application of knowledge, from the Creator, which God grants unbegrudgingly to all who sincerely ask."

"Scones?" Maya asked, passing them out to all who wanted.

"The way I understand it," said Murmur, "In the beginning, Genesis 1:1, God the Father, created the Son of God with Holy Spirit, His active force. Time began, so it's called the beginning. You see, nothing means anything without two or more. That's the power of two. God created the heavens and the Earth. John 1:1 has to explain it a little clearer, all was created by, for, and through the Word, Logos, Jesus, as a Master apprentice. No one else is given this distinction that Jesus is given. Now, Satan was given a vital job as the worship leader and adornment of beautiful colorful lights or gems. But that wasn't good enough for him. The Argument began between Satan and God. Satan challenged God's sovereignty on Earth. He was envious of God's authority over humans on Earth. Instead of being satisfied as the main worship leader, he was jealous of the honor and adoration given to mankind. Humanity was made in God's image, not Satan's. Satan knew mankind was destined to be a little higher than the Angels. That's

why because of his covetousness of the position and purpose of man, Satan started to hate humans. He propositioned and pestered God to allow him control over the Earth and earthling man. He asserted that God could merely colonize other planets in other solar systems with other humanoid beings. God admonished Satan that he could never handle that level of responsibility. It wouldn't work. It would be a dismal abysmal failure. Therefore, God got sick of hearing Satan's stupid suggestions and requests. To settle the argument, he proposed to let mankind decide for themselves whose rule they would long to be under. God's Kingdom or Satan's World. They all had free will! The right to choose. So, he set up the Tree of Knowledge of Good and Evil. That's Satan's tree. God set up in another area of the Garden of Eden, the Tree of Life, in case they decided to obey and choose the glorious life that was ordained for them by God. God told Adam and Eve, 'Trust Me, why learn everything the hard way?' Do you want to cut your arm off in a bandsaw to find out how much it hurts? Do you want to find out the hard way what will happen if you pound a nail into your forehead?"

"Ha-ha! Brilliant," declared Fred. "How did you figure out such a thing? No one can measure the depths of God's understanding, but you effectively psychoanalyzed Satan and his followers."

"I know how they think," replied Murmur. "When I was about five or six, my parents were separating. They wanted a divorce. My mom packed up to go, and since she was a housewife and stay-at-home mom, I was closer to Mom than Dad. He was the workaholic breadwinner and selfish

philanderer. Papa was a rolling stone. She packed all her essentials and put them in Gramma and Grandpa's station wagon. Naturally, she had me hop in the back seat so we could flee his drunken abusiveness. Then Dad was out under the walnut tree having a confrontation with Mom. The argument escalated. Unexpectedly, Dad opened up the passenger-side door and Mom opened the driver-side door, and they both fought over me, pulling my arms apart like a wishbone. Then one said, 'This is ridiculous. Let him decide which one he wants to go with. I chose to go with Mom for about two weeks but then return home with Dad and the surrogate family for the next two weeks."

"And Satan's a great salesman," added Tom. "Notice how he made the choice seem so appealing to do what God told them *not* to do. Eve could have just said, 'Well hold it just a minute. We will discuss this with God first so as not to upset Him. Do a little research. Since they were divided, such as in an interrogation, she hadn't waited to discuss it with her husband first, either. Then, when Adam realized what his wife did, he went ahead and did it too, to see what would happen."

"Yes!" agreed Murmur. "It is said 'It's a sin to tell a lie.' But did you know that it's a sin to willfully believe a lie? That's what Adam and Eve did with the original sin. For God wouldn't lie, but Satan is the Father of the Lie. Now people question if the world is a round globe saying that's a conspiracy theory, believing instead that it's a flat pancake. People question if we actually sent a man to the moon, believing instead it was all an elaborate hoax from a Hollywood movie set. People constantly question and reexamine anything known

to be true. They question their true identity in Christ, and instead believe who Satan says they are. He's the accuser. From personal experience, I can honestly say that humiliation arises from Satan, along with hatred and doom. God is not out to humiliate you or embarrass you unless you're already haughty, full of yourself, and devoted to destruction. We're not. We're on God's side. For if our God is for us, who could ever stop us? And if our God is for us, then who could stand against? We've become an unstoppable force. For eye has not seen nor ear heard that which God has in store for those who love Him…us!"

"Devil's worst nightmare…US!" quoted Tom. "That's from a song.[11]"

They all laughed. "Do you guys want some biscotti?" offered Maya. "I picked up some from the bakery." The guys said "Sure!" Cindy and Marcie were in the kitchen. They were making up some deviled eggs.

"The way I understand it," said Murmur, "people get too self-conscious. In the Garden of Eden, Adam and Eve were cool walking around nude in the cool of the day, chilling with God whenever He showed up to talk to them. When they bought the line Satan, playing the snake, sold them, their eyes were suddenly open to what was right and wrong, good and evil. They looked at their bodies, which were now suddenly ugly and disgusting. That's when they felt the need to cover up. They

---

[11] Social Club Misfits. (2018). Nightmare [CD]. On *Into the Night*. Daniel Steele, Wit.

learned the hard way. Think about it! Whenever the Bible talks about exposing someone naked in front of everyone else for them to laugh and scoff at you, why would you be ashamed, embarrassed, and humiliated if you were a gorgeous couple with perfect bodies, Eve having perfectly shaped curves and supple breasts, Adam having chiseled lean muscles and huge, impressive penis? No, childbirth was suddenly painful and terrible, and Eve and women since began to have periods, and Adam and men since then needed to be circumcised because as you might guess when old men try to stretch their penises with weights, it only stretches the foreskin and not the internal parts which shrank, and likewise the woman's birth canal was much smaller and less flexible to get a baby out of it. Today when kids get too self-conscious about their bodies, they have all sorts of problems like body dysmorphia, anorexia, bigorexia, bulimia, or gender confusion. All because they question everything and start questioning the truth, over and over again. It's like OCD. All since Adam and Eve ignored God's advice and took the Devil's."

"Not only that," agreed Deere, "they had too much trouble growing good food; fruits, and vegetables, but invasive weeds took over."

"I imagine," contributed Tom, "that's because either God took his maintenance of their land, healing their land, away… Not just that God or Satan necessarily cursed everything, but then again…outside of the Garden, they had burrs, thorns, mosquitos, hornets, gray aliens, and things Satan might have been able to make because remember, the magicians in Egypt tried to emulate all the bad stuff of the plagues, only always inferior

in quality to what God was able to make. And as far as the Tree of Life, there in Revelation, are multiple trees for the future on both sides of the river, for mankind to eat from, and be restored to perfection so they can live forever on paradise Earth. Some people will choose to live forever in heaven and some will live forever on Earth, like God's original purpose for them. No compromises. God's will and Kingdom come. That's what I'm excited about."

"The meek shall inherit the Earth," said Deere, "that certainly hasn't happened yet."

"Yeah," said Murmur, "Satan had the authority over them so why wouldn't he want the worst for people? Their motto is plainly, 'Only the strong survive.' I ascertain that Satan and the fallen angels were like, 'Leave us alone! We're fine without God's intervention. We can have a utopia on our own,' which always became a Negative Utopia, because they were dismal failures, like Communism, Socialism, Monarchies, Oligarchies, Dictatorships, and Tyranny. Through their hatred for everyone, many died a horrible death—many exterminations and genocides. Jesus loves everyone. As followers of Christ, Satan no longer has authority over us. God does not desire any to be destroyed but to come to a full understanding and healthy relationship with God. For God loved the world so much that He gave His only begotten Son that whosoever believeth in Him may not perish but have eternal life. Literally, and they will."

"Yeah, and you know what?" asked Tom plaintively. "Everything was easy at first. Nowadays, if it isn't super-easy, you're doing it wrong. Oh yeah, we have troubles in this world, we were forewarned of that. We have opposition. But

take heart because Jesus overcame the world. He conquered death. Pain, suffering, fear, and outcry will be no more. He will wipe away all our tears. Tears that he collected in a vial. We have our names written on His hand. We are chosen, wanted, loved, and important. Lions will play with lambs, and a mere young boy will lead them and play with all the formerly wild, formerly dangerous animals. You tried to force things to happen. When the college kicked you out, you couldn't accept that. You had a conniption. That roadblock might have been to help steer you into another more lucrative and valuable field. You chose revenge. God said vengeance is mine. He would handle things. You were trying too hard, and too many things unnecessarily."

"I never thought of it that way," confessed Murmur. "I felt God was using me to exact His holy vengeance upon them. Come to think of it, you tried too hard too. Iron sharpens iron, my brother."

"Touché, bro," concurred Tom. "I was just so successful meeting and dating hot women. It gave me more confidence. I felt that I could do anything. Not everyone is so lucky at that."

"Me too," confided Murmur. "I didn't know I'd be any good at driving a semi-truck tractor-trailer rig, but I gave it a shot. It was very challenging, but I did it. I overcame adversity and persevered until I was an expert. That gave me tremendous confidence. It's like JFK said, 'We choose to go to the moon and do these other things, not because they are easy, but because they are hard.' *Nothing succeeds like success* is the title of a Bill Deal and the Rhondels song, and one of my mottos."

"Yep," said Tom.

"Tom," said Murmur, "one more thing I've been meaning to ask you about. Why don't you settle down and get married? Can't you pick one really great woman who is best suited to you? Don't you believe God has one picked out for your soulmate, your twin-flame?"

"I've narrowed it down to Gianna and Desiree. I've always felt since the divorce that it wasn't my fault my wife cheated and left me. I felt since I prayed and prayed for her to come back to me, and it wasn't God's will, God was giving me a free ride ticket to date and make love to whomever I pleased. I'm a stallion. I'm a stud. God's gift to beautiful women."

"That's not very Christian," Murmur said. They all started laughing and chuckling around the room.

"Speaking of stallions," Maya said looking at Murmur, "didn't your family have horses growing up?"

"Yes, I remember my brothers setting me up on our horse, Flicka's back when I was a toddler. They didn't put the saddle pad and saddle on. They just were teaching me to ride bareback. They said hang on tight, don't fall off, and one of them was riding Blackie, the other set out on foot. When we got out in the field, something spooked Flicka and he went running as fast as he could back into the barn for safety. I got off-balance, shifted to the right side, and fell on my back just before the threshold of the barn door which was made of cinder block. My life didn't flash before my eyes, but in that moment, time seemed to slow down to a crawl. I was lying on my back watching the horse's feet galloping and flying overhead and past me. I had a

sense of peace about it and remember that moment in time the rest of my life, because instead of dying by my head being stamped in, I lived. There's been thousands of times I could have died since then, but I survived."

"Wow, my love!" said Maya.

"When we sold Blackie," Murmur explained, "the buyer did not have a horse trailer available but had to stuff him in the back of a Volkswagen Beetle. Out in the middle of the corral, there was a patch of weed trees. Later, I was able to identify them as poke sallet. We must have tried everything to get rid of them, cutting them down with a scythe, burning them out, you name it, but they kept coming back."

"Bummer," said Deere.

"What a drag," said Fred.

"I remember we had a giant old oak tree with a tire swing hanging from the first branch, which was about 20 to 25 feet up. My brothers would put me on and push me about as far as they could, but no matter how they attached the rope, it would always break. It was like the Sky Wheel almost, and we never knew when it would happen but sooner or later, even with the heaviest rope it would create enough friction with the branch and I would be sailing, free flying through the air. Time seemed to stand still, and it was a great fun feeling…until I eventually hit the ground. Then it hurt."

"Cool," said Fred.

"I would sit under the tree, and eat the Good 'n' Plenty, and Chuckles my dad had brought me. I didn't like them, but it was the thought that counted, so I ate them anyway. He must have heard me

making fun of the radio commercial for the Ronald McDonald coloring calendar, because he got me one for a present. I made the best of it and colored each page of the calendar whether I liked it or not. He wasn't a great dad, but I learned a lot even from his bad examples. I learned what *not* to do. I know what not to do as a parent. When it came to school, I was very conscientious. I found a crayon on the floor and went around to every one of my classmates asking if they had lost that crayon. Anyone else would have kept it they said."

A fly was buzzing about as if spying on them. The women kept swishing and shooing it away from their faces. "Did you know the bigger animals the slower heartbeats in general. Elephants have a slow pulse, and a rabbit has a fast heartbeat. Pet rabbits can have a heart attack if chased by a dog. Caffeine is a natural pesticide because it revs up an insect's heartbeat, causing it to fail and explode. You know different animals and creatures experience time differently. A sloth experiences time very slowly and has slow movements. It lives up to forty years. A fly experiences time very quickly and has a short lifespan. It lives 25 days to two months. They have compound eyes, but their drawback is, they can't notice something approaching if it is moving very slowly." The fly landed on an end table. Murmur slowly put his hands closer together surrounding the fly, then quickly clapped his hands. The fly flew up and was smashed in his palms. It made an electronic zapping sound. "Hmm. That was weird," exclaimed Murmur. He went and washed his hands.

Deere stood up and said, "Hey my mom's here!" He got up to greet her. They shared a loving

hug. Everyone else came in from the pool party and sat somewhere in the room. "Hey where's your dad?" asked Tom. "We lost track of him. Probably gallivanting around the country," said Deere.

"They never were very close for long," Sarah said.

"Yeah, the one thing I remember him teaching me is how to recycle. That's why I'm to this day, so into recycling. Gramps taught me the rest, about the hard work on the farm."

"He means *my* dad," said Sarah.

"The way I see it, Deere, you have nothing to complain about, and especially no right to be depressed or sad, with all you have in life to be grateful and thankful for," said Murmur.

"You're right," said Deere, "I'm turning over a new leaf."

"Fred, you now know that money, wealth, material things, they're not what's important. It's not greed you need. Your best friends, awesome times like this. You start storing up your treasures in heaven, now," said Murmur.

"Yes, agreed," said Fred.

"And you know what? Jesus thinks you're smart," said Murmur.

"How do you know? Did you hear him speak?" said Fred.

"Matthew 7:24. Anyone who listens to my teaching and follows it is wise, like a person who builds a house on solid rock,[12]" said Murmur.

"Thank you. I needed that," Fred said.

---

[12] *New Living Translation*. (n.d.). . Tyndale House Publishers Inc. LTD

Tom found himself spending more time with Gianna. He found they were more compatible with each other. He announced that they would get married soon, when they returned to Florida together. Everyone cheered them on.

Chapter Twelve, Bad People:

The next day, Deere was outside in the flower garden sitting on the bench listening to *I'm Beside Myself* by Frabjoy and Runcible Spoon in his earbuds. Murmur woke up early and walked into the kitchen. Tom was seated at the dining table drinking beer for breakfast. "Hey bud, you want to come sit in the new Challenger? I traded the LTD in for it."

"Sure thing," said Murmur. "Let me have a beer." They walked out and opened the hood and examined its power plant. They sat inside the interior listening to the music, like Compliance by Muse.

"Why in the world would you want to go to college and get into psychology and mental health counseling?" asked Tom. "What a tremendous waste of time!"

"I know that now," admitted Murmur. "I had some conflicts when it was time for the practicum and internship. Actually, it was that witch Dr. Jacqueline Paarsens. The professor for the practicum which I knew was trouble when they started talking about 'gatekeeping' and 'gatekeepers.' She was on a conference call with the group of students, and I could sense her disdain for conservative Christians, and hillbillies down South. She related her experience working with some folks who were supposedly so inbred that they had several rows of teeth, which she likened to shark teeth. That was really biased, stereotypical, and derogatory. Finally, after having so much trouble securing a practicum site, they said I was ***DISMISSED FROM THE PROGRAM!!!***" (Murmur rocked his head from side to side and used

a profusely exaggerated cynically hoity toity mocking tone of the arrogant Bluhm) "I personally got into it because of my best friend, Johnny who always seemed like a pretty cool dude. He was having bad luck with everything, bad times with his woman, he embarrassed himself in front of everyone he was doing jobs for, as a failure who could no longer do anything right, he was pathetic, everything was going wrong for him in his life at that point. He told me one day that he was going to kill himself and that there was nothing that I could say or do that would make him change his mind… I tried to reason with him, saying I wish he would reconsider and that I was there for him if he needed anything. He just said he had his mind made up…"

"He killed himself," said Tom.

"Yeah, man, overdosed on Antabuse, turned blue and dropped on the floor while on the phone with 9-1-1. DOA," said Murmur, "and there were many other loved ones I couldn't save or prevent from dying. I was sitting listening to Type O Negative, Everything Dies. I just stood up and decided to try and go into the helping profession. Try to help people. Plus, I was interested in psychological stuff anyway. Everything fell into place; it was as if all the doors were opening for me. Ultimately, at the end, all the doors went slamming shut. Then I started thinking about how Timothy Leery was a professor who changed his mind about academia; got disenchanted with it, and told people to tune in, turn on, and drop out. When he died, he was totally happy. His last words were 'Why not?' and 'beautiful.' So, I decided to become a spiritual warrior, and *really* help people. Because the dark forces, powers and principalities, couldn't get to me

directly, they started getting to me through other people."

"I might need your help, too, buddy," confided Tom. "I got anger issues. I'm afraid of my thoughts. I scare myself. But that mindfulness, counseling, therapy; all the crap they taught you in college don't work. I've tried everything."

"I'm going to do my best, buddy," said Murmur. "The therapies and meditation *can* work but they have to be applied in the right context. In the context of being helped by the Lord.

Deere and Fred came out and joined them in the back. They each had their own beer.

What would you do if you had your own private practice, Murmur?" asked Deere.

"I'd probably try neurofeedback. I'd use rTMS, repetitive Transcranial Magnetic Stimulation. I'm interested in low-dose ketamine therapy. But you know a lot about natural supplements from your training?"

"Yes," said Deere. "I like ginseng, all forms, like Ashwagandha, Indian ginseng. I like Maca, Muira puama, stuff like that.

"I'll come work out at your gym, Deere," said Tom. "I want to have the ultimate male physique. It always makes me feel great. There are no weirdos in your gym, are there?"

"No, I screen them," said Deere. "If there are those kind of people around who aren't serious about doing the work and achieving their best selves, I don't want to have any part of it. They can go get balloon implants, fake muscles. There could be a brain-dead zombie apocalypse, and they would have strong muscles and overpower us. How frightening is that?"

"I'm not afraid of anything! I fear no evil," mentioned Murmur. "Fearing evil means you have faith in it. The only thing we have to fear is fear itself.[13] Phobophobia.[14] It applies even today.[15] People are usually scared of mental illness because of the unpredictability, as in the fear of the unknown."

"Like, what's the worst cases you've gotten into?" asked Fred. He passed a joint. Murmur thought for a fleeting moment.

"At the youth homes…the kids often self-harmed, cutting themselves. Suicide watches around the clock, checking in on them in their rooms every fifteen minutes. They were self-loathing. One kid I knew of found a hammer and was hitting himself on the head with a hammer. I mean a claw hammer."

"Which end?" asked Tom.

"Huh?" said Murmur.

"Which end of the hammer? The claw end or the hammer end?" asked Tom.

"Does it matter?" pondered Fred.

"I don't know, the hammer end," returned Murmur. "It seems too…severe…to use the claw. Although, either end is an arduous task. He was just trying to knock himself out, I imagine. Anyway, I took the real hammer and confiscated it. I gave him back a plastic toy hammer and we always joked about it after that."

"Did he say anything while he was hitting himself in the head?" asked Tom.

---

[13] https://www.fdrlibrary.org/first-inaugural-curriculum-hub
[14] https://www.healthline.com/health/phobophobia
[15] https://poemanalysis.com/franklin-d-roosevelt/nothing-to-fear-but-fear-itself/

"Something like; Shut up, stupid brain! I don't work for you; *you* are supposed to work for *me*!"

The guys couldn't stop laughing, but it could have been from the effects of beer and cannabis. At least they didn't start using it until they were adults.

"Poor kid," continued Murmur. "He just wanted to turn his brain off, he kept saying. The voices in his head wouldn't shut up and let him have peace."

They played some songs on the radio; *Brain*, *Look at the View*, and *Never Ever* by The Action, *Man in the Teapot* by The Fire, *Oh Happy Day* by Mahalia Jackson.

"Evil forces couldn't seem to get to me directly. I had protection from the Lord, like I asked for. They could only affect me through other people. But bad associations spoil useful habits. I couldn't stand all their toxic negativity. Too much drama, cussing and swearing, complaining all the time, and extreme stupidity. They take all the joy out of life until there's nothing left," said Murmur.

"But *who* are *they*?" asked Fred.

"Bad People," answered Murmur. "People like Bryn Dimpleton. You know what? When Nik Wallenda crossed the 1,500-foot Grand Canyon tightrope, she told me she hoped to see him fall because he was praising Jesus for his success. She said that would be more exciting for her to watch."

"Oh," said Fred.

"The type of people who put razor blades in an apple, or as I've heard on the news, people put pins or needles in strawberries being shipped out, because of their hatred for humanity. They have no idea who might bite into one, nice old lady, pretty

young girl, innocent young boy, regardless of nationality, ethnicity, or skin color. My pastor said these are the hardest people to love. We're supposed to hate the sin but love the sinner. What about the unlovable? We're supposed to pray to love the unlovable. We're supposed to hate what is bad. What if there is so much bad in them, there is no good at all left?"

"Hmm," said Fred.

"I was delivering supplies to the old-folks home in Ashland," said Murmur. "I heard a discussion on the radio about a particular disturbing video. One of the world's most disturbing videos of kids destroying a benevolent man with common tools and various inexpensive objects. They said it was impossible to get it out of their heads. It was like being on a rollercoaster with wave after wave of a crescendo of emotions. They would have nightmares and feel as if they themselves were performing these inhumanities, the savage brutal attacks, upon the well-meaning man. The viewers would see the man's pitiful face begging them for mercy, whenever they closed their eyes, because the camera man did nothing to help. They became the camera man, who did nothing to assist. It was like full-blown PTSD. There was also a video called Destroying Daisy. Nobody should watch these. They'll be scarred mentally. Trust me. Take their word for it. Yet there are police investigators who have to review them. Did you know lawyers have one of the least life satisfaction, and highest suicide rates among professions? And cops, there are good ones, and there are evil ones too, of course. They know too much, they can't unknow, see too much they can't unsee. Things you can't undo. Things

that should never occur… Never be *allowed* to occur. In this situation, maybe there's truth in the phrase 'ignorance is bliss.' The mind is your greater consciousness, awareness, thinking, and feeling. It's experiential, assembling meaning and order from the chaos outside. The brain is your body's computer. You know what they said about computers, garbage in garbage out."

Deere lit up another doobie. They all smoked it.

"All too often, we can't control our thoughts, we can't help but think about all the badness. Can't see the good through the bad. But God's thoughts are higher than our thoughts. His ways are higher than our ways. The conundrum is that God sees everything, but for the sake of the argument, won't intervene. That way we can see true evil. Know that it exists. That's the way the Devil wants it."

"He gets it," whispered Fred.

"All because of that stupid tree," announced Deere. "The Devil's tree. Let me give you a tour of the property."

Tom started his car and Deere showed him the way to his golf course, the farm, his fishpond, and the garden. At that point, Garden of My Mind by The Mickey Finn was playing on the car stereo. After that, Dream in My Mind by Ruperts People played.

"My aunt Samantha is buying this all from me, and moving mom back in. It'll be difficult for her to get an ID, I suppose, since she had a death certificate and was resurrected. I'm coming with you guys. I'm selling most of my possessions and

becoming a minimalist. I'll give most of the proceeds to charities and good causes."

So, they stopped back in the house to say goodbye and to pack up and go. Diva was napping in her My Pillow pet bed. "We're all off to spread the Good News of the Kingdom," said Deere. "Let's put on our shoes of the spreading of good news, our helmets of salvation, breastplates of righteousness to guard our hearts, shields of faith, swords of the word of God, and belts of truth[16]. I used to work in a full-body armor manufacturing facility, but that is all I can say about that. I signed a non-disclosure agreement. Are you all ready to go? Got all your supplies?"

Deere hugged his mom, and they kissed each other's cheeks. "I will be back to check on you from time to time. You got my cell phone number on that new phone I got you."

"Yes, I do," said Sarah. "I really appreciate everything you guys! You've been so good to me. Anytime you want to visit California you just come right out. We'll hold the fort down."

"We can't take all the vehicles," reminded Tom. "What with Biden's high gas prices and all. We'll have to carpool."

"But we'll have to take more than just one vehicle to fit everyone," added Murmur.

"I have the bus ready to go," offered Deere. I had it fitted with its own pool table, so we don't get bored on the road."

"Cool, dude," said Tom.

---

[16] Ephesians 6:11-18; Retrieved from BibleTools.org

"Yeah, man!" said Murmur. "We're taking the whole crew?"

"Yeah, man," said Tom.

"Yeah, man," said Deere.

"Yeah, man," said Maya.

"Yeah, man," said Cindy.

"Yeah, man," said Marcie.

"Yeah, man," said Gianna.

"Yeah, man," barked Diva in her dog language. Her tail was wagging as she did the playful bowing pose, she always does, that's similar to the downward-facing dog yoga pose.

"Me and the guys figured out the meaning of life, and the secret to happiness, Mom!" said Deere. "It's to have a good time with the Lord. In other words, rejoice with the Lord always, again I say rejoice[17]. Delight yourself in the Lord[18]. In a word, Love is the secret to happiness. Having a purpose from The Creator. He has a plan for everyone ever born. According to a Discover magazine article,[19] there are six secrets backed by science: nurturing your relationships, performing random acts of kindness, surrounding yourself with happy people, practicing gratitude, smiling more, and looking for daily experiences of awe. Everything that pops into your brain from the world can be either ignored or your brain attaches importance to it. Meaning is

---

[17] Phillipians 4:4-8 NLT Retrieved from www.tyndale.com and www.bible.com

[18] Psalm 37:4 ESV Retrieved from biblehub.com

[19] Orlando, A. (2023, January 16). Try these 6 science-backed secrets to happiness. Discover Magazine. www.discovermagazine.com

instilled by the impossibility of us even being here; the miracle of us being alive at this moment."

"That's lovely, dear!" Sarah turned to look at the new couple. "Remember, don't forget to remind me not to forget to come to your wedding, Tom and Gianna," said Sarah.

"Remember that song Simple Man by Lynyrd Skynyrd? Mom used to not only say that to me, but she'd sing the actual song! She had me listen to Greatest Love of All by Whitney Houston. That's like…you love yourself and you love God. God is inside you! God is life. God is love. Whitney did some great Gospel songs too. I'm going to make everyone some organic non-GMO buckwheat pancakes with amaranth flour and ancient einkorn wheat flour, the only wheat that's never been hybridized or messed with by bioengineering or tampered with by wicked Monscanto[20] with its poisonous and highly toxic Glyfoolsafe that definitely does kill people dead."

"That's for certain," said Murmur. "Everybody knows GMOs mess up all your DNA and insert their diabolical mRNA.[21]"

"Speaking of which," inserted Tom. "Have you ever noticed how fiercely and ferociously people or organizations try to refute and cover up something they are hiding, some inconvenient facts implicating themselves or their cronies? Say somebody hands The Weather Channel, NPR,

---

[20] Kuti, S. & Egypt 80 (2011). *Rise* [Digital download *Rise*]. From the album, From Africa with Fury: Rise. Produced by Brian Eno, John Reynolds, Sean Kuti.

[21] https://www.drrobertyoung.com/post/god-has-written-his-name-in-every-strand-of-your-dna

CNN, or MSNBC a huge stack of cash and tells them talk about Covid, talk about global warming and climate change as if it were a real thing. Or you tell Fakebook, I'll give you this wheelbarrow of cash to refute anyone who is trying to alert citizens about the dangers of chemtrails or that these horrible deadly storms are actually caused by geoengineering."

"Tell me about it," Murmur rolled his eyes. "The JWs were fearful of Covid. They were one of the first denominations to cower to the establishment's orders and shut down and start using Zoom for virtual meetings. And despite Zoom's widespread security concerns they said it was God's providing for them for the pandemic, to keep them safe. That's when I stopped conversing with them completely. Most Christians kept their churches open and disregarded the test from the governments. I was an essential worker, so it didn't affect me or change my life one iota. Leftists on the coasts were sabotaging church parking lots by putting out nails to try to puncture tires and wiping infected rags on the church door handles. The latest variant Omicron is an acronym for moronic."

They all ate their pancakes and other breakfast items and then hit the road.

They headed back to Bois Blanc Island, in a small caravan of vehicles, stopping frequently along the way for gasoline and potty breaks. The bus Deere drove led the way, the stereo system played *Egyptian Tomb* by Mighty Baby, and some songs by Big Star. It played Captain Beyond and Captain Beefheart, but no Captain and Tennielle. The 50-disc CD changer did have The Carpenters and The Poppy Family with Terry Jacks. Next in line was

the Challenger, and after that the 1970 GSX. They sometimes changed vehicles so that they could take turns playing billiards on the bus.

"Will you be my Janis Joplin?" Tom asked Gianna.

"Of course!" Gianna said.

"You know Gianna's from Newark, Ohio originally," Tom told Murmur.

"Wow, I know where that is," said Murmur.

"She might even be willing to have children with me," said Tom.

"That's incredible," said Murmur.

"Yeap!" said Tom.

"Maya and I are trying for a baby too now. We're going to have to mentally prep for the End Times, too," said Murmur. "Not be just regular preppers, like have been prepping for decades without anything big really happening."

"Yeah, man, now it's *really* getting bad," said Tom.

"The guys were telling me about your negative, unwanted thoughts. Cognitive dissonance. Stinking thinking. Repetitive thoughts. I forgot to tell you, thought suppression doesn't work[22]," said Murmur.

"I know," said Tom. "Maybe we can meditate together sometimes."

"Maybe we can also go do battle with demonic cryptids, sort of like Ghostbusters. We can't use regular weapons on them, like shotguns, because they're supernatural," said Murmur.

---

[22] https://www.verywellmind.com/thought-suppression-and-ocd-2510480

"Although shotguns are good for blowing zombies' heads off," said Tom.

"Yes!" said Murmur.

"You know," said Tom, "all those social influencers get paid to go spread garbage misinformation and lies around. We aren't going to get anything for telling the truth to people. I wouldn't have it any other way."

"Yeah, they know so much that isn't so," said Murmur. "Makes you ponder the ethics of influencing others, except for spreading the truth. It's immoral to influence others with falsehood."

"Why don't they consider that at the college level?" asked Tom.

"They're ungodly," said Murmur.

"So, what do we say to those academics who always explain things in terms of evolution and Big Bang theory? They state it as fact, but creation is not even a consideration. They regard it as unscientific," said Tom.

"I believe God used evolution for biological and ethnic diversity," said Murmur, "especially since the flood. Antediluvian era had dinosaurs, according to Ray Comfort. A few small dinosaurs would have been on the Ark. After the flood there would have likely been a mini-ice-age and they just didn't make it through with the sparse vegetation available to them. Besides, enormous dinosaurs which were obnoxious and burdensome to civilization had long been targeted for extermination by man. God, only, made it possible for them to be destroyed by us. It was what everyone wanted. By the way, covfefe means 'in the end we win.' This antediluvian phrase was not understood by the worldly fake news outlets, and it

was interesting to see how they rushed out an explanation of the unexplained to satisfy watchers, listeners, and readers. What they hear first by their trusted outlets is what they tend to believe. That's why they slander their political enemies by accusing them of what they themselves are doing or have done. It's like opposites day. You know who did that first. Satan said the opposite of what God told Adam and Eve. He contradicted God. Just like Bryn always contradicted me."

"I sense you have some real animosity toward the Enemy," said Tom.

"Truth is, Tom, I have been directing my anger and hostility toward the Devil. I mean I haven't gone out into a field and shouted the worst cuss and swear words at him, like my friend did. Nothing happened, but he knows the Devil has no power over us. I want revenge on the Devil…for everything he stole from me: Everything that came up missing, and I never found again: All the loved ones that died of cancer and unfortunate circumstances, all the many series of unfortunate events, and all the great things he destroyed. He always killed my favorite pets growing up, repeatedly…until one day I just started acting like I didn't care about pets anymore. I didn't have any more favorite. I never had an animal that lived as long as Diva has. I have no toys or possessions left from my youth. Who knows where they all went. God only knows."

Murmur played *Goin' Back* by the Byrds for Tom. The first leaves started to fall. Soon it would lead to the fall color tour. "This is a great song," said Murmur. I also like *The Christian Life*, and *Draft Morning.*

"You know," said Tom, "Satan only does all that stuff to you because he knows how much it bothers you. He knows how aggravated and agitated you get. When you don't let it bother you and listen to Gospel and Christian music, he hates that! Do that more instead."

"Okay," said Murmur. His lips began to form a smile. Gradually it became not a fake smile, but a real, genuine smile, one that showed his teeth. They had been straightened and whitened by an orthodontist.

They drove up to Bois Blanc from the Ambassador bridge again in Detroit. They took each vehicle on the ferry. All passengers got out once at the storage yard to stretch their legs. There was no attendant around. Tom looked at Deere and Fred. Fred and Deere looked at each other and then at Tom. They had weirdly worried expressions on their faces. Fred said, "Hey, bud, why don't you let me and Marcie handle getting this back. Our favor to you. Just head back in the bus and take a nap, you look awfully tired from the trip."

"Nonsense," said Murmur. "Maya can drive it back, while I drive the GSX. She's fully competent as a great driver."

"Or maybe let Cindy and I drive it back; we'll take extra loving care of it for you. You two deserve a break."

"Nonsense," said Murmur. "I insist. I can drive some more. I am used to driving the big trucks, and cars, cross-country. Maya and I will stop often and rest." He went to open the hood. "Check this out Maya."

Tom swooped around to get in his way. "Don't look under there."

"Under where?" said Maya.

"Ah-hah! I just made you say underwear!" laughed Tom nervously and pointed at him.

"Ha-ha-ha," said everyone.

"Out of my way," said Murmur. They gasped as he opened the hood, and a nice impeccably clean 440 was where the 383 used to be. "I had my friend put this in for me."

"Oh," said Tom.

"Oh," said everyone else, sighing with relief. Crisis averted.

Fred rubbed the back of his neck. "Let's go."

"Where to next?" asked Deere.

Fred's cellphone rang. "Hello!"

Maya and Murmur hopped in the Polara and started it up, revving it a few times to hear the motor purr. They started giggling and making out in the front. Everybody could see them. They didn't care of course.

"Hey, guys," Fred knocked on the driver's side window and Murmur rolled it down. "Do you guys mind if we all head out to upstate New York? My aunt Ethyl bought another house to flip, and it appears to be haunted. Besides a hoarder lived there and it needs a good clean out. She's willing to let us in on the profits. Around five grand she said she's willing to pay us for our help."

Maya and Murmur whispered to each other and talked it over. "We'll go if you can talk everyone else into it."

"Thanks man," said Fred. "I really appreciate it. I'll see to it that we have plenty of money. You won't regret it."

"You're welcome," said Murmur, and the couple went back to passionately and romantically making out in the front of the Polara. They were steaming up the windows. In about fifteen minutes, everybody piled in the vehicles. They followed Fred who was driving the bus. He decided to go through Canada. The bus went about 666 kilometers to a restaurant, Northstar Public House, 202 E Falls St, Ithaca, NY 14850. Following his GPS, Fred drove up to 401 East, to 403 East and I-90 East, to NY-318 E, took exit 42, and merged onto 401 East, to 403 East, to exit 64 for Lincoln M. Alexander Parkway East, to Red Hill Valley Parkway, to Queen Elizabeth Way. They continued onto ON-405 to I-190 South, to exit 16 for I-290 East, to I-90 East toward Albany, (they had to pay tolls). They then took NY-14 South, NY-96A South, NY-96 South, and NY-89 South.

When they all stopped to get out, Fred motioned to them to come in, to the Inn to eat. "I'll call Aunt Ethyl that we're here, she can come meet and eat dinner with us and afterward she'll show us the way to the house we have to work on."

It didn't take long for Aunt Ethyl, since she was already close by and expecting them to arrive, little more than ten minutes. She whipped in the parking lot with a new silver Porsche 911 Turbo S Cabriolet. Her long gray hair shimmered in the breeze. "Here she is now, guys," called out Fred.

"How's it going?" greeted Aunt Ethyl. "This place isn't as big as I thought it would be. Wow, are these all your friends?"

"Yeah," said Fred, "Mortimer Murray we call Murmur, he's from around the Detroit metropolitan area, originally.

"Howdy, Ma'am," said Murmur.

"Nice to meet you," said Aunt Ethyl, shaking his hand heartily.

"My new wife, I don't think you've met her, right here, Marcie."

"Hi there," said Marcie.

"Pleased to meet you!" said Aunt Ethyl.

Murmur said, "And my wife, Maya."

"Hi," said Aunt Ethyl.

"Hi," said Maya.

"Tom, and Gianna," said Fred. They nodded and waved.

"Deere Muff and Cindy Muff," said Fred. Ditto.

"Chuck, Marvin, Cardy Flowers, that's our band members. My friends from New York City; Martha, Aimee, Dorothea, Tony, Richard, Martin, Tonya, Janet, Todd and Beth. More of the groupies: Millie, Desiree, Holly, Carrie, Candy, and Dolly… and who are you?" Fred asked those he didn't know the names of.

"Alley," said one.

"Kristen," said another.

"Leah," said another.

"Trish," said another.

"Kendra," said another.

"Sandy," said another.

"Becca," said another.

"Valleri," said another.

"Oh, I didn't even see *you* there," said Fred.

"I'm new," said Valleri. "I just now joined up here in town."

"Cool beans," said Deere. Cindy gave him a dirty look.

"I mean, uh, we're all cool," said Deere.

"Seems like you got enough help," said Aunt Ethyl.

"Tell me more about the job you need us to do," said Fred.

"Okay," said Aunt Ethyl, "well, I bought this house in town, like I told you; and I didn't know this when I bought it, but apparently a previous owner went missing a few months ago, and was a Satanic priest, who officiated a local Satan church, the bank foreclosed and there's still a lot of satanic relics and memorabilia all over inside, especially in the attic."

"What denomination?" asked Murmur.

"Probably theistic Satanism," said Aunt Ethyl.

"Oh, so they were pretty serious," said Tom.

"Serious as a heart attack," said Aunt Ethyl. "But I really need that junk completely cleared out and a cleansing done so it won't be haunted. That would definitely be a drawback for any potential home buyer. It's a beautiful old house when all fixed up."

"Sounds good, take us to it," said Fred.

"Follow me, I'll lead the way," said Aunt Ethyl.

"Wait! We've got to eat first," said Deere with his tray of food.

"You're right," said Fred. "Everybody, get you some food. I'm buying." Everybody was starving. They took at least an hour to eat.

"One of their websites said something about FREE ABORTIONS!" said Aunt Ethyl.

"That's because they want the baby alive for satanic ritual sacrifice," said Murmur. "Of course, they might never admit to that, but that is what's

done, at least by some of the hardcore groups. If you can imagine it, it's probably been done. There is no new thing under the sun. Except maybe an old thing with a new modern twist."

"But they do that to adults too, right?" said Fred.

"Yes," said Murmur. "Outsiders, but you have got to understand their mentality. When an innocent beautiful baby is traumatized and dies a horrible sickening death, it releases adrenochrome, which the evil spirits crave. Plus, they love torturing and killing anything that is super-cute and pure. They have videos online showing them feeding the cutest baby animals to a big snake or a giant centipede. They're cruel barbaric sadists at heart. Undercover eyewitness visitors they're trying to initiate, have reported them cutting off a baby's head on the altar, holding them up by the leg and letting the blood drain out into a basin and then drinking it from a goblet. They tried to get the inductee to do it themselves, so they'll incriminate themselves and not tell anyone. They'll be too afraid to tell. That's why it's all sworn to secrecy. If it wasn't a big secret the authorities might put a stop to it, unless they're in on it too, like in *Young Goodman Brown*."

"Yep," said Tom. "The deep state is in on it. The military industrial complex, secret societies. Millionaires, and billionaires. They've got pedophilia rings, drug lords and kingpins, human traffickers, all the awful stuff in the news right now. The news as we know it." *The Night of the Sadist* by Larry and the Blue Notes played on the outdoor speakers on the patio.

"Hear that? They're listening to us," said Fred. "Let's go."

It was early evening in the early fall, they followed Aunt Ethyl's Porsche through the burgeoning fall color tour to the house she had bought.

They drove up the lengthy driveway and parked. It was a beautiful brick home with a tall tan roof. "Wow," said Tom to Murmur, "it looks like the Devil blessed this guy."

"No," said Murmur. "The Devil isn't capable of truly blessing someone of his people. To do that in the traditional sense he would have to love someone, and he's incapable of loving his followers. Only God can bless. The Devil tries to indicate God is the epitome of evil, but it is Satan that is the epitome of evil. Remember it's like opposites day, every day with him."

"Ah," said Tom. "Let's have a look inside."

They walked up the magnificent stairs, checked out the bedroom, and took the fold-out ladder to the attic. There were musty boxes of stuff, and not much room to walk or get around. Most of the rest stayed out in the yard and vehicles. They went to look in the basement. It was similar to the attic but had more room for walking through.

"This is too much to start now. We'll sleep first and start work in the morning. I need at least ten hours of sleep from being on the road," said Tom.

"I agree," said Murmur.

"That's fine by me," said Aunt Ethyl. "I've got extra sleeping bags and cots in the corner of the main living room if you want them."

"Some of us might opt to sleep inside the bus," said Deere.

"Sounds about right," said Fred.

The next day, about noon, almost everyone was awake. Aunt Ethyl had a roll-off dumpster dropped off in front of the house. They split up to tackle different rooms, and the basement. Fred, Deere, Tom, and Murmur took care of the creepy attic. They sat in old chairs with boxes in front of them.

"Take a look at this," said Tom. There were tracts and literature promoting Satanism. It appeared nobody wanted them, so they were never used. "Garbage," said Deere. He pulled out a Ouija board. "Garbage."

"We better burn the stuff," said Murmur, "Do we have a burn barrel?"

"I saw a chiminea on the back patio," said Fred.

"That'll work," said Fred. "Hey look at this…" He held up a satanic mask. "It's real ugly!"

"It was probably used in his ceremonies," said Murmur.

"Can we desecrate it? I mean they *say* the Devil is not mocked," said Deere, "Is that true?"

"The Devil *is* mocked," said Murmur. "God is not mocked."

Deere took the mask and rubbed it against his buttocks and farted on it. He got a static electric shock from it. "OW!" He threw it against the floor and stomped on it. "Let's dunk it in the toilet, and poop on it," said Deere, "then we'll burn it all in the chiminea."

"We could do worse than that," said Tom, winking and smiling.

"Ha-ha-ha!" laughed Fred.

"Okay," said Murmur, "but remember this, it's probably not a good idea to unnecessarily taunt and ridicule Satan and the demons more than we have to. They can bother and harass us; better to let God rebuke them. God will deliver us from all evil." So, they did all that and burned the offensive items in the chiminea.

An hour later Maya came out to see them. "We got all the junk cleaned up and disposed of in the roll-off," she said.

"Already???" said Fred.

"Yeah," said Maya, smiling.

"Okay, then, one more thing," said Murmur. "We have to cleanse and bless this house. Everyone went around holding hands and praying, cleansing, and blessing the entire house and property.

"Great job, guys!" exclaimed Aunt Ethyl.

"Five Grand! Not bad for a few hours' work," Fred said as he collected the money from Aunt Ethyl. He split it up equally between all of them.

"Where to, now?" asked Deere.

"Everyone is cordially invited to Florida to attend our wedding," invited Tom.

"Good," said Deere, "I am going to move there."

"Me too," said Fred.

"Me too," barked Diva in her dog language.

"Me too," said Murmur. "I think we *all* are!"

In a while, everyone was ready, and they embarked on the final leg of this journey, stopping often for potty breaks and to gas up. They went 1,225 miles, and it took almost 19 hours, via US-15 South, and I-95 South. Tom and the girls were

motoring along in the Challenger. Murmur and Maya were following in the Polara, but Alley, Kristy, Leah, and Trish were in the 1970 GSX, with Alley driving.

Once at Tom's house, everybody was able to sleep for about ten hours, or as long as they wanted. Tom woke up first and made his guests a huge feast including the vegetarian foods some required. Murmur, Deere and Fred woke up next. "So, you guys are moving to Florida?"

"Yeah, man," said Deere.

"Yeah, dude," said Murmur.

"Yepperz," said Fred.

"Y'all can stay here until you've found your own house," said Tom, "but don't take too long. I'm not a bed and breakfast. I'd have to start charging you."

"Cool, thanks man," said Deere.

"Yeah, thanks," said Murmur. "I appreciate everything."

"Thank you, Tom," said Fred. "I can help financially."

"And I can help marry you two because I am an ordained minister through Universal Life Church,[23]" said Murmur.

"You never said that before," said Deere.

"Yeah, I just remembered," said Murmur, "and I want to print out a phony diploma saying I graduated from Harvard or something."

"You don't have to do that," said Fred. "I own a university now, called Tantamount University. I can give you an honorary degree."

---

[23] https://www.ulc.org/training/ordination-training

"No one can know it's an honorary degree, though. It's got to be an actual degree like I earned it," said Murmur. "Look, Diva won't take a treat unless she's actually earned it." He gave Diva a treat from the bag, and she acted like she didn't want it. Then he had her do 'sit,' 'lay down,' and 'roll-over,' and after that she happily ate the treat.

"Deal," said Fred.

"Tha's pretty amazing," said Deere.

"Do you have a church home, or do you do home church?" Murmur asked Tom.

"I haven't made the time for it really," said Tom. "I'm sort of a spiritual vagabond, going to whatever church in the area fits my mood at that time."

"Well start looking for a church we can do the wedding at," said Murmur.

"Okay," said Tom. Deere called all his friends and relatives from California to get them to come for the wedding. Tom called all his friends and relatives, and so did Gianna. Practically everyone else was getting the word out too. It was going to be huge! They set a date for Thanksgiving Day, so they would have a holiday as an anniversary date, ensuring they would always get their anniversary day off work. It gave them over a month to plan and get ready. Tom and Gianna looked day after day and attended churches in the area, but they always found they disagreed with some of the doctrine, or the type of people there were disagreeable. There were a lot of heathens and heretics they ran into. Often times, the people would argue with them as they were sharing the Good News of the Kingdom. Some would act possessed and talk in possessed multiple voices. After a week

had gone by, the other guys helped look while sharing the Good News also.

"You're all missionaries," said Murmur. "I know you all don't have a lot of experience and didn't go to seminary school or a Christian college, but you are Bible scholars. Jesus didn't pick his apostles from a group of graduates with a lot of experience. I call it 'being and becoming,' for example, you're playing basketball 12 hours a day training so that you can become a professional basketball player. That is your aspiration, and you're dedicated to it, you're an aspiring basketball player, but you're also a basketball player until you hit the big time as a star."

"It's like me being a millionaire, and becoming a billionaire with commercial real estate," said Fred.

"Yeah," said Tom. "Just like God saying, 'I am what I am,' or 'I am what I shall prove to be,' in Exodus 3:14. It's a good example to follow…"

"It's just like being and becoming a musician," said Deere. "We picked up our instruments with good intentions and were able to become what people came to listen to, with God's good grace. We always knew we were musicians from day one, not just something we could be one day if we were good enough to go pro. Just like we were chosen from day one to be Christians, since we were saved. We were destined and pre-destined to do it. We're improving, doing more and becoming more every day. Day by day."

"I think I see what you're saying," said Fred. "People shouldn't think they aren't good enough to do God's will. They shouldn't be pathologized. They should '*JUST DO IT.*' God gave us everything

we need to live a life pleasing to Him. God gave us a spirit, not of timidity, but of power, love, and self-discipline, or self-control.[24]"

"Yes," said Murmur.

"I agree," said Deere.

"Amen," said Tom.

"Be bold for God," said Murmur. "Be confident. Have pride in a job well-done. Take pride in yourself, maintaining your health and cleanliness, for being alive, for having knowledge of God. That's what you *can* boast of[25]. It's the good kind of pride. The bad pride is just when someone is full of themselves without God's help. They're arrogant, insolent, haughty, and cocky. Loving only themselves and *not* God[26]. We are not that way, but as though we've had some assertiveness training."

"All hell can't stop us now," said Tom.

Time rolled on and as there were now only two weeks left and a growing number of people showing up who were living in tents out front and back yard of Tom's place, Tom and Gianna began to look for a vacant church to buy. Fred offered to help pay for it. Soon they found the perfect one that was in the country near St. Pete.

"It's so cute!" said Maya. "Look at the little bell tower. Just a traditional church like I've always dreamed of getting married in."

"I love it!" said Gianna.

"Yeah, Awesome!" said Tom. "It could use a couple coats of pearl white gloss exterior paint. Let's buy it."

---

[24] 2 Timothy 1:7
[25] Jeremiah 9:23-24
[26] 2 Timothy 3:2-4

"How much are they asking?" asked Fred.

"250,000 or best offer," said Murmur. "For sale by owners."

"I'll talk to them and offer 200,000. What's their number?" asked Fred.

"Here it is," offered Maya. Fred whipped out his cell phone and called the number. "Hi. My name is Fred. I'm calling about your little church you have for sale. I'm over here now, are you nearby and can stop out?" Fred paused to listen to their reply. "Yeah, I have cash and would like to offer 200,000 today. Okay, see you then." He pressed end saying, "They'll be right out. It's an old couple retiring."

"Well, good for them," said Gianna. "I wish them happiness."

"Just like we're so happy, honey," said Tom.

"Mmmm, yeahhhh," said Gianna as they began to smooch.

The old couple, George and Donna, pulled up in a gold 1934 Deusenberg SJ Torpedo Phaeton. They smiled and waved as they got out and acted friendly. They accepted the offer for $200,000 cash. Everyone immediately started helping out to fix it up and make it look better.

Fred also surprised Deere with a gift of his own gym where he could be a trainer. Deere gave as many as wanted a grand tour and identified all the muscles of the body on a chart. He described many of the wonders of the human physical body, saying we are fearfully and wonderfully made. Fred then surprised Murmur with a private practice building where he could help others. "I'll have to show you guys my auto body shop," said Tom. All of them went out to see it. There was a lot of memorabilia,

antique signs and petroliana. He also had several cars, many of which were a work in progress.

As Tom and Gianna were driving to the church the next morning, they were deciding what they might call the church. Then as they pulled up into the parking area, they noticed a vandal had spraypainted in black the words “The Hippie Cult” on the side of the church. He phoned Fred to come on out and look. Fred looked and laughed, “No problems, we’ll just call the friends and paint over it. It needs to be repainted anyways. Don’t sweat the small stuff.”

“What should we call our church? Forever Church? Our band can play worship songs there,” said Tom.

“Church of Eternity?” suggested Gianna. Murmur and Maya stopped out with Diva to help.

“Church of Jesus,” said Fred. “That should be fine.” Their people had it perfectly painted in a few hours.

Later, Murmur was unpacking boxes of books at his new private practice. “What Cha got there?” asked Tom in a hillbilly accent wearing a cowboy hat, cowboy boots, and Men’s bootcut jeans.

“I got a book about Maslow’s idea of Transcendence[27]. Hey, have you ever heard of the Silva Mind Control Method[28]? He started everyone talking about the Gamma, Beta, Alpha, Theta, and Delta brain waves. That’s this book. Hippies were

---

[27] Kaufman, S. B. (2022). Transcend: The new science of self-actualization. Sheldon Press.

[28] Silva, J., & Miele, P. (2022). The silva mind control method. Gallery Books.

influenced by it. Now the newest ‘in thing’ is Psycholytic Therapy in lower doses more often than Psychedelics[29] and since Covid when people were isolated in quarantine there has been a rise in loneliness, and mental illness including depression and anxiety, and plant medicine acceptance is increasing in the West encompassing mind, body, and soul, where traditional medicine largely ignores the spiritual aspects[30]. So, I am very interested in each part of the brain, brain mapping. Bipolar which includes manic depression occurs up here,” pointing to a spot in his forehead, “in the Prefrontal cortex, the limbic system starting with the amygdala with more activity in the left hemisphere and less in the right, and the ventrolateral prefrontal cortex, gray matter in the frontal, temporal, and parietal areas, and Hippocampus with its role in emotions and memory. According to WebMD and MedlinePlus, schizophrenia involves structural changes in the frontal, temporal, and thalamus. They’ll have a thinner cortex in the frontal lobe. They may have a reduction of gray matter here in the left temporal lobe.” He pointed to the side of his head. “And mutations in the dentate gyrus. They may have chemical imbalances of neurotransmitters; glutamate, dopamine, causing delusions and hallucinations, putting them out of touch with reality. Genetic predisposition can arise from

---

[29] Butler, J. A., Herzberg, G., & Miller, R. L. (2024). Integral psychedelic therapy: The non-ordinary art of psychospiritual healing. Routledge, Taylor & Francis Group.

[30] Read, T., & Papaspyrou, M. (2021). Psychedelics and psychotherapy: The healing potential of expanded states. Park Street Press.

duplicate or deleted material from a chromosome such as chromosome 22."

"Very interesting," said Tom.

"Fascinating," said Deere.

"Great insight!" said Fred.

"I would like to help train the subconscious brain for my clients, so that they might become experts in all their fields," said Murmur.

"Like a Jack of all trades, master of all of them?" asked Fred.

"No," said Murmur. "Some people have told me it takes 5,000 hours to achieve mastery. Malcom Gladwell estimated 10,000 hours. That could take as much as ten years or at least 2.6 years. Now we can train the brain in optimal conditions to reach that goal in half the time. According to Indeed there are 72 trades or more. Almost nobody in the world has trained optimally and if they took just 2.6 years, that would be 187.2 years from the day they were born. Therefore, anyone (younger than 190) who said they or someone they know is a 'jack of all trades, and a master of all of them,' is a liar, or perhaps a liberal who knows so much that isn't so. In that case they are trying to impress someone else or being facetious."

"Do you ever notice how the leftist Democrats pander to every one of their constituents?" asked Tom.

"Is that the same as patronizing?" asked Deere.

"No," answered Murmur. "Pandering is when you say something that all your listeners can agree because it's pretty obvious, like the family values of the Mormons, the sanctity of life by the Catholics, the right to life, liberty, and pursuit of

happiness by American patriots, and then they are on board with you for everything else. You then influence them to reinforce the negative behavior. Patronizing is like my dad talked to me in baby talk, and I wanted him to talk to me like everyone else. He talked down to me, appearing to be kind and helpful, but feeling superior he came off as unwittingly condescending, and behind my back he would downgrade me saying bad things about me to others. That's how the Democrats treat the voter base, assuming they are not as smart as they themselves are."

"What if someone truly evil like Shifty Schiff, Gates, or Soros repents and is saved and enters the Kingdom, while we work hard doing the right thing to get there?" asked Maya.

"Most likely they won't because it's too hard for them to break free from their true main identity. Let the unrighteous be unrighteous still, and filthy to be filthy still. Let the righteous continue to do righteousness still[31]. I think of it as inertia; it tends to let an object at rest stay at rest, and an object in motion to stay in motion, unless otherwise acted upon," said Murmur. "Anyway, they treat you like a little kid, because you're in a nanny state."

"That makes sense," said Tom.

"The simplest explanation that makes the most sense," said Murmur, "is probably right."

"Sounds about right," said Fred.

"Right on," said Deere.

---

[31] Revelation 22:11

The Wedding was just a few days away, the hippie groupies got some fabric to make the wedding dress for Gianna from the Hobby Lobby in Clearwater. Fred's friends helped Tom by lending him a tuxedo that fit. Deere's mother and aunt showed up. They stayed in Deere and Cindy's little living space at the back of the gym. However, his fitness followers from California did not have enough room and were living in tents or in their vehicles for the time. Deere's mom made the wedding cake from scratch. Murmur was staying in the living space above his private practice clinic. He also did massage therapy, with aromatherapy. Maya helped.

Deere and Cindy drove out to the little church in the morning mist, surrounded by bald cypress trees and tweeting birds. Many of the friends were watching out on security shifts to keep vandals, thugs, and would-be contaminators away. Murmur met them there, and said he was working on the speech for Tom and Gianna. "You should be spontaneous, off the cuff, and improv.," said Deere.

"Normally I would," said Murmur. "It's just that I never officiated a wedding before. I want it to be perfect."

"It will be," said Deere, "just pray about it and then it's already done for you. Believe it and you shall receive it."

"You're right," said Murmur.

"I know I'm right," added Deere.

"I just have to feel it," said Murmur.

"This is beautiful; this little church," said Cindy.

"Wish it was a *big* church like that *Joel Osteen has*," said Deere. "He's so abundantly rich. What with that prosperity gospel and all."

"Deere," said Murmur, "I hate to say this to you, but you're *envious*. Don't **do** dat. You see the grass as greener on the other church ground. Just be grateful he's helping with the Great Commission, and the positivity, and charisma. The harvest potential is great, and the workers are relatively few. Pray that more workers be sent out into the mission field. Pray for your enemies. Love your enemies, it's like piling hot coals on their heads."

"Why on earth would I want to pile hot coals on their heads if I learn to love them?" asked Deere.

There was a long silence. "I don't know," said Murmur, "but you won't be the one doing the piling. Your enemies will have to answer for their own sins because you did the right thing. Never ever give up the good fight!"

"Guess what, dude," said Deere.

"Uh…you're going away to join the circus?" guessed Murmur.

"Uh, *NO!*" Deere said with a sideways glanced quick headshake and exaggerated sarcastic tone. "I got Cindy pregnant!"

"Wow!" said Murmur. "That's great!"

"I'm so happy for you two!" said Maya.

"Guess what," said Murmur.

"Your personal pronouns are It, That, and THE?" guessed Deere.

"Don't be ridiculous," said Murmur. "I got Maya pregnant!"

"GREAT!" said Deere.

"Yes!" said Maya. "It's true!"

Tom and Gianna drove up in the Challenger and hopped out.

"Guess what, dudes," said Tom.

"You're starting a professional nose picking business and need to borrow my drill?" guessed Murmur.

"I got Gianna pregnant!" Tom said, and at the same time:

"I'm pregnant," said Gianna excitedly.

"Awesome," said Murmur and Maya.

"Groovy," said Deere and Cindy.

Fred and Marcie showed up on their way back from a romantic walk. They were all smiles. "Hey, guys, guess what?"

"Marcie's pregnant too???" they all said.

"Wow…How did you guess?" said Fred and Marcie together.

"God given intuition, like Silva talked about," said Murmur.

"Praise God! Thank you, Jesus! It's an answer to our prayers," said Fred.

"Yes, the almighty! Creator of life! He created life through us! It is so amazing," said Cindy.

"Right," said Maya, "God is the wisest being in the Universe and we have a direct line with him. You know how difficult it is getting to have supper with Adragon De Mello, Terence Tao, or Marilyn Vos Savant. Well, the ONE with the most knowledge and wisdom of the Universe, because He *made* everything, you get to approach in prayer and ask Him questions. You know how hard it would be to get a hold of someone as rich as Bill and Melinda Gates, Jeff Bezos, or Warren Buffet. But God owns everything, so He is the richest. Just think what all

He does for us already! You get to make a request to Him. Isn't that a lot more reassuring than trying to win the lottery, or a sweepstakes?"

"Yes!" said Murmur.

"Amen," said Tom.

"You bet!" said Fred. Everyone else nodded.

They wanted to go to church on that Sunday, the 19th. The women had washed all the wood down with Murphy's oil soap. Artisans within the bunch repaired the stained glass windows. It was ready to hold attendance inside. Deere needed his motorcycles from California brought out. He called on his biker friends to get them there. "I've got an Indian and a Harley."

"What's your code to get in?" asked Bruno Belcher.

"8170, and don't make off with them. I know where your parents live," reminded Deere with a chuckle.

"You can count on me, dud, I mean dude," said Bruno.

"Really?!?!" said Deere.

"I haven't let you down yet now, have I?" said Bruno.

"You haven't had the chance to," laughed Deere. "Why don't you bring the whole gang? We're having a wedding and playing worship songs in the church band."

"Oh, the Forever Church Band?" said Bruno.

"Yes," said Deere. "The Forever Church of Jesus. You'll love it."

"Way cool!" said Bruno.

"So, I'll see you guys here in about two days," said Deere, "and please bring me the rest of my vehicles. Thank you."

"Sounds good," said Bruno. "See you then."

"Bye," said Deere.

"Bye," said Bruno.

"Hey guys!" said Deere as he tapped end. "The bikers are coming; the bikers are coming!"

"They're not Hell's Angels, are they?" asked Tom with alarm.

"No," said Deere. "They don't need to have to be members of an obnoxious group of evil biker freaks, who callously hurt people, to prove they are cool. They're just regular guys who happen to be really cool and friendly anyway. Most of them don't even have tattoos. Maybe they never had the desire to call attention to their bodies by torturing themselves with needles, indelible ink, and stupid obscene artwork, like I don't…hey, where'd this come from? Must've happened when I was high."

The church speakers were playing *Why Did I Get So High* by The Peanut Butter Conspiracy, as the bikers rode in on their choppers and Deere's Indian and Harley that Saturday evening. "Welcome brothers and sisters." Then Deere had the church's sound system play *I Couldn't Get High* by the Fugs. They had a cookout and drank a lot of beers. "Hey, we need to go fishing down here in Florida!" said Fred.

"That's a good idea," said Tom. "I know some people with boats. Teach a man to fish, you know."

"Yeayahhh!" said Murmur. He was getting slightly inebriated. "But not tonight, we got to get to bed early, we got church in the morning."

Charlie, one of the bikers with a chopper, walked up and extended a hand to shake. "Hello." He was wearing a regular plain leather jacket without markings. "I can't believe you guys aren't in a biker gang," said Murmur.

"Yeah…we're not followers groveling for acceptance, just a bunch of friends who like to ride and be cool," said Charlie.

"Well, you'll love it here then," said Murmur. "We're jamming some worship tomorrow morning in the church with our band and then having some testimonies, and if anybody needs baptism, and be born again, we have an old fashioned tub in the back now. That was donated."

"Awesome, man! We'll rock out and have a good old fashioned revival," said Charlie.

"Then on Thanksgiving Day you're all invited to dine with us," said Murmur. "The cooks among us are making a huge banquet. Also, Tom and Gianna are getting married. I am officiating the marriage." Deere checked out his bikes and vehicles. There wasn't any damage. "Let's head down to the beach and show you guys around."

Bruno, Charlie, Steve, Deano, Tim, Pete, Sandra, Mick, Evan, and Earl walked out to the splashing waves. "I always wanted to be a beachcomber," said Deano. "Nice," said Evan. "I'm sleepy," said Mick. "I don't ever want to go back to work again," said Bruno. "It's mind-numbingly boring. I tune out and my brain goes on autopilot, and I just want to turn my brain off and have someone wake me up when it's over. I'm going to seriously think about moving out here and do whatever y'all are doing." Murmur looked him in the eye and smiled and said, "Fred can help you

find your best career niche. He'll hook you up! You can be your own boss." They made a bonfire that night and roasted hot dogs and marshmallows and made S'mores. They all managed to find a place to crawl off to bed somewhere for the night.

The next morning, Murmur woke up before sunrise. He did his daily devotionals in the morning watch. He meditated mindfully in The Lord. Praying, he prostrated himself on the floor with the window and curtains open. He focused on the molecules; the atoms; the fractals with which God created everything. He knelt on the floor and looked up at the heavens out through the window: at the quantum mechanics of the cosmos. Tom woke up with a beer and rang the church bell 30 times. They were still so groggy from not going to bed early enough.

Deere, Murmur, and Fred met Tom out in the front of the church. "Doesn't it seem like God, spirits, and the Supernatural are in another dimension?" mused Murmur. "I know I said there aren't any more dimensions as far as measurements go, but I mean realms. There are other realm dimensions it seems."

"Yeah, man!" said Tom.

"Dig," said Deere.

"Far out!" said Fred.

"Now let's go get some exercise," said Deere. They ran out to Deere's gymnasium and worked out until it was almost time to go to church. Then they ran back.

The band equipment was already set up in the church. People were pouring in and filling the seats. They got up on stage and started playing, mostly Christian and Gospel songs. The choir was

there too. They played and sang five songs together. Then they had prayers and testimonies.

Murmur took up a microphone and said to the crowd, “K.I.S.S. Keep it super-simple. Be honest with yourself; don’t pander or patronize others. Don’t patronize yourself. Stand up for yourself. Don’t let anyone treat you like a little kid, acting like your parent, or else you will *be* a little kid, by implied consent. Whether they be a boss, a supervisor, a government official, whatever…They act like Nanny McPhee. You’ll be insecure, vulnerable, unsure of yourself, pathetic little dweebs, under control of manipulative government and authority. On the other hand, my dad gave me a birthday card once that said I had class! I took it to heart. Labels matter. If you’re out in the world; maybe on the road, an imbecile in a big vehicle flips you off, do not make eye contact. Ignore them. You are better than that. They’ll try to make you a slave to fear. It’s a culture of fear[32]. Anybody who does self-trepanation, or self-immolation; it is an act that is inherently evil. Extreme evil, because you’re hurting or killing someone that God loves. Just like self-harm and suicide. Powers that be that follow the powers and principalities of darkness love to hate. They love to abort babies because it amounts to genocide. They say we need to maintain access to abortion in case of rape and incest, but I say we need to go to the source of the problem and put a stop to rape and incest for good. Our two stepdaughters were rescued from it, who are right over here! We come against those evil forces now.”

---

[32] https://www.youtube.com/watch?v=ApK0kcy7U0Q

Tom came forward with his microphone. "My good friend Mortimer, you put love back into my heart. God bless you." The guys hugged. "I was playing the Sims 4 when I was dating a lot of women, having a lot of recreational sex. I pretended I was a Sim, and I had a wonderful Sim wife and made love to other Sim women as well. Then I went back and tried to make woo-hoo with my first wife, but I noticed she was crying and lonely for me because she missed me when I had been gone. My heart broke. It was so sad. It took all the fun out of polygamy, namely polygyny. I knew if people have multiple families, it steals away the quality time with another spouse. You helped show me the light. The way, the truth, and the life through Jesus. The truth that sets us free. You explained things to me in words that even a brute like me could understand."

Murmur said, "You've helped me tremendously, too. You showed me how not to hold a grudge, that vengeance belongs to the Lord. I need your help with forgiveness. Let's just say a relative borrowed $500 when his baby was being born. He swore up and down that as soon as he got the money together, he'd pay me right back. Then when my life depended on it, he refused to pay it back even a year later. The punk called me every name in the book after I demanded it back, and used every cuss word and profanity. Then I saw he was living it up, and partying hard extravagantly with his family on Facebook. I told him I was going to sue him, and he blocked me on Messenger. I never heard from him again. By now the statute of limitations has run out. I guess it was worth it for him to burn the familial bridges. Then a female friend laid a sob story on me about needing $500 for nursing school

tuition. I read in a book that if you type up a promissory note, they will have to pay you back. Totally false. It's as worthless as an IOU. I never saw the money again."

"Let it go!" said Tom. "You paid *me* back, setting a good example. Just breathe in good fresh clean oxygen through your nose, wait a second, then let all the bad air and bad vibes out through your mouth. Fred will help us earn all the money we'll ever need. So, let…it…go…"

"Thanks Dude," said Murmur.

Deere walked forward with his microphone, smiled and patted Murmur on the back. "And you guys showed me I just have to be grateful and thankful just to be alive on this glorious planet at such a time as this. Not to be envious or jealous of anyone else. We're all having a tough time in these last days. You really helped me learn to love my neighbors as myself."

"I have some advice for you," said Murmur to Deere. "Love every day!" Murmur winked.

"Thanks, I will. Some very amazing things happened on our spiritual journey, like my mother being resurrected. Stand up. MOM!"

His mother stood up in the audience. She got a standing ovation.

"Now I know I don't need drugs to get high," Deere said. "I get high naturally on life. I get high on God. I get high on Jesus!"

There was a huge round of applause from the audience, many of whom were walk-ins.

"I don't need beer for breakfast anymore," said Tom. "I can take it or leave it." More applause.

Fred said into his microphone, "I used to be really into the love of money. Now I'm not. I finally

feel rich with all of my friends, and my wife. I feel like one of the luckiest men on earth. Money is just a way to facilitate buying and selling of goods and services by having a standard of worth and value, on a price tag. But what if there's unfair pricing? Within a community like ours where everybody's like family and loved ones, we can barter and trade and not get ripped off. We don't have to take the mark of the beast to buy or sell that way. I tell you, it's all underway with the cashless society and one-world universal currency. They're getting people to embrace the identification chips in their hand or forehead to pay for things and be employed at certain workplaces like in Britain. I'm going to help everyone here to develop their talents and spiritual gifts, so we can build up treasure in heaven and not just on earth where rust or moths consume it, and thieves break in and steal it. We're going to have to be mentally tough, so there's an app I downloaded that helped you develop mental strength."

Everyone else gave their testimony and shared biblical teaching. They did two more songs and concluded the Sunday service.

"I almost forgot to mention, Murmur," said Tom, "if you're letting your little Diva out to go potty, make dang sure an eagle or other bird of prey don't pick her up and make off with her, and watch out so gators won't eat Diva."

"I know," said Murmur. "Thanks for the reminder, buddy. Do you and Gianna have your marriage license?"

"We have an appointment this week," said Tom. "We're also taking a licensed marital course so it will be cheaper. There's no officiation registry requirement."

“I know,” said Murmur. “We need a place to race our vehicles, like Daytona.”

“I know some tracks we can go to,” said Tom.

“Great!” said Murmur. “I also want us all to go fishing now that we’re all here.”

“Fishing in Florida,” said Tom. “There’s Flounder, several types of Groupers, Ladyfish, Permit, and Pompano this time of year. A little farther North there are Bass, Bonito, Flathead and Blue Catfish, Red Drum…”

“Murder spelled backward?” asked Murmur.

“That’s another name for Redfish. Flounders, more Groupers, Speckled Seatrout, Sheepshead, Snapper, and Triggerfish in November.”

“Cool,” said Murmur. “I can’t wait.”

Deere drove up with his little VW Beetle. He used his pen-cutting plotter to make his own decals on the back window. One had Calvin peeing on a horned devil. One had Calvin peeing on the name Satan. Tom and Deere looked. “Like them? Made them myself.”

“Yes,” said Tom. “I would buy one from you.”

“You know,” said Deere, “Uncle Ted has the right idea. He always has a sharp witted reply for silly celebrities, Hollywood actors, and liberal leftist musicians, Stupid Hippies! Not their fault, they’re just uninformed. Ignorant. Don’t want to mention names. Love them. Love not what they do.”

The four of them and their wives all went fishing for the rest of the week. They had a great time. Everyone laughed and frolicked.

Finally, it was Thanksgiving Day. Many of them watched the Thanksgiving Day parade in the morning. Like a potluck, everyone participated and brought wonderful entrees so they could have Thanksgiving dinner with plenty of food around noon. There was turkey and ham of course, but Deere also make a vegetarian turkey and tofurkey. There were mashed potatoes and groovy gravy, rolls and biscuits with butter, jellied cranberries, green bean casserole, sweetcorn, creamed corn, candied yams, sweet potato pie, potato salad, macaroni salad, and custom salads, Better-than-stuffing authentic Native American frybread, which Deere called pan bread, it was from his mother's secret recipe. Everyone raved that his butterscotch brownies were better than sex. Oreo pie, peach cobbler, strawberry rhubarb pie, strawberry shortcake, coconut cream pie, banana cream pie, banana splits, ice cream sundaes, blueberry pies, donuts, and no-bake cheesecakes, Southern pecan pie, nut butter and chocolate pie, cupcakes, root beer floats from homemade root beer, apple pie, apple crisp, and ice cream cakes were also available if anyone still had room. All ate until they were stuffed. Then they gathered around the church for the wedding.

The bridesmaids were the two stepdaughters, and the girl from the abortion clinic was in attendance. Fred was the best man, and Deere was the photographer and videographer. Going to the Chapel played on the loudspeakers. Murmur did the speech, "Allow me to read from First Corinthians 4:3-7. Love is patient, Love is kind. It does not envy, it does not boast, it is not proud. It does not dishonor others, it is not self-

seeking, it is not easily angered, it keeps no record of wrongs. Love does not delight in evil but rejoices in the truth. It always protects, always trusts, always hopes, always perseveres. Love never fails. Tom and Gianna, a beautiful couple. You will now become one flesh. Tom your body belongs to Gianna, and only Gianna. Gianna, your body belongs to Tom, and only Tom, forsaking all others. You will become a three-ply chord that is not easily undone. You are married not only to each other, but to God, with these rings. Tom, please put the wedding ring onto Gianna's ring finger. Now, Gianna, please put the man's ring onto Tom's ring finger. Thank you. Does anybody object? If so, keep it to yourself; nobody cares. By the power invested in me, I now pronounce you man and wife. Go ahead and have a great honeymoon, you two! Live EPIC[33], be fruitful and multiply and fill the Earth. Now is the cool of the day[34].

Everyone helped throw rice into Tom and Gianna's hair, while *Rice is Nice* by The Lemon Pipers, who were from Oxford Ohio, played. Outside were tin cans tied to the back of the car and Just Married written on the back car window. Everybody watched them ride off into the sunset in their Challenger to go on their honeymoon.

---

[33] https://genius.com/Sherrod-white-epic-lyrics
[34] https://www.youtube.com/watch?v=mfVRXCXeShw

Love

Appendix:

When I was growing up, I submitted a few cartoons to the local newspaper, The Monroe Evening News. I had one that depicted extravagant toilet paper with genuine gold leaf smiley faces on each section and captioned it as "toilet paper no one wants to use." They of course rejected my submission saying they were a "family paper" and their readers would not appreciate "toilet humor and bathroom jokes."

Hi-way Overpass painters Helper!
NO MORE OF THIS!!
Hey!
1-888-888-8888
CALL NOW!
Hey!
WOW!
ONLY $29.95
LUV u BAE
Mirror, extra.
Beep Beep

Stupid
Nonsensical
grafiti
figures on
train car
NOT Art...
Blight!!

This is my original character conceptualization sheet.

Diva, AKC registered, pedigreed Shih-tzu, in the sleeper of a truck on a long-haul trip. She was from Amish country, bought as a runt puppy at Berlin Pets.

Diva, the perpetual puppy.

Coming soon; Book 2 and 3 of the series.

I hope you enjoyed this book. All the glory goes to God Almighty. If you didn't like it, it is probably my fault, although I did put so much time and effort into getting it done, over thousands of hours throughout many years. I told my wife after I write the characters' story and do all the editing a month later, they come to life and become real (in effect). She said that if I really believe that, she was going to have me committed (to an asylum). But seriously, what happens when a writer for television or the movies creates characters in their minds, at least for fictional stories, they find actors to play the parts and the actors actually try to become and think like the people they had in mind. They have sex if the role requires it, and thus they had actual sex in their own lives. If they glorify senseless violence, it portrays violence in a favorable way among audience's minds, setting a bad example. The same with explicit language. Some watchers or readers may be able to handle this well, such as playing Grand Theft Auto, or first person shooter games. However, someone with a weak or vulnerable mind can be negatively affected and decide to act out

among society based on the encouragement from what they have seen or heard.

Hint: In the next two books we will be exploring controlling other human minds for political power and gain, and role reversal for the inmates to get out of prison, while the innocent people are imprisoned. The sane will be committed to asylums, while the truly insane are released.

www.ingramcontent.com/pod-product-compliance
Ingram Content Group UK Ltd.
Pitfield, Milton Keynes, MK11 3LW, UK
UKHW021937190726
13853UKWH00004B/1498